# MAKE TIME FOR LOVE

# MAKE TIME FOR LOVE

## FORWARD IN TIME, BOOK ONE

## LOUISE CLARK

Book and cover design by eBook Prep
www.ebookprep.com

February, 2019
ISBN: 978-1-64457-011-1

*ePublishing Works!*
644 Shrewsbury Commons Ave
Ste 249
Shrewsbury PA 17361
United States of America

www.epublishingworks.com
Phone: 866-846-5123

# CHAPTER 1

Faith Hamilton stared into the empty office and tried to figure out what to do next. She needed the occupant, a computer genius by the name of Cody Simpson, to abandon the work he'd been hired to do and help her keep the office computers in working order. So far that hadn't happened, which was why she was standing in the doorway to his office on a mission to convince him that when she called with a problem, he needed to snap into action.

She looked around. The hallway was still, the office definitely empty. There was no point in sticking around. She'd have to leave a note asking for a meeting and hope that Cody saw it and responded. Not that she expected him to. He never reacted to her telephone messages. Why would he pay attention a written note?

She hadn't brought a pen or paper when she came up to his second floor fortress from the first floor bullpen where she managed the company's office staff. She hoped she'd find something on his desk.

She stepped into the doorway.

A rustle of sound behind her alerted her that she was no longer alone moments before an amused male voice said, "Hey good-looking, to what do I owe the pleasure?"

The voice was a rich, silky baritone. Faith felt heat creep into her face and flush her features. She turned slowly, knowing who was in the corridor behind her and absolutely furious at what he'd said. "Well, well, well, it's Cody Simpson. You don't answer your voicemail."

He grinned at her, unrepentant. "I try not to." Several inches taller than Faith's leggy five-nine, he was able to look down at her.

That annoyed her, as did her appreciation of his looks. His face featured blue eyes fringed with black lashes, a straight nose, and a wide sensual mouth. His body wasn't too shabby, either, with a lean, muscular build that wouldn't go away. When? She thought. When did he have the time to keep his body in shape? As far as she knew he spent most of his waking hours at a computer.

She raised her brows and said in the coolest voice she could muster, "Have you heard about Sue's accident?"

Sue Green was the company's computer troubleshooter. If an employee had a problem that couldn't be fixed by a simple restart, Sue emerged from her second floor office to do a house call. Sue was a wonder with computers. She'd coax and caress, talking to them in husky, silken tones while her fingers played the keyboard. There was hardly a machine she couldn't fix and Faith was convinced it was because she seduced each and every one of them.

Sue reported to Cody Simpson and she thought he was the best boss in the world. Faith thought that was probably because Cody paid little attention to Sue or the tasks she performed and let her manage her time in her own way.

His very engaging smile faded. "Yeah, I heard. Tough luck. Some drunk ran a red and slammed into the side of her car. She'll be okay, but for now she's got broken ribs, lacerations, and internal bruising. She feels pretty miserable."

Surprise made her say, "You talked to her?"

He raised black brows in an expression of surprise, as if he wouldn't consider any other course of action. "Of course. I called the hospital as soon as I heard."

Embarrassed color washed Faith's cheeks. Though Sue didn't report to her, she was always friendly and Faith enjoyed working with her. She should have checked on Sue herself. That was a mistake and she hated making mistakes. It didn't matter that Sue reported to Cody. Faith made a mental note to send Sue some pastries from the café where they often went to have coffee together. Sue swore the cinnamon buns were the best in town and ate hers with an almost sensual appreciation. She'd enjoy the treat.

Cody's marvelous blue eyes narrowed, then suddenly he smiled in a mischievous way that hinted at naughty behavior to come. Faith was still trying to figure out exactly what that look signified when his hands caught her around the waist and he picked her up as easily as he would a ten-year-old child.

She shrieked. "What are you doing?"

Those marvelous blue eyes of his still wickedly amused, he spun her around, then put her down a couple of feet away. "You were blocking the doorway to my office," he said, as if manhandling a woman was an everyday occurrence. "Come on in." He sauntered through the door, obviously expecting her to follow.

Faith considered her options. Cody Simpson might be gorgeous to look at, but someone needed to talk to him about his social skills. He couldn't go around calling a co-worker 'good-looking' then pick her up as if she was a cute little pet. Come to think of it, someone ought to tell him that voice and e-mail had been invented to make communications easier, not to shut them down completely.

Which brought her back to why she was standing in his doorway. She'd come with a problem. If she refused to talk to him now and stomped off in a huff, she'd never get an answer from him because she'd have to start voice and e-mailing him again and he didn't answer his voicemail or e-mail messages. Which was why she'd come up here in the first place.

Swallowing her annoyance, she strolled into the office, her gaze sweeping the room in what she hoped was a coolly critical way. "Not too shabby," she said, aiming for just the right amount of disdain. It wasn't easy.

The office was big, far bigger than Faith's. In fact it was the size of the executive offices and had a view of the Charles River, with the city of Boston beyond. She coveted the office for its size, its view and for the appealing way it had been decorated. The furniture was gorgeous, solid mahogany that gleamed deep molten russet in the sun. A Persian rug woven in rich tones of sapphire, ruby, and gold disguised the beige industrial carpet that covered the floor in all of the offices. There wasn't a file cabinet to be seen, but there were three computers and they were all on. Clearly, the office was a reflection of Cody's position in the company.

The company was Networking Innovative Technologies, or NIT for those into acronyms—which seemed to be just about everybody in the high tech world. Just under a year ago it won two substantial contracts and obtained a government grant to support its innovative research. It soon became evident that the original staff didn't have the time or experience to deal with all the work the contracts brought in. New employees were hired, including Cody Simpson, Director of Network Services, whose job was designing the software for the new technologies. The specialized software Cody created was essential to the success of NIT. Faith figured that he could pretty much ask for whatever he wanted and he'd get it. A big fancy office was just the tip of the iceberg.

Another hire was Ava Taylor as COO, and Faith's boss. Ava was a detail and procedure oriented person, and she was the reason Faith was standing in Cody Simpson's office now.

Cody glanced around the office as if seeing it through Faith's

4

eyes. "Thanks." He headed over to one corner where a small bar fridge sat. Perched on top was a coffeemaker that produced individual cups. He pushed a cup beneath the spigot and loaded a pod then set the machine going. "Want a coffee? Or a pop?" he asked as coffee gushed into the cup.

Faith leaned against the doorjamb and tried hard not to be jealous. The personal coffee machine was strictly against regulations. Ava had decreed that all NIT employees use the coffeemaker in the lunchroom for their caffeine intake. Supposedly that was to ensure people from different departments got to know each other and to generate a sense of belonging to the organization. Faith figured it allowed Ava to tally how many cups of coffee each individual drank and the cost to the company. Cody's personal coffeemaker indicated that either Ava didn't journey up here much or he was too valuable to NIT to force him into the mold the rest of the staff was expected to fit.

The small bar fridge, which presumably held the pop, was another no-no. Faith shook her head, a little resentful of his successful flouting of the rules Ava had imposed. Cody must have thought that she was responding to his offer, for he shrugged, pulled the cup from the machine, and sauntered over to his desk. There he leaned against the edge, which put him with his back toward the window and gave him an advantage, for the mid-day sun was streaming over his shoulder into Faith's eyes.

As she stationed herself so that she no longer longer looked directly into the sunlight, she couldn't help but notice the way his position drew the fabric of his jeans tight against his muscular thighs. She swallowed and resisted the urge to sigh in appreciation. Cody Simpson might be great to look at, but so far he had proved to be a real pain to work with. Something she'd be well advised to remember.

He gestured to an over-stuffed chair covered in cream-colored leather that would be suitable for an upscale living room. "Have a seat."

"No, thanks." The chair would put her back in the sunlight's path. Besides, she was here to do battle and that was better done on her feet. "If you haven't heard my voicemail," she said, "did you by chance read my e-mail?"

He stared over the rim of his cup as he sipped, his blue eyes glazed in thought. Then, quite suddenly, his brilliant gaze focused on Faith's face. "The network problem."

Well, that was a positive sign. "That's right. But the glitch seems to have spread. Now Angela's terminal is completely frozen." Angela's computer problems were a regular issue and Sue swore they could be sorted out by Angela herself if she was given time, responsibility, and a bit of tech training. Sue had confided to Faith that when she'd suggested to Ava that the clerical staff be empowered in this way, Ava shot the idea down. So Sue continued her regular visits down to Faith's area. With Sue gone it was now Cody's turn to sort out Angela's glitch.

His eyes lit up and he looked intrigued by the idea of a frozen terminal for a brief moment. "Really? That's odd. Are you sure it isn't operator error?"

"Angela's pretty competent. She believes it's in the software. Or perhaps in the computer itself."

Cody put down his mug. "Okay. I'll get on to it."

Surprise flickered through Faith. She'd expected a hard fight. After all, Cody hadn't responded to any of the phone messages she'd left, or the e-mail's she'd sent. It shouldn't be this easy. Still, she might as well be gracious. Maybe Cody Simpson was one of those people who liked to have face-to-face communication before he acted. No harm in playing along. She smiled at him. "Thanks, Cody. I appreciate this."

He raised black brows. "No problem. Remind me tomorrow,

okay?" His eyes gleamed. "Come up and visit again. I can't guarantee I'll be any better at listening to voicemail tomorrow."

Feeling as if she'd just had all the air punched from her lungs, Faith said faintly, "Tomorrow?"

"Yeah. It's lousy timing, but I think I'll be able to break long enough to fix the problem. Should only take fifteen minutes or a half-an-hour and I can manage that."

"Tomorrow isn't good enough!"

"It's the best I can do."

He sounded disgustingly cheerful about it. "You just spent fifteen minutes talking to me! If you'd listened to your voicemail you could have used this time to come down and fix Angela's problem."

"If I hadn't discovered you hovering outside my office when I came back from the operations center I would have been working on my own projects. I wouldn't have had fifteen minutes to spare. Besides, if Angela is as experienced as you say she is, she can probably fix the problem herself."

"That's not her job!" The certain knowledge that there was nothing she could do to force Cody Simpson to do what he was supposed to do had her voice rising.

"It's not my job either," Cody said, sounding perfectly justified and annoyingly calm.

"It is while Sue is ill!"

He picked up the coffee cup again, holding it in both hands. "You've been talking to Ava Taylor."

There was something in his voice that warned Faith there was more to come. A coldness that had her saying warily, "I report to Ava."

He contemplated the interior of the coffee mug for a minute. When he looked up those marvelous warm blue eyes of his had cooled to the pale, chilly blue of polar ice. "Let's get this straight.

My job is writing software and developing the network protocol for this company. If I have time I will pitch in for Sue while she's off, but that's it. I'll help if all other attempts to correct the problem have failed, but I am not the company's computer troubleshooter."

Faith's temper rose. It wasn't her fault that Ava had decided differently. She hated conforming to regulations that she didn't think made sense and she really hated being in the position of defending them. It made her grumpy, if not downright snarly. She had to get out of here before she said or did something that would make working with Cody Simpson impossible. She stomped to the doorway. There she stopped and turned back to face him. "A lot of good you are. So what am I supposed to do when problems come up?"

"Cope," Cody said.

"Jerk," Faith retorted, completely forgetting her good intentions. She slammed the door as she left and hoped that the force would be enough to shake the illegal coffeemaker off its perch on the equally illegal bar fridge.

# CHAPTER 2

*W*hat a day! Faith pushed open the front door of her home. Located in Lexington, one of the suburbs in the greater Boston area, the house was nearly two hundred years old. Designed in the traditional gracious New England style, with a white clapboard exterior and black shutters on the sash windows, it was an inviting remnant of a time long past. She stood for a moment listening to the quiet and appreciating the stillness before she entered the beautifully proportioned hall. She tossed her keys on an antique half table in the Chippendale style that sat against the robin's egg blue wall, then slipped out of her shoes. The smooth old hardwood floor was cool under her feet. Her tension eased immediately. She dropped her purse beside the table, then ran lightly up the wide staircase to the second floor.

The house was located on what had once been the extensive farm of Andrew Byrne, a well-to-do and influential landowner prominent during the Revolution, and one of Faith's ancestors. The nineteenth century equivalent of an in-law suite, the house had been built in 1815 for his widow, Mary Elizabeth, in a wooded area that had been one of Andrew's favorite places.

The economic and social changes of the twentieth century had forced Faith's family to sell off Andrew's land, piece by piece, as Boston grew and the suburbs sprawled away from the center of the city, until all that the family owned was this old dower house and the main house, located more than a mile closer to the centre of Lexington. When Faith was growing up, her grandparents had lived in the old farmhouse while her parents, Chloe and Daniel, lived in the dower house with their two daughters, Faith and Elizabeth. When Faith's grandparents died, Chloe and Elizabeth had moved into the old farmhouse, leaving Faith in the dower house.

Faith quickly changed into a t-shirt and light pants that hugged her hips. She often came home tired at the end of the day, but not only had this day been busy, it had been emotionally taxing as well. First there was her argument with Cody Simpson. Then, when Cody Simpson refused to help out, Angela decided she might as well try fixing her computer glitch. She fiddled happily for a while but somehow deleted her printer protocol, making her computer problem worse. At that point Faith decided she couldn't leave Angela to solve the problem alone. Between them they found the cause and corrected it, but the cost had been two hours of frustration and a lecture from Ava Taylor when she noticed Faith working on Angela's computer.

Ava had been good enough to summon Faith to her office for a little 'chat', rather than chewing her out in the bullpen, but that small mercy was all she allowed. She reminded Faith that fixing computers was Cody Simpson's job, not Faith's. When Faith had tried to explain Cody's position, Ava looked at her in a no-nonsense way and said simply that Faith must find a way to work with Cody.

With a sigh Faith headed down the stairs, on her way to the kitchen. She loved her job, really she did, but there were times when she felt she would never fit in. Sooner or later Ava would notice that Faith wasn't quite right for NIT's new corporate culture, that she was a little odd. Then her job would be in jeopardy and the normal life she was trying to build would collapse around her.

To ensure this didn't happen Faith worked hard at being the best she could be. There were days, like today, when the strain took its toll. That was why she loved this old house. It was the place she felt free to be herself.

It was also the bond that tied her to her eccentric and often annoying family.

In the kitchen she crossed the tiled floor to the fridge, which stood on one side of the big room. Opening the door, she pulled out a bottle of spring water. She took a swig, then held the cold plastic against her flushed cheek. What was she going to do about Cody Simpson? The man was as impossible as he was gorgeous. He wasn't going to rush down if she called, the way Sue Green did. He probably wouldn't come down at all, making her do all the computer fixes. Yet if she spent the weeks of Sue's recovery being the company computer troubleshooter she'd never get anything done.

Look at today. The two hours she'd spent at Angela's computer had snowballed, so that she ended up getting behind on her to-do list. That meant she was going to have to go in tomorrow to catch up. After all that had gone on today, she wanted to do nothing more than to have a quick dinner, then sit in front of the TV for an hour or so before she crawled into bed. Unfortunately she was expecting her mother and sister for dinner along with her most eccentric relative, Uncle Andrew.

An hour and a half later, Faith, her sister Elizabeth, better known as Liz, and her mother Chloe were crowded around the circular oak table that filled the central portion of the big country kitchen staring dubiously at a freshly baked loaf of bread. The crust was a beautiful golden brown, the shape a perfect rectangle with a smoothly arched dome.

"I've gone wrong somewhere." A young looking fifty-six, Chloe poked at the loaf with her fingertip. Nothing happened. The bread was rock solid. "This will not do! I don't have the option of producing dud loaves of bread. I'm going into a war zone—"

"Perhaps you interfered with the rising process when you brought the dough from your place to mine," Faith said.

"I started late," Chloe said. "There's a lot to do to prepare before I go away. I lost track of time." There wasn't a hint of defensiveness in her voice. The statement was an observation, not an excuse.

"Let someone else do the baking," Liz suggested before she headed over to the counter. Like the other women, she boasted strong cheekbones and blond hair, but she lacked the long legs of her mother and sister.

"The problem with these old cookbooks is that they aren't precise. The recipes say things like 'a pinch of salt,' but how much is a pinch? Is it an eighth of a teaspoon? A sixteenth? Then there's 'a handful of nuts.' What's a handful? Your father's handful? My handful? A child's handful?"

Faith made her hand into a fist and tapped on the loaf of bread with her knuckles. The solid 'thunk' could have come from a two-by-four. She flipped her long, golden hair behind one ear as she grinned at her mother. "I think it's a process of trial and error, Mom. Anyway, you'll be a visitor. No one will expect you to do the chores."

"Who knows what hardships Mary Byrne has had to endure? And since I must be with her always during my visit, I will have to endure them too."

Liz returned to the table, cutlery in her hand. "Faith, we're using the good silver tonight, aren't we?"

Faith nodded. "We'll use the bone china dishes too. You know

Uncle Andrew, Liz. He loves to visit, but he's not quite ready to accept twenty-first century manners."

"Not surprising," said Chloe, a trifle tartly, still staring balefully at the loaf of bread, the symbol of her failure.

"I think Uncle Andrew puts on all that old world charm," Liz said. "Give him a t-shirt and jeans and he'd be just another good-looking guy."

"Not quite." Resignation bound together with resentment sounded beneath Faith's words. Uncle Andrew was not just an eccentric relative who lived in the area and liked to come to dinner, he was a man from the past. The year seventeen seventy-two, to be precise. And Faith was the reason he was able to move from his time into hers.

Faith was a beacon. Her light shone brightly into the past and the future. In his own time, Andrew was a traveller, able to see the light and walk into it, and so into the future. The skill existed only within their family. Chloe was both a beacon and a traveller, but not all family members were endowed with the special talent. Liz was neither traveller or beacon.

"Yeah, well—" Uncomfortable, Liz turned away. She began to lay the cutlery onto woven placemats. Opposite her, Chloe was hefting the loaf of bread up and down as if she was lifting weights. Liz shook her head. "You're obsessing, Mom."

Chloe's green eyes sparkled with annoyance. "I am an educated woman. I teach history at Harvard University. I am renowned in my field. Why is it impossible for me to successfully bake a loaf of bread?"

"That's why bread machines were invented, Mom," Faith said as she rummaged in the fridge. "Let's forget the homemade bread with dinner idea and concentrate on steak and salad instead. With winter over, but summer harvest not yet begun, Andrew always appreciates fresh meat and veggies. Bread is something he has aplenty."

"Why can't I master a simple process, one my ancestors did without thinking? I'm an intelligent woman. I'm a good cook—"

"That's why you can be the one to barbecue the steaks, Mom," Faith said, handing her mother a large packet of beautifully marbled beef.

"Faith, didn't you say you had a can of artichoke hearts?" Liz asked. "I thought I'd combine them with some of your spinach and make a dip for the corn chips."

"Check the pantry." Faith drew spinach, butter lettuce, tomatoes, sweet peppers, and a cucumber out of the fridge.

"Corn chips have transfats," Chloe said gloomily as she pulled the plastic wrap off the disposable tray holding the prime rib steaks. "Andrew's body is used to heavy doses of saturated fats in the meat he eats." She plopped the well-marbled beef onto a plate. "We're altering the man's normal diet. We're probably ensuring that he'll die before his time." She rubbed seasoning salt into the meat.

Faith looked pointedly at the steak on which Chloe was now shaking a light coating of cayenne pepper. "You think heavy doses of spices are part of Uncle Andrew's normal diet?"

"He uses spices when he can get hold of them," Chloe protested, wiping her hands on the bib apron she wore to protect her brightly patterned dress.

"These are organic corn chips," Liz said, busy with her dip. "They aren't fried with hydrogenated oils. They're baked. Uncle Andrew will be fine."

Chloe looked at her watch. "It's six-thirty. When do you think he's going to want dinner?"

Faith cocked her head, listening. "I don't hear the shower. He's probably primping in the bathroom by now. He told me he wants to be home by eight o'clock, so why not aim for seven, Mom."

Liz shot her a questioning look. "That's pretty early for Uncle

Andrew to leave—usually when he has dinner with us he stays for a longer visit. What's up?"

"There's a dance or something tonight and he thinks his new neighbors from Boston will be going." Faith paused for effect, then added, "He wants to flirt with the daughter."

"Oh," said Chloe, sounding intrigued and wise at once.

Liz laughed. "Do you think—"

Faith nodded. The three Hamilton women stared at each other, eyes bright with amusement and anticipation.

Liz said, "Oh, wow."

They were all laughing when a good-looking young man sauntered into the room. His long dark hair was damp, tied at the nape with a black velvet ribbon. The style should have looked effete, but with his muscular build he was able to carry off the fashion. Besides, it went with the black velvet breeches and fine linen shirt with the lace ruffles at the wrists.

"Well met, Miss Elizabeth," he said, kissing her cheek. She hadn't yet arrived when he'd shown up earlier.

"Hey there, Andrew." Liz returned the kiss, then stood back to gave him a visual once over. "I hear you're going to a party tonight."

He nodded, smiling a wolf-grin of anticipation. "All the landowning families in Lexington plan to attend. I will be the best dressed there. Thanks," he added, "to Faith's bathing accommodations and cleaning facilities."

Chloe stiffened. She shot her daughter an accusatory look. "You took Andrew's suit to the dry cleaners?"

"He dropped it off last week." Faith met her mother's gaze with defiantly raised eyebrows.

"I have been planning this evening for some time," Andrew said. There was a gleam in his eyes that suggested he wasn't about to be stopped.

Chloe rinsed her hands in the sink and dried them in an agitated way. "You know we cannot interfere!"

Faith put her hands up, palm forward. "Look, Mom, I didn't think it would hurt. I mean, I feed Uncle Andrew most Fridays and he washes with my cranberry soap when he showers. Where do I draw the line?"

Chloe stared at her eldest daughter from beneath her brows, a look she'd perfected when the girls were small and needed to be disciplined. Then she relented. Shrugging, she said, "Balancing past and present is an art, not a science. You must do what you think is right."

Uncle Andrew smiled broadly. "I am much relieved to hear you say that, Madam."

Chloe shot him a fierce look. "You," she said, wagging her finger at him, "are not to lead my daughter into mischief."

Andrew inspected the fall of lace at his wrist the way a man wearing French cuffs might check the set of his cufflink. "You may depend upon me, Madam."

"Yeah, right," said Liz.

Uncle Andrew laughed.

Chloe said stiffly, "I certainly hope so, Andrew."

Faith sighed. "This is all way too complicated."

# CHAPTER 3

"I'm late!" Chloe Hamilton breezed into Faith's office, a small cubicle that boasted a window overlooking the parking lot and a solid panel door that closed it off from the action in the bullpen and gave Faith a privacy she valued greatly.

Faith logged off her computer. "Only by an hour, Mom."

"I'm sorry, honey!" Her hair drawn back in a smooth bun that exposed the lovely bones of her face, Chloe was dressed in a tailored jacket and floor-length skirt in subdued grey wool. Though the clothes were a far cry from her usual choice of vivid colors, the costume could do little to hide the energy that radiated from her.

Faith hugged her, loving the warmth and life that was so much a part of her mother. "Come on, let's get going. I'm starved and I know you've got a deadline to keep." She slipped a light jacket from a hook on the back of her door. "When does your flight for Washington leave?"

"At four o'clock," Chloe said as they walked through the bullpen to the exit.

"That means you'll get into Washington at rush hour. Lucky you. It will probably take longer for you to get downtown than to fly in from Boston," Faith said as they emerged from the NIT suite.

"Probably. Thank heavens I'm not taking any luggage. That would really hold me up. Still, I've got plenty of time. Mary Byrne has promised to join me at the special place at eight o'clock. I think I'll have dinner at a nice restaurant before I meet her."

They walked down the corridor toward the lobby. "You know, Mom, I'm not comfortable with you going to DC for this trip. What happens if there's a problem? What if Mary Byrne isn't there? Or there's a pile up on the highway and traffic backs up so that you can't make your meeting on time? What do you do then?"

"I get a hotel for the night and then I try again the next day. It's all been arranged, Faith. Trust me!"

Easy to say. Chloe was travelling back into the past to Washington during the Civil War years. She would be completely out of touch, reliant on their ancestor from that time to protect her. Anything could happen and there was nothing Faith could do to stop it.

They reached the lobby. It was a small area, hardly more than a widening of the hallway. On one wall were two utilitarian elevators and an open stairway that led to the second floor. Between the elevator doors was a signboard identifying the building's tenants. "I do, Mom. It's just that—"

Footsteps sounded on the staircase. Faith closed her mouth on what she'd planned to say as a male figure emerged from the upper level, running lightly down the stairs. Seeing the two women he hesitated briefly, then he flashed a grin and said, "Hi."

Black hair, blue eyes, muscles in all the right places, Faith knew that her mother would approve of Cody Simpson as a man. She might even consider him prime son-in-law material. That made Faith uneasy, because Cody was not only the sort of man she avoided socially, but he was the worst kind of coworker. Angela's computer had broken down twice since she had gone up to his office to ask for his help and twice he hadn't responded. She'd had to risk raising Ava Taylor's ire by fixing the machine herself.

"Hi," she said back, hoping her mother wouldn't notice the reserve in her voice and question her on it.

He swept Faith with a look that catalogued every part of her, from head-to-toe. "Nice day, isn't it?" Then he deliberately looked from Faith to Chloe, his eyebrows raised.

Very much aware that the slacks she was wearing did little to minimize her height and that her blond hair had started to stray from the restraints that kept it in a tight chignon, Faith wished she knew some way of escape. She didn't want to introduce Cody to her mother, who she knew would be intrigued by him. She also knew Cody expected to be introduced and that he wouldn't understand why a casual, 'Cody this is my mother, Chloe. Mom, this is Cody Simpson,' left her frozen in terror. Each and every one of the good manners drilled into her from the time she was tiny was actively demanding she make the simple introduction. Every survival instinct was fighting back, just as intensely, telling her that she'd be a fool to open that door, even a crack.

She swallowed hard, avoided Cody's eyes, ignored the surprised curiosity emanating from her mother, and said, "Yup."

Cody raised his brows, then shrugged. "See you later, then."

"Sure," Faith said, hoping she wasn't blushing.

Cody nodded and headed off toward the NIT offices. Faith shoved open the door.

Outside Chloe said cheerfully, "What a gorgeous male. Who is he?"

Faith shrugged. "Our new systems guy. He lives upstairs so we hardly ever see him."

"You know him then?"

Faith debated telling her mother about the battle she and Cody were having, then decided now was not the time. She shook her head. "Not really." A wash of heat told her that now she really was blushing.

Chloe didn't seem to notice. Or maybe she did, because she laughed and said, "Well from his expression I think this Cody Simpson would very much like to know you better. Much better."

"Mom!"

Chloe chuckled again. "You may not want to admit it, my beautiful daughter, but you have had boys falling over themselves trying to get you to notice them since you were five years old. This one is no different."

Faith shot her mother a sideways look as they headed toward The Sandwich Hut, a favorite hangout for the NIT staff. "Mom, I was a wallflower in school. Liz was the one the boys all fell over themselves trying to attract. Remember? Let's talk about something else."

Chloe paid no attention. "Not so! I saw what you would not, my darling daughter. You scared those boys off. Males look at the package. If they like it, they probe further. If they don't they move on. Your package is very nice, Faith. You have beautiful skin, gorgeous long, blonde hair, and beautiful grey-green eyes a man could drown in—"

Faith squared her shoulders as she stared straight ahead. "I am so not comfortable with this conversation."

"With you, men look, then they want to sample," Chloe continued, mischievous amusement now coloring her voice. "It's not until you've snapped or growled at them a few times that they decide, nice as the wrapping is, it's too much like work to discover what's inside. That's why they abandon the effort."

"I'm not a package, Mother! I'm a person and deserve to be treated as one."

"Oh, don't give me the feminist line! I'm a child of the '60s, remember? I was a pioneer in the feminist movement. I've lived the feminist philosophy. That doesn't stop me from realizing that sex motivates all of us, but it motivates men differently than women. That gorgeous male animal we just spoke to is intrigued by your package. Play your cards right and he might want to tear off the wrappings to see what lies beneath."

The Sandwich Hut loomed, growing closer with each step. Faith groaned. "Mom, could we talk about something else when we get to the restaurant? Just in case someone from work happens to be there. Or comes in while we're eating. I don't really want to become the latest hot topic in the office gossip mill."

Chloe sighed. "I'm not trying to embarrass you, Faith, but I'm going into a war zone. I might not come back."

"Mom! We've been over that. Washington was safe. It was never invaded. Nothing is going to happen to you."

They reached The Sandwich Hut. Chloe took hold of the door and pulled. "I have to be realistic, sweetheart. We don't know what my future is. You may be right. In fact, you probably are. But I want to make sure that my daughters are okay. That they have happy lives. Liz will graduate soon, but she has to build a career before she thinks of having a family. You, on the other hand, have a settled path. It's time for you to start looking back at all those boys who like to look at you."

"What will you have ladies?" asked Jake, the bald, pot-bellied owner of The Sandwich Hut. There was a twinkle in his eyes as he stood behind the counter, waiting to take their order. Evidently he'd heard part of Chloe's 'mom' lecture.

"I'll have the Southwestern Chicken Wrap," Chloe said, "with lots of extra hot peppers." She added cheerfully, "I don't think they'll do hot and spicy where I'm going, so I'm stocking up on flavor before I head out."

"And where would that be?" Jake asked in a friendly way as he assembled the sandwich.

"Washington—"

"Hey Jake! I'll have a big bowl of your broccoli and cheese soup."

"Broccoli and cheese soup. Sounds good. I'll have some too since I'm not sure how scarce food will be."

Faith could have groaned, but Jake apparently hadn't paid enough attention to Chloe's conversation to think further comment was necessary. Or maybe he was too polite to say that Chloe sounded like a woman way out in left field, because there was no scarcity of food in either Washington DC or Washington State.

"Okay, ladies. Find yourselves a table." He grinned, apparently deciding his comment was a witticism since only two tables were occupied and there was plenty of free space. "I'll bring your meals when they're ready."

Faith led them to a table in a corner where she positioned herself so she could sit with her back to the wall and watch the rest of the room, not to mention the doorway.

"I want to see you happy," Chloe continued, refusing to be diverted. "You are twenty-six years old. You're settled in your job. You need to open yourself up to new experiences in your personal life."

Jake emerged from behind his counter, carrying a tray. Faith watched him head their way. "Yeah, okay, Mom. I get the point."

Chloe rolled on, as unstoppable as an avalanche. "You need to let nice young men like that good-looking systems expert get to know you."

Jake hovered just behind Chloe's shoulder. "Ah...Mom—"

"To unwrap your package..." Jake plunked the tray on the table. Chloe blanched and for the first time hesitated. "...so to speak."

Jake's lips twitched, then he winked. "Enjoy."

After that Chloe dropped the subject, much to Faith's relief. They were just finishing up when the door opened and Ava Taylor breezed inside.

"A ham sandwich to go, Jake, and make it quick. I've got a conference call in fifteen minutes and I need something to eat fast." As Jake worked on the sandwich, Ava looked around restlessly.

Faith was able to pinpoint the moment Ava noticed her. She was an attractive woman who dressed impeccably whatever the occasion and she looked a lot more approachable than she was. The impatient expression on her round, sweet-featured face tightened with curiosity that was quickly covered by her usual polite social mask. She strode across the room. "Faith! Hello. Who is this?" She scrutinized Chloe, then smiled. The expression lit up her face in an appealing way. Her eyes remained cool and assessing. "A family member, I'll bet." She tapped her cheek. "Let me see. Your mother. Am I right?"

Chloe held out her hand. "Quite right. I'm Chloe Hamilton."

"The history professor." Ava shook her hand. "I've heard of you."

"You have the better of me, then, I'm afraid."

"This is Ava Taylor, Mom, our new COO," Faith said.

Chloe retrieved her hand. "Of course. Faith has mentioned you."

Ava shot Faith a look that was hard to interpret. "Has she? I must say, Mrs. Hamilton, Faith is wonderful to work with. She manages the office beautifully—"

"She should." Chloe pushed her plate aside and threw her crumpled napkin on top of it. "My daughter has an MBA from Harvard. She is more than capable of doing any management job she chooses."

Ava's eyes narrowed and for an instant her features hardened dangerously, then she was smiling again so that Faith wondered if she'd misinterpreted the fleeting expression. "I depend on Faith. It's because she is so effective in handling the day-to-day that I'm able to be more involved in marketing and sales, which is what I'm most interested in. Ah, there's Jake with my sandwich. I've got to run. Faith, I'll talk to you later. Mrs. Hamilton, nice to meet you!"

The door closed behind her with a soft thump. Chloe pushed back her chair as Faith finished the last of her ice tea. "What's Ava like to work for?"

Faith tossed her napkin on her plate as she prepared to leave. "She's okay. Why?"

Outside they saw Ava's hurrying form disappear into the building that housed the NIT offices. "I'm not sure," Chloe said slowly. "She just makes me think it would be a good idea for you to watch your back."

That was advice that was easy to accept. "I already do, Mom."

Chloe was parked on the street, halfway between The Sandwich Hut and the NIT building. When they reached her car she wrapped Faith in a big bear hug. "I'll see you in a couple of weeks, sweetheart. Wish me luck!"

Faith hugged back. There was no point in suggesting Chloe shouldn't go. When she was set on her path, nothing would stop her. "I love you, Mom."

"Oh, I love you too, sweetheart. I'll miss you!" She kissed Faith, then opened the car door. "Now remember—be more open! I've got to go!"

# CHAPTER 4

Faith studied the spreadsheet on her computer screen. There was a discrepancy here, she was sure of it. She hadn't found it yet, but she would. Part of her job was to check the expenses of the various NIT projects, ensuring the budget for each was followed. She also chased down suppliers, kept track of the staff and performed a myriad of other duties. Pretty much anything that had to be fixed went to Faith. And today that meant figuring out why a major project was two hundred thousand over budget at such an early point in its existence.

The variety in her job was what she loved best about it. That and the authority she'd been given when she started and the respect she'd earned since being hired straight out of college by the company founder, Ralph Warren.

She had graduated with high marks, but little experience, a lot of enthusiasm and an enormous desire to contribute. On her first day Ralph had met her enthusiasm with a whole mountain of his own, told her she needed to create a filing system and asked her to hire an accounting clerk who could also be the receptionist. As an afterthought he asked her to okay a salary range for the new hire with him before she made an offer.

In those early days there were no job descriptions at NIT and damn little structure. Everyone did what had to be done for the company to survive. Salary was a combination of a monthly paycheck, annual bonus and, when things were really tight, shares in the company in lieu of hard cash. In those days you had to believe in NIT to stick around.

Faith stuck. So did the woman she had hired in that first week. June McGuire was now more of Faith's assistant than a clerk-receptionist, but she still kept an eye on staff comings and goings.

Faith tapped the desk with the tip of one finger. She still hadn't found out how the project was so far off target. Budget estimates were what NIT used to create a project bid. If they won the contract they were expected to stick to their bid totals, unless the customer requested significant changes.

Maybe that was it. Maybe there were new requirements that were more costly. She contemplated the staff telephone list pinned to her bulletin board. Who was the project manager again? Oh, yeah, it was—

There was a tap on her door. Pulled from her reverie she looked up to see June hovering in her doorway. Perfect. "June! What do you know about the ArcPAC job?"

June slid through the door. Standing with her hand on the handle, she said, "They're on time and over budget. Herb thinks they can make up the budget difference in the second leg of the project."

"Two hundred thousand, June. That's a lot over budget."

June glanced out into the general office, then deliberately closed the door. "Herb says that his estimates were rounded down before the bid was submitted."

That explained why June had shut the door. When NIT was preparing a bid, project managers created an action paper that included project strategies and outcomes, as well as a detailed budget. The executive committee, consisting of Ralph, the Chief Financial Officer, the Director of Sales, and Ava as the COO, then reviewed and sometimes revised the action paper.

Evidently a mistake had been made in the ArcPAC project during the review process. That June felt she had to close the door to mention it spoke volumes about the way NIT was evolving as a company.

"Okay, we'll keep an eye on it. If the project continues to be over budget I'll have to talk to Ava or Ralph."

June nodded. "Faith, have you got a moment?"

Faith sat back. June leaned against the door, her hands behind her, evidently still holding the handle. "Of course I do." Faith pointed to a chair. "What's up?"

June left the door and began to pace. "It's Angela. Her computer went down this morning just after we got in...

Faith nodded. "I called Cody Simpson to ask him to check it out."

"I know. The thing is, he hasn't come yet and Angela has filed her nails, gone on a long, long coffee break, called her mother, and her boyfriend, and her best friend, and who knows who else, and now she's playing computer chess on her cell phone." June's hands clenched into fists that she punched, one against the other. "So far she's had four opponents and she's beaten each of them. It's bad enough that she's playing games during office hours, but she's also wasting our time bragging about how quickly she won the games. Now she's even got a couple of the girls watching over her shoulder."

"Wow," Faith said. "It's only eleven o'clock. Angela sure gets a lot done when she's not working."

June stopped her pacing. She stared at Faith for a moment, then uttered a choked bark of laughter. Faith grinned at her.

June sank down into the chair. "I called Cody Simpson three times," she said, with a sigh. "His voicemail was on."

"Ava doesn't want us doing anything to fix the computers," Faith said, tapping her desk with a pen. "She says it's Cody's job and it's not efficient for us to do it ourselves."

June snorted. "How efficient is it for Angela to be filing her nails?"

Faith dropped the pen as she threw up her hands. "Not efficient at all. But I suspect there's more to this than fixing computers. I think Ava's making a point, establishing her authority, all that kind of stuff. So we're stuck with this regulation. Sue is gone for six weeks. We can cope for that long. Let's figure out a strategy to make this work."

June thought about it. "My frustration is the result of watching Angela goof off when there's a lot of other stuff she could be doing."

"Right," Faith said. "And if you're annoyed about it, so are other people. What we need to do is find things for her to do. Have her file for you, or input data on another terminal."

"I'll organize that," June said, looking brighter.

"Good. The second thing we need to do is to keep on top of the repair issue. Whenever Angela's machine goes down I want updates on the status." June nodded. Faith hesitated a moment, then plowed on, "I can't expect Angela—or anyone else—to spend half their day unable to do their job. Once the repair call is made I'll give Cody a couple of hours. If he doesn't respond by then I'll fix it myself."

"What about Ava's ultimatum?"

Faith raised her eyebrows. "What about it?"

By lunchtime Cody still hadn't arrived and Angela had filed the stack of contracts and contract correspondence June had given her. Faith sent her to lunch and decided to deal with the crisis herself. She waited until she saw Ava head out with Ralph, probably for a business lunch, then she settled at Angela's terminal and set to work.

She was still there when Angela came back from lunch and, wide-eyed, asked what Faith was doing. Faith ignored the question, instead demanding details on what Angela had been doing when the problem initially occurred. Angela told her, then parked herself on the edge of her desk and chattily told Faith what else she'd done to try and fix the computer before and after she'd called Cody Simpson.

"You've been at this for an hour," June said, from her desk nearby. She indicated the office entryway with a wary nod.

Angela cocked her head in an interested way. "What hour?"

"I gave myself an hour to get this done," Faith said. She had a sense of falling into a hole, then dug in a little deeper. "I asked June to let me know when my time was up."

Angela hiked herself further up on the desk, then crossed one leg over the other. Swinging her ankle back and forth, she said, "So it's a time management thing?"

"You could say that." Faith glanced at the doorway. Ralph and Ava could return at any time. Although she'd been nonchalant about her decision to flaunt Ava's rule, she really didn't want a confrontation with her over it. She could feel sweat beading on her forehead. "Okay. I think I've got it. I'm going to switch off your computer. Restart it, Angela, and let me know if everything is okay. If it's not I'll have to update Cody Simpson and see if he can suggest any other options."

Angela hopped off the desk. "Okay."

Faith stood up and eased away, wanting to run, determined not to.

She'd made it back to her office when June entered. "Angela's terminal is working fine. Ava came in just after she got it up and running again, so Angela looked busy and efficient." She grinned and gave Faith a thumbs-up sign. "Good work, boss."

29

After she'd disappeared from the doorway, Faith closed her eyes and resisted the urge to curse Cody Simpson to an eternity in a blast furnace.

~

By FRIDAY EVENING Faith was stressed over the Cody Simpson situation and needed to decompress. Friday was Andrew's night to visit and this week Liz had decided to join them, so instead of the lazy night she craved, she was entertaining. Again.

Liz arrived before Uncle Andrew and together they prepared lasagna, one of Andrew's favorites, and organized a spinach salad. While they worked Liz talked about the summer job she'd secured on a paleontological dig in China, which had recently fallen through. "Funding cut," she said, her expression drooping gloomily. "Not only would it have been an awesome experience that isn't going to happen now, but I'm going to have to scramble to find another position."

"That's tough." Liz was a graduate student in evolutionary biology at Harvard, where their mother taught American history. Unlike Faith, who had decided to go into business, Elizabeth was headed for a career as an academic, much to her parents' satisfaction. Her field was competitive, though, and she needed the on-site experience to get ahead.

Liz spent another minute brooding, then her green, almond-shaped eyes brightened. "Do you remember the paper I told you about last semester?"

Faith nodded as she shoved the lasagna into the oven.

"Well, my professor suggested I submit it to the annual dinosaur conference. I didn't think that it had a hope of being accepted but today I found out it was picked to be a poster paper! The presentation will be in New York in October."

Faith was genuinely pleased for her sister. Though they were competitors by choice, they were sisters by blood and in the end they stuck together. "What fabulous news."

"It doesn't make up for the China dig, but it helps." They settled at the big kitchen table to wait for the lasagna to cook. Liz said, "Okay, enough of my news. Let's hear what's up with you."

Faith didn't want to ruin the evening by talking about work, but Liz might be hurt if she refused to confide, so she shrugged and said, "I'm having a problem with a guy at work, Cody Simpson."

"Who's he? I don't think you've ever mentioned him before."

"I haven't. Cody is a mathematician and software engineer. We don't interact much. Usually I deal with Sue Green if I have any computer problems. But Sue was in a car accident, so now I'm supposed to go to Cody for help."

"So?"

Faith made a face. "So Cody Simpson is a jerk who is impossible to work with."

"What makes Cody Simpson so difficult?" Liz asked.

Faith opened the bottle of red wine she'd brought to the table and poured each of them a glass. "He won't do what I want him to."

Elizabeth began to laugh. "Is that all? Welcome to the real world, sis."

Faith bristled. She couldn't help it. There was far too much snap in her voice when she said, "Cut it out, Lizzy. This has nothing to do with the real world and everything to do with a pampered geek who has never had anyone tell him he can't!"

Liz did stop laughing, but her eyes were still brimming with amusement as she said, "Wow, this guy really has gotten to you, hasn't he? Now why would that be?" She tapped her chin, pretending to ponder deeply. "Aha, I've got it! You don't like his glasses!"

"Who said he wore glasses? Actually, he has gorgeous blue eyes with thick black lashes," Faith said before she could stop to think.

Her sister's eyes opened wide and she sat up straight. "Faith, are you attracted to this guy? Is that what this is all about?"

"No, I am not and it is not," Faith said crossly. She wrapped her hands around her mug, seeking warmth and comfort. "Honestly, Liz, give it up! My problem with Cody Simpson is that I'm supposed to be delegating work in his specialty to him and he's supposed to be doing it. Instead, he's not and I am. And because I am and he isn't, I'm getting into trouble with Ava Taylor."

"I should have known Ava the Tyrant Lizard was involved somehow." Liz put her mug on the table then shook her head. "That woman plays you like a trumpet, Faith. She blows and you honk."

Faith thought, rather uncomfortably, that her sister might just be right, but she couldn't let her know it. "I do not!"

"Oh, did I misunderstand? Ava isn't in some kind of power struggle with this Cody Simpson and she hasn't put you in the middle of it?"

Faith sighed. "It's not that simple, Liz."

"What isn't simple? Cody Simpson didn't do his job, forcing you to cover for him. Who is at fault here?"

"I am. It's my job to get the best out of the employees. I'm supposed to motivate and direct them. I didn't do that with Cody Simpson."

"Does Cody Simpson report to you?"

"No."

"What is his job title then?"

Faith sipped her wine and took a long time answering. She could see where Liz was heading and she wasn't sure she wanted to go there. Finally she said with a sigh, "He's Director of Network Systems."

Elizabeth dove in for the kill. "Sounds pretty impressive. I'll bet he's even above you in the company hierarchy."

Faith sipped again, giving herself time. "The company doesn't believe in rigid management structures. The NIT philosophy focuses on teamwork. Each member of the team has equal weight and merit."

"Sounds like something Ava the Tyrant Lizard would say. When push comes to shove, who makes decisions? The mail clerk or the CEO?"

A little desperately Faith said, "The mail clerk is empowered to take responsibility for his own area, within the limits of his job description—"

Liz pounced. "My point exactly! Cody Simpson is not taking responsibility for his own area! He's refusing to cooperate with the rest of the team so he is the one at fault, not you! I rest my case."

She sat back looking so smug that Faith had to laugh. "The longer you go to university the harder it is to win an argument with you. You may be right. Cody Simpson could be the one at fault, not me. But the reality is that Cody Simpson is brilliant. He's important to NIT. Cody Simpson, the individual, would be difficult to replace. Faith Hamilton, on the other hand, is one part of a team. If I go, the team covers for me until someone replaces me. And I can be easily replaced. So Cody Simpson has to be coaxed into doing stuff he doesn't want to, while I..." She broke off, lifted her glass with careful deliberation, took a sip, savored the flavor. "I am expendable."

Liz captured her sister's free hand. "Sweetie, you are unique, way more than Cody Simpson is. If the people in your stupid company had any idea of your abilities—"

"They'd run screaming from the building." Faith gave her sister's hand a squeeze. "Thanks for your support, Lizzy, but I don't want anyone at NIT to know about my special...talent."

Sighing, Liz said, "You don't know how lucky you are, Faith. I would love to be able to do just a tiny bit of what you do."

Faith ran her finger over the rim of the coffee mug. "Liz, I want to be able to succeed in the real world. I don't like making mistakes—"

"Mistakes are one thing, Faith. What happened today is another!"

Faith held up her hand. "Perhaps getting chewed out by a superior doesn't matter to you, Liz. You're normal. You see the world differently than I do."

Liz's expression tightened. Regret, anger, and not a little jealousy lurked in her eyes and added an edge to her voice. "I know that."

Faith softened. "Yes, I know you do. Look, let's just leave it at that. I've got to figure out some way to make Cody Simpson work with me. A way that doesn't make waves but gets the job done." The oven timer beeped, alerting them the pasta was done. Faith glanced at her watch and frowned. "Uncle Andrew's late tonight."

"You're right." Liz stood up to get the salad, while Faith went to pull the lasagna from the oven. "I wonder what's up?"

"Well, at least we know he hasn't been in an accident on the interstate," Faith said lightly. "He's due to get married this year and he'll be survived by three children. Whatever is keeping him is just a minor problem."

"Like Cody Simpson!" Liz said, pouncing on Faith's last comment.

Faith made an unladylike sound. "Will you give it up, Liz? I get the picture."

"Well, you don't or you wouldn't be stressing about this guy."

Faith opened the oven door. While she was pulling out the pan she heard Elizabeth say, "Hey, Andrew! What's up, man?"

"Speak of the devil," Faith said, turning. "We were just talking about you, Uncle Andrew. What kept you?"

# CHAPTER 5

*A*ndrew dropped the leather satchel he was carrying onto the floor. Then he sauntered over to the table, pulled out one of the oak saddleback chairs and sank into it like a man familiar with his surroundings and comfortable in them. "Is that wine you're drinking, lass?" he said. When Liz nodded, he added, "Why then, I'll have a glass, if you would be so kind."

"I'm on it," Liz said. With a little sigh, Andrew leaned back in the chair and closed his eyes. He didn't notice when Liz set the full wineglass in front of him.

As Faith brought the lasagna and serving implements over to the table she observed her relative and decided he looked tired.

He also looked dirty. Come to think of it, he smelled a little ripe.

Andrew was a fastidious man. That was why he came to her house once a week to use her shower, the fine soap, and the special shampoo, not to mention the electric razor she'd bought for him. He regularly dropped his suits to be dry cleaned, much to the fascination of Faith's cleaners, but she drew the line at doing his laundry.

In return he brought her organically grown fruits and vegetables packed with flavor Faith had never found in modern factory farmed produce. When the harvest came in Faith and Liz would eagerly await his arrival and Andrew would laugh as he watched them wolf down his offering.

At the sound of the pan settling on the table Andrew opened his eyes and sat up, visibly shaking off his fatigue. He noticed the wineglass and picked it up. A man from a more formal age, he thanked Liz with practiced ease before he drank. He expected certain rituals to be observed, no matter what the time or place. "Ahh," he said after taking a sip. "So civilized. Thank you, lass."

"You're late tonight," Faith said. She nodded toward her sister. "We were just talking about it."

"One of the cows was in calf, early I might add. It put a crimp in my style, as you lovely lasses say." He drank deeply and sighed again. "Birthing a calf makes a man's bones ache, it does."

"Think of how the cow feels," Liz muttered.

Andrew flashed her a wicked grin, his gray eyes sparkling with mischief. He wagged his finger at Elizabeth. "Mind you don't mock your old uncle, now, when you've no notion of what he must endure in his own time."

Liz wiped a nonexistent tear from beneath her eye. "Ah, poor Uncle Andrew."

Andrew wagged his finger again, pretending to be stern. The sleeve of his white linen shirt, which had been rolled up to the elbow, loosened. As it slid down to his wrist the flounce that took the place of a cuff fluttered around his hand. He lifted the wineglass, but before he sipped, he said, "Mind your manners, girl. Without me you wouldn't be here."

For a moment, as he observed them over the rim of the glass, Faith had a sudden uncomfortable memory of Cody Simpson watching her over his much more pedestrian coffee mug that day she went up to his office. The two men were of an age—she knew Andrew was just past his twenty-eighth birthday and she guessed Cody was somewhere between that and thirty. Physically they were completely different, however. Cody was tall and lean, while Andrew was medium height and stocky. There was something in that look, though, something that linked the two men in a way she couldn't quite pinpoint. A sense of confidence, perhaps? Of knowing yourself and feeling comfortable in your own skin?

Unsettled, she stood up to get herself a refill on the wine. She brought the bottle over to the table, then sliced the lasagna and dished squares onto plates. "So how is the cow?" she asked as she passed around the plates.

"A proud mother. Both cow and calf are doing well," Andrew said in a satisfied way. "Did you replenish the liquid soap, Faith, the way I asked you to last week?"

Faith laughed. "What if I forgot? Would you go home and use the basin in your room to wash instead of my shower?"

Andrew placed picked up his cutlery as he sent her a disappointed look. "Now you know I enjoy the use of your wonderful bathroom, girl. It's a luxury to me, truly it is. The cranberry soap is just…a little bit more of a luxury."

Faith shook her head, but she was smiling. "Andrew, the next thing you'll tell me is that you come visit me for the pleasure of my company, not to use the bathroom."

"We've been friends for years," he said, a little defensively. He sliced his pasta and popped the piece into his mouth. "Delicious!"

"I was thirteen when you traveled here for the first time," Faith said. "I can still remember thinking you were wearing funny clothes."

"And I thought you had long hair like a girl's," Liz added.

Andrew looked down at the white linen shirt and the brown

breeches below it, and said, "What's wrong with how I dress? My clothes proclaim me for the substantial landowner that I am."

"You're a farmer," Liz said.

"There's nothing wrong with what you are wearing." Faith smiled at him mischievously. "Unless you're traveling through time and you've come two hundred and forty years into the future. Then you look a little odd."

Andrew rubbed his cheek, which was dark with evening stubble. In addition to his shower, Andrew usually shaved when he visited. "You've a point there, lass. Still, I don't leave your house, so no one is the wiser." He nodded, satisfied he'd dealt with that issue. He turned to Liz, now prepared to answer hers. "In 1772 it is not your occupation that makes the difference, but the size of your property. And mine," he added with considerable smugness, "is extensive."

Faith regarded her ancestor seriously as cut into her own lasagna. "Which is why no one is surprised that you wash frequently with soap delicately scented with the tart fragrance of cranberry. We hope. Andrew, isn't this regular trip to the future dangerous? Don't you ever worry that people will start to wonder what you do on Friday evenings when you disappear from your house?"

Andrew impaled her with a sharp, assessing gaze that made her think, once again, of Cody Simpson. "Are you trying to tell me something I am not supposed to know, Faith?"

*You must never reveal the past.* Faith could hear her mother's warning ringing in her ears as clearly as it had the day Chloe Hamilton had watched her best friend and distant ancestor return to her own time and a certain death from an infection that could be easily cured in the twenty-first century. The weight of knowledge, the despair of a loved one lost, were there in Chloe's voice and they echoed in Faith's mind now. She shook her head. "I don't hint, Andrew. We've been friends too long for you to think that I would."

He grinned at her, unrepentant. "A fellow can try, can he not?"

Faith raised her brown at that and conversation dwindled as they focused on the meal. When his plate was clear, Andrew stretched with the satisfaction of a well-fed cat. "I must make my ablutions and be off, Faith. Otherwise, you may find me nodding over my plate."

"Because of the cow, no doubt," Liz said dryly.

"Ah. Well now, not quite."

She leaned forward and made a waving motion with her hand. "Come on, give. What's up?"

Andrew looked from one sister to the other. Then he too leaned forward and whispered in a conspiratorial way, "I was trysting with Mary Elizabeth Strand last night. A fine, bonny lass she is and I believe she is quite taken with me, though her father disapproves."

"Who is her father?" Faith asked, carefully casual.

"George Strand. He is an agent of the King, collects the taxes in Boston town." Andrew sniffed, making his opinion of George Strand's occupation clear. "Bought himself a section of old man Abnernathy's farm adjacent to mine and moved his wife and daughters there a month ago."

"Were the Strands the neighbors you mentioned last week?" Faith asked, hoping she only showed polite interest.

"Aye, they are." He added in a disapproving tone, "I think Strand's got himself a mistress in Boston town and wants his family safely tucked away while he plays." He cocked an inquiring eye at Liz, then Faith. "I've no proof of that, mind." Both women kept their expressions bland. Andrew sighed. "Well, it's not as if I'm gossiping, now, is it? Neither of you ladies can tell the neighbors what I've said."

He stood, picking up his bag. "Time to bathe and be gone. I thank you for the dinner, Faith, lass."

Faith and Liz cleared the kitchen and talked about weekend plans until they were sure the shower was running and they could hear Andrew singing lustily under the spray. Then Liz turned to Faith. Her eyes were dancing with excitement. "We were right! Mary Elizabeth Strand is the woman he marries, isn't she?"

"Yup."

"Oh wow," Liz said. "And if history is right, while he's busy trysting with Mary Elizabeth..."

"Her tax collector daddy is arranging for his daughter to marry someone who works for the King..."

"And not an independent colonist like Andrew. So daddy sets his thugs on Andrew..."

"But Andrew escapes his pursuers, proposes to Mary Elizabeth..."

"And they elope to New York City where they are married."

"They have three kids and also bring up his sister's children—including our great, great, great, grandmother—when she and her husband die from an unnamed disease." Faith concluded as she finished the loading the dishwasher.

Liz handed her the box of dishwasher powder. "This is it, then," she said, flashing a grin.

Faith nodded. "It's all begun." She switched on the dishwasher.

A half-an-hour later, Andrew wandered into the living room where Faith and Liz had settled. He was wearing a freshly ironed linen shirt, tied at the neck with a black band and ornamented by a fine lace fall. Over the shirt he had donned a white silk waistcoat. His breeches were black, the buttons at the knees gleaming silver. He crossed to Faith. "Thank you, my dear, for the use of your delightful bathing chamber."

"I thought you were tired," Liz said, as she watched him kissing her sister on the cheek.

He straightened. "The elegant surroundings have revived me."

Faith watched him as he sauntered to the center of the room. His square jaw was clean-shaven, his dark hair still damp from the shower, and he smelled tantalizingly of cranberry. There was no way poor Mary Elizabeth would ever be able to resist him, even if she wanted to.

"I have left my breeches and two fine shirts in your bathroom, Faith. Would you mind having your cleaners see to them?"

"No problem."

"My thanks." He stepped back and shrugged into the coat he had on his arm. It was dark green velvet picked out with silver braid. "How do I look, ladies?" he asked, as he flicked the ruffles that finished his shirtsleeves free of the deep cuffs of the coat.

He looked what he was—not just a hard working farmer, but a prosperous eighteenth century gentleman fashionably dressed for an evening out. The clothes should have looked ridiculous, but they didn't. They suited him, giving him a devilish air that was extremely appealing.

Liz shot him a glance that was close to a leer as she watched him pick up his bag. "I think you've got a hot date with Mary Elizabeth again tonight."

Andrew shot her one of his roguish smiles. "Or something." He executed an ornate bow that involved much bending and hand waving. "Your servant, ladies," he said.

"Bye Uncle Andrew," Liz said, blowing him a kiss.

Andrew grinned.

Faith said, "See you next week, Andrew."

He nodded, turned, took two steps...

And disappeared.

Faith sighed. "That man is heading for trouble."

Liz laughed. "He is so great. He makes me wish I was born in the eighteenth century, just to meet a guy like him."

Faith sighed again. "Don't get me wrong, Liz. Andrew is a very dear friend, but he's why I can never be normal."

"Why would you want to be normal, Faith? You have a special ability. You're a Beacon. Enjoy it! In fact, think of me. I'm the only one in the family who doesn't have the ability and I wish I did."

"Dad doesn't have it."

There was an uncomfortable silence. Faith's ability to guide people through time was a family talent she'd inherited from her mother. Her father, Daniel Hamilton, had never been comfortable with his wife's talent and when Faith reached her teenage years and proved that she too was a Beacon, the fragile bonds that kept the marriage together broke. Daniel walked away from his eccentric family, keeping in close touch with his normal daughter, Elizabeth, but limiting contact with his odd ex-wife and equally strange older daughter, Faith. The pain of that abandonment still haunted Faith and was at the center of her need to fit in.

Liz leaned back in her chair and scrutinized her sister. "Okay. You'd prefer not to be a Beacon. So what are you going to do about it?"

"What can I do about it?"

"Good question. I don't think anyone has ever tried to stop being a Beacon, sis."

"Or if they have, they haven't explained how they did it," Faith said gloomily.

"Cheer up. Life with Andrew is about to get pretty interesting."

"So is life with Cody Simpson." Faith groaned and closed her eyes. "I feel like I'm in a car with no breaks. My life is suddenly out of control and there is nothing I can do about it."

Elizabeth came over to the sofa to give her a hug. "I've got to be off, but listen, don't sweat it. Everything will work out."

"Sure," Faith said, not believing it for an instant.

After Elizabeth had gone, Faith returned to the sofa and curled her legs beneath her. Propping her elbow on the arm, she rested her chin on her palm and stared unseeing at the fireplace. As long as she continued to have her ancestor travel through time to visit her she would always feel different from those around her.

Hell, she didn't just feel different, she was different!

So if she wanted to stop being different, if she wanted to fit into the normal world, she must stop Andrew from visiting her.

She sat for a long time with only the light from the hallway to relieve the darkness of the room. The gloom matched her mood. Andrew was a friend and in his way, he depended on her. What she was thinking of doing was a betrayal. Yet, if she didn't stop being a Beacon she would never have a normal life.

There was no easy answer. She hadn't expected there would be.

# CHAPTER 6

Faith stood at the bottom of the square, modern staircase that led to the second floor, looking up. She rubbed her temples with the tips of her fingers. It was mid-week and Angela's computer problems wouldn't go away. There had been incidents on both Monday and Tuesday, which Faith had sorted out when Cody didn't respond to requests for assistance. Each time had Faith looking over her shoulder, watching nervously for Ava Taylor to appear. So far she'd lucked out. Ava hadn't noticed.

But this had to stop and today was the day she was going to make that happen. She could do this. She would do this.

She started up the stairs. Got to the landing where the staircase broke to change direction. And stopped.

It would really be much easier to fix the problem herself. It would only take an hour or so. Maybe. She turned around, heading back down the steps she'd mounted.

"Looking for me?"

There was amusement in Cody Simpson's voice, curse him. He knew he was running her ragged over this computer stuff, but he didn't care. Oh no, he thought it a great joke. She had undermined her position with her staff, watched productivity fall, worked late to make up time, all because Cody Simpson refused to fulfill his responsibilities. Worse, he'd put her in the position of skulking around to avoid Ava as she defied the COO's edict that Cody was to fix all the computer problems that came up. And now she was here, on the stairs, in the embarrassing position of being caught obviously chickening out on her decision to climb up to his lair to confront him.

Slowly she turned. He was standing on the landing, effectively towering over her. To look him in the eye she had to tilt her head back to the point where she figured she'd fall over if she leaned back any further.

It was tough to exchange loaded comments with a man who was not only taller than you, but was way taller. In fact, it was hard to talk at all with her neck bent back so far. She straightened up, squared her shoulders and said, "When you come down a step and stop standing over me like some avenging male deity, I'll answer that." Heavens, she sounded bitchy.

Cody raised his brows, but he came down to the step she was on. "Is this all right, or would you prefer I go down another couple?"

Now that sounded like a good idea. Much as she wanted to stay grumpy, Faith couldn't. The thought of Cody's dark head coming up to her chin tickled her sense of humor and she laughed. "I certainly would prefer it, but I doubt you'd be quite that accommodating."

He leaned against the builders' white wall, his broad shoulders emphasized by a t-shirt on which 'Red Socks Rule!' was written in bright red letters, while his dark hair and blue eyes were vivid above the navy color of the shirt. He shoved his hands into the

45

pockets of worn, rumpled jeans. "An interesting reading of my character."

"You're not exactly my favorite person right now."

He frowned. "Why? I haven't talked to you since last week."

"Exactly. I've been covering for you, Simpson. Fixing all the spreadsheet, word processing, and database problems you won't!"

"Thanks."

"Is that it? Thanks?"

He shrugged. "Should there be more?"

From the way his brows rose and his eyes frosted to an icy blue, he'd just uttered a challenge he didn't intend to back down from. Briefly Faith wondered if she was ready to meet him word for word, then she consoled herself that doing battle was not her style. Though Cody Simpson brought out confrontational elements in her personality she didn't know existed, she refused to sink to his argumentative level.

"There should be," she said coolly, "but I don't bother with expectations that can't be met."

The ice in his eyes frosted further, then amusement warmed and darkened the blue. "Well," he said, "that certainly puts me in my place."

Faith almost gasped. Almost. She was very proud that she managed to stifle the sound before it popped out. Cody Simpson was absolutely the most annoying man she had ever had to deal with, and that included that eighteenth century chauvinist, Andrew Byrne, and her constantly disapproving father. "I am tired of working late," she said. What she really meant was *I'm tired of looking over my shoulder*. That was an admission of failure she wasn't prepared to make, though.

"It does get to you after a while, doesn't it," Cody said in a way that suggested he felt a certain kinship with her statement. "Come in late the next morning if you can. It makes it easier to handle."

As if she had that luxury! Her job description said she had to be in the office by eight-thirty and stay until four-thirty. As the supervisor of a dozen support staff she had to lead by example. How could she expect her staff to arrive on time if she waltzed in halfway through the day? "Fascinating advice. My point is that I do not intend to continue covering for you, Mr. Simpson—"

"Doctor."

His gently spoken interruption stopped her mid-tirade. "Excuse me?"

"If you want to be formal I'm Doctor Simpson. I have a PhD in computer science."

Of course he did. That was probably in his job description. This discussion was going from bad to dreadful. She glanced at her watch. "Point taken, *Doctor* Simpson. It's been nice talking to you, but I have to run." She trotted down the stairs, well aware that he was following behind her at a more reasonable pace. Good manners and corporate policy said she ought to slow down and walk with him making pleasant small talk, but she just couldn't handle it. Not today, not with Cody Simpson.

It wasn't until she'd reached the security of her office, that she finally felt able to breathe a sigh of relief. When would she learn to listen to her instincts? The next computer that broke down, she'd fix. And the next, and the next after that. Ava Taylor could drop loaded hints about protocol and productivity into infinity if she wanted. Faith would handle her. She could not handle Cody Simpson. The less she had to do with that gorgeous, annoying—frustrating—male, the better.

CODY COULDN'T CONCENTRATE. He was meeting with Ralph Warren about the status of the network redesign and the new piece of software he was developing and he couldn't concentrate. Well, maybe that was because Ralph was cheerfully describing every stroke of his most recent golf game. Cody had never had much interest in golf, although he supposed a certain amount of mathematical precision would be needed to ensure the ball got to the pin. As well, it was a solitary sport, something that appealed to him, but it was usually played in groups, something that did not. Cody got his exercise jogging, swimming, and skiing, and he lifted weights to keep up his muscle strength. All were activities that he could do at his own pace, in his own time, and on his own. He didn't like the boundaries and ties that groups put on individual choices.

Ralph had whacked his way through the first nine holes and he was deep into his story. As he talked he occasionally patted the top of his nearly bald head. Once upon a time, at the beginning of the computer revolution, Ralph Warren had been a high tech guru. Part hippy, part geek, he'd sported long hair and brightly flowered shirts. He'd worked at a think tank that paid him lots of money, but didn't treat his ideas with the passion he expected. When the opportunity came, he'd slipped the traces of academia for the pure joy of creation and moved into the practical world where his ideas would have more immediate applications. The flowered shirts and long hair disappeared as he navigated the corporate world and by the time he started his own company he'd been all but bald and wore a suit and tie to work.

Ralph Warren rarely did any research now, but that didn't stop him from appreciating the kind of work Cody did. His scientific background combined with his corporate viewpoint also made him well aware of the benefits scientific breakthroughs could bring to his company. That was why he had hired Cody, provided him with a nice title, a big salary, and no responsibilities other than doing what he did best—research and development.

When the golf game was over, he and Ralph would spend the next two hours talking in the mathematical language both of them loved. In the meantime, Ralph's eyes gleamed as he described his weekend foursome. Clearly he had transferred the intensity he brought to his company onto his golf game. Cody figured he should be listening attentively, but he couldn't. There just wasn't enough thought-provoking material to keep his mind from wandering. Ralph was a decent guy, though, so he made the appropriate noises to indicate interest as he let his thoughts drift to more interesting places.

Or more interesting people. Like Faith Hamilton. An image of her on the stairs, her head tilted up, her deep-set gray-green eyes blazing, made him grin—almost. It wasn't the right place to laugh in Ralph's ever-lengthening story.

Faith Hamilton was a gorgeous woman. She was tall, just a few inches shorter than his six-two, and curved in all the right places. Her slacks had hugged her nicely rounded hips, while a knit top showed off her breasts and emphasized her narrow waist. He'd wanted to reach out, catch her around that waist and pull her close, then tilt up her heart-shaped face with its sexy, determined chin and kiss that wide, generous mouth until her full lips relaxed and responded under his.

Nice fantasy, but nothing more than that. Faith was far more likely to look down her straight, narrow nose at him, even though he was taller, than she was to kiss him back. She needed to loosen up if he was going to be seriously attracted to her.

Giving himself a mental shake, Cody also indulged in a rueful silent chuckle. Faith Hamilton was just about the most uptight woman he'd met since he left the computer software company where he'd worked before he earned his PhD. He knew her type. She was career-focused to the extent that all else took a back seat. She made rules and demanded that they be kept, then gave no quarter if they were not. She followed a rigid schedule and liked it. Orderly and punctual, she didn't have time to pause for a good laugh or to help another human being in trouble.

She was everything he was not.

Ralph was rambling toward the end of his story now. He was at the sixteenth hole and was six shots above par. That was pretty good, Cody thought, so the punch line should be coming up soon. Either Ralph won the foursome he was in by achieving some hugely difficult shot, or he ended up saving some poor sod from humiliating himself, causing Ralph to lose dramatically as a result of his good deed. It had to be one or the other because Cody couldn't see the CEO telling a story in which he ended up being less than the best.

Time to start paying attention to golf and stop thinking about Faith Hamilton. He knew women like Faith and he knew he couldn't compete with the structure they created around themselves. He didn't—couldn't—no, wouldn't—fit into their orderly lives and they weren't willing, or to be fair, weren't able, to change them. The type of woman who appealed to Cody was a free spirit who didn't object to chaos around her, who was loving, passionate and deeply committed to what mattered—people, especially the people she loved.

Faith Hamilton didn't fit that description and the eighteenth hole beckoned. He had another few weeks of having the woman on his tail, demanding he pay attention to software problems, then Sue Green would be back and he'd be off the hook. He could hang on until then.

Just.

THE NEXT COMPUTER problem occurred at nine-forty on Monday morning—Angela's computer again, of course! Faith was beginning to think that perhaps Angela's computer was suffering a nervous breakdown and needed to be replaced. After her run-in with Cody, she was damned if she was going to call him and ask for his help fixing the problem, though. She'd just do it herself and save the grief.

Disaster struck as she sat at Angela's desk, muttering under her breath and fighting frustration. Angela was peering over her shoulder offering suggestions and helpful hints that weren't helpful at all. Suddenly the secretarial bullpen became quiet as Ava Taylor walked up to Angela's desk and slowly came to a stop. "Faith! I did not expect to see you here."

What she actually meant was, *You're supposed to call in Cody Simpson to do this sort of thing. Why haven't you?* Faith could hear the words in every nuanced tone, beneath every innocuous word.

She straightened slowly as she abandoned the computer and its glitch. Angela would have to fend for herself. "Hi, Ava."

"I called your office, Faith. I wanted to talk to you." *But you weren't there. You were here doing what you are not supposed to.* Nuance said so much more than a simple word could.

Faith lifted her chin. "Then let's go to my office now and we can discuss what you came by to see me about. Angela, call Cody Simpson and ask him to come down and help you with this."

"But he won't come. You know that, Faith."

Faith glanced at Ava, wondering if she was getting the picture about Cody, but Ava's expression showed nothing but polite interest. Although her eyes...yes, her eyes burned with an expression that could only be called greed. Ava wanted to hear the company gossip. Heaven knew what she'd do with it once she had it. It was a scary thought.

"Try Doctor Simpson," Faith said. "I'll check back with you later to see how it's going." She rose before Angela could come up with another protest and led Ava back to her office.

"I thought you were going to alert Cody Simpson whenever there was a problem with one of the computers," Ava said as soon as the office door closed behind them.

"He's busy, Ava. It's easier to do it myself."

"I'm disappointed in you, Faith. That is not the kind of team spirit I know you are capable of."

That was a low blow. Faith could feel heat rise in her cheeks. "Ava, I am thinking about the best interests of the company. Dr. Simpson is doing important work. Why bother him with stupid little problems that are way beneath his skills?"

"I am well aware of the value of the work Cody Simpson is doing, but he is the head of our computing department and as such repairing the computers is his responsibility."

That surprised Faith, though she supposed she should have expected Ava to be rigid where Cody Simpson was concerned. "I take your point."

Ava peered at her from under furrowed brows, as if she couldn't quite believe Faith was giving in so easily. "So what will you do the next time one of the clerical staff has a computer problem?"

There were moments when Ava was too cute to swallow. Faith gritted her teeth and resisted the temptation to say that she wasn't a naughty preschooler. Instead she replied as politely as she could, "I'll call Doctor Simpson and ask him to fix it."

Ava nodded. She bared her teeth in a smile that could kill, but her tone was confused when she said, "Why do you keep calling him Doctor Simpson?"

"Because he told me that is how he should be addressed." Not quite true, but close enough.

Ava shot her another under brow look. "We are all on a first name basis at NIT."

"Of course," Faith murmured. She was not about to admit that she was the one who had decided to be formal with Cody Simpson. Let Ava assume what she wanted to.

"I believe you and Cody Simpson need a counseling session to help you work through your differences."

Alarm shot through Faith. The thought of sitting in a meeting room on one side of a table with Cody Simpson on the other and Mona, the Human Resources Manager, between them, telling them they needed to express their anxieties and be open about their conflicts, was truly terrifying. Or was it just too absurd to be contemplated? Faith didn't know. All she was certain of was that she didn't want to do it.

Ava must have been watching Faith's face and read her dismay. "There may be another way to handle the problem. In fact, it's the reason I wanted to talk to you this morning."

There was a tense silence until Faith finally said, "And that reason was?"

"You haven't replied to your invitation to the company picnic."

She hadn't? Could that be? She was certain she must have replied. She always went to NIT events and responded to the e-mail announcements as soon as they came into her mailbox. Ava had probably lost her reply and wasn't willing to admit it. Since she didn't want to get into an argument, she said, "Sorry about that, Ava," in as positive a tone as she could muster.

"Well?"

*Well what?* Faith searched her mind for Ava's meaning then suddenly realized she was talking about the invitation. "Oh, yeah. Am I coming to the picnic?"

Ava bestowed an indulgent smile on Faith. "Exactly. I think you should, Faith. You need to build more positive relationships with your fellow workers."

The last time Ava had given Faith a pep talk, she'd said that Faith was management and as such had to keep herself separate from the support staff she supervised. It would be nice if Ava could sort out her priorities.

Unaware of the negative thoughts running through Faith's mind, Ava continued on, "The picnic is an excellent setting in which to do this. The mood is relaxed, people are enjoying themselves, they are willing to see a side of their fellow staff members that they might not otherwise notice. I do hope you will reconsider your decision."

There was nothing to reconsider. Faith had planned to go to the company picnic all along. "Of course I'll come, Ava. I look forward to it."

Ava beamed. "Excellent! I know Cody Simpson will be attending too. I'll make sure you two have ample opportunity to get to know each other." She paused, tapping her lips with her forefinger as she thought. "Perhaps you could pair up in the volleyball tournament. That way you could work closely together as a team. Hmmm, I'll have to think about that. Hot dogs or hamburgers?"

Faith had been visualizing Cody Simpson dressed in shorts that showed off his long legs and a t-shirt that molded his chest in a very attractive way. The sudden change of subject left her bemused. "Excuse me?"

With an airy wave of her hand, Ava said, "Would you like hot dogs or hamburgers? I'm tallying the numbers today so that we can purchase the food. "Pop or juice? Salad or chips? Cheesecake or apple pie?"

"I'd like one hot dog, apple juice, salad and cheesecake, Ava. Anything else you need to know?"

"I think we've covered everything." Ava stood and headed for the door. There she paused and smiled, her hand on the knob. "Do try to work more effectively with Cody Simpson, Faith. I know you can do it, especially when the stakes are so very high."

# CHAPTER 7

*F*aith wondered about Ava's comment for the rest of that day and into the next. On the surface it sounded as if Ava was trying make Faith feel positive about a difficult situation, but the longer Faith considered it, the more she thought Ava's words sounded like a threat. But what kind of threat? Would she be demoted to the bullpen if she didn't have Cody Simpson do the computer jockeying? Or would Ava actually fire her?

*You're being paranoid,* she told herself. Of course Ava was not threatening her. Why would she? Ava was responsible for ensuring that the staff utilized their time as effectively as they could and she was just reminding Faith that there was someone else who would be better suited to fixing the bullpen computers. That was all. It was Faith's own need to do her job perfectly that was making her look over her shoulder.

Maybe that was it. Maybe she just needed some balance. On the one hand she had Ava demanding utter conformity to procedure. On the other was Cody Simpson whose organizational style seemed to be benign anarchy. Somewhere in between was Faith, who believed in empowering people and flexibility. With two powerful personalities, each with a conflicting style, pulling at her from either direction, she wasn't in a position to achieve balance on her own. She needed input from outside. She chose Liz.

They met after work on Wednesday. "Great idea to take in a movie, Faith," Liz said as they stood in line outside the multiplex theatre. She flexed her shoulders, rolling them back and forth with a sigh. "I've been analyzing dinosaur footprints all day, trying to determine behavior patterns and how they relate to modern herd animals. There was a moment this afternoon when I realized I'd been sitting hunched in the same position for over an hour. I thought the muscles in my shoulders and back had frozen into one solid block I was so tense. A night away from technical details is just what I need."

Faith laughed as she bought the tickets. "I'm a little tense myself. There's so much stuff going on at work I sometimes wish I could just disappear."

Fifteen minutes later, burdened by extra large buckets of popcorn, liberally spiced with assorted seasonings, and waxed beakers of high-calorie pop, they settled into the perfect seats. Dead center, three rows from the front, the location provided the maximum sensory overload and had been the sisters' favorite theater seating since they'd been old enough to go to the movies on their own.

Faith slumped in her chair, leaning her head back so she could look up at the screen, which was only showing advertisements at this point. She stretched her feet out and began to munch her popcorn.

"So what's up?" Liz said, turning to view Faith as she popped a handful of popcorn in her mouth.

Faith glanced at her, then stared at an image of women's high fashion sandals, available only—so the ad said—at a national chain of popular shoe stores. Seen on the movie screen, each shoe was enormous and, with the high spike heels, vaguely phallic. Faith wondered if the makers of the ad had really intended for the product to relate to people on a sexual level or if her over active imagination was seeing something that wasn't really there. She certainly seemed to be thinking about sex a lot these days.

An image of Cody Simpson on the stairs, leaning against the wall, his torso beautifully filling out the dark blue t-shirt, slammed into her. She sat up abruptly. Her drifting thoughts had brought her to an unexpected place, one she didn't want to go to. "I think I'm losing it at work."

Liz raised her eyebrows. "Sounds dire."

Faith laughed at her sister's dry tone. "Doesn't it? I suppose it's not all that bad, but you know, Liz, I'm making mistakes. I've got Ava Taylor telling me we all have our job descriptions and mine doesn't include computer troubleshooting. Then I've got Cody Simpson, who's supposed to be troubleshooting, not doing it. And then there's Angela, whose computer should probably be replaced, but hasn't been, and that's out of my hands too. I feel like my department is falling apart and I'm not doing my job properly. I hate that."

Music blasted out of the sound system as the pre-movie entertainment shifted from the advertisement about shoes to one promoting the soundtrack of the film they would soon be seeing. Liz glanced at the screen, ate popcorn until it was quieter, then said, "Ava the Tyrant Lizard has been harassing you since she was hired, but what's Cody Simpson been up to? Fill me in."

Faith shot her sister a disapproving look. "I've never described Ava as a tyrant. Or a lizard."

Liz laughed. "I like to call her that because she reminds me of the largest of the dinosaur predators, good old tyrannosaurus rex. He was big and dangerous, but not as smart as the raptors, which were half his size. That's the way I see Ava, mean and ruthless, but not very bright, like some corporate hatchet man out of the eighties. I thought those types had died out with the turn of the millennium."

"She's not a hatchet man—person," Faith said, not quite sure why she was defending Ava.

Liz grinned mischievously. "I guess that means she's mutated into another form, like birds evolving from dinosaurs. Now she's the company tyrant."

Faith snorted. Liz laughed again. "Tell me something. Does Ava have a computer background?"

"No. She's got a business degree, like I do."

"Ahh," Liz said, tilting her head back and dropping popcorn in her open mouth. Faith thought she looked remarkably like a baby bird being fed by its parent. Liz washed the popcorn down with a sip of pop. "Ava the Tyrant Lizard must hate that."

Faith shook her head. "You're not making any sense, Liz. What would Ava hate?"

"Being different."

"Get off it! She's not different, not the way I'm different! She just has different skill sets than Cody Simpson's. Why would that make her so insistent he has to be the one to do what amounts to a technician's job? It doesn't make sense."

"Back up a step," Liz said. "How important is Cody Simpson to NIT?"

Faith frowned, then shrugged. "Pretty important, I guess. Ralph used to do a lot of the software design, but he's focused on sales since Cody was hired. I don't get into the technical details, but we've expanded and I know that there was hot competition for at least one of the contracts we recently won. Whether NIT got the contract specifically because of Cody's work, I don't know. I'm not part of the executive committee."

"But Ava the Tyrant Lizard is." Trailers for the movies appearing on other screens in the multiplex were now being shown. It wouldn't be long before the movie began. Urgency added impact to the rest of Liz's words. "Sounds to me like you've got yourself into the middle of a power struggle between the big guys. My suggestion to you?"

The in-complex trailers shifted to ones for upcoming films. The movie was next. Once it started their conversation was over. Faith nodded. "Tell me."

"Act like one of those cute little rodent-sized mammals from the dinosaur age. Burrow deep and keep your head down. Let the overgrown tyrannosaurs fight it out between themselves."

As advice went it was pretty sensible stuff. The trailer ended. The screen flashed dark. In the moment of silence before the new images began, Faith said quietly, "Cody Simpson isn't a tyrant. He's a pain, but he's not like Ava."

"Whoa!" said Liz. "Where did that come from?"

The screen burst into life as the movie started. Faith was relieved she wouldn't have to answer her sister's question.

Because the only answer she had was a disturbing one.

She wasn't constantly thinking about Cody Simpson because he refused to do the job Ava had assigned to him. She was aware of him on another level, a personal level that had allowed physical attraction to slip past her barriers.

Not a reassuring scenario. So how should she handle it?

As the credits splashed across the screen, she slumped down in her seat. Maybe Liz was right. Burrow deep and keep her head down.

THURSDAY WAS ALMOST over when Angela appeared in Faith's doorway. From the chagrined expression on her face Faith guessed she'd done it again. "What's up?"

"I typed the letters you assigned me into my computer." Angela's pale features didn't register an expression, but she leaned her body against the doorframe with a lazy sensuality Faith had never noticed before.

She gave herself a mental shake. Last night she was fantasizing about spike-heeled shoes. Today she was looking at one of her clerks and seeing her in an entirely different way. Angela was one of those people who never stood out. Her straight hair was a true, pale blond, but it lacked vibrancy. Her body was the same way, not too tall and not too short. That pretty much defined her manner as well—pleasant, undemanding, unassertive. If there was any sensuality in her movements, it was because Faith had imagined it, not because it was really there.

Dragging her thoughts back to Angela's comment, Faith said briskly, "Good start. I assume there's more?"

Angela straightened. Clasping her hands together and holding them in front of her in a prim way, she said, "I was going to print them off, but..."

"Let me guess. Your computer froze. It lost the letters. It exploded in a hail of shrapnel that took out all the lights in the office and there was a major panic..."

Angela's eyes widened to round saucers, then she giggled. "No one was hurt!"

"That's good to hear." Faith shot her a considering look. "So what happened?"

"Well, you were right, sort of. My computer refuses to print them. I've tried everything I can think of, but still it won't work. Can you fix it?"

With Ava's sweetly uttered command still fresh in her thoughts and Liz's practical advice to keep her head down, Faith was not about to allow herself to become involved in fixing what sounded like a reasonably simple problem. "I'll call Cody Simpson and ask him to come down."

A sudden intelligent gleam brightened Angela's eyes. Evidently she didn't expect Cody to show up anytime soon. "If he doesn't come can I go home early?"

"Do you have any time owing to you?"

Angela shook her head.

"Then no. Take the opportunity to clear up your desk and see if there is any filing to be done around the office."

Angela's plain, undemanding features screwed up into a temperamental expression that on another woman Faith would have described as a pout, then she stomped back to her desk in a way that looked remarkably like a flounce. Faith reflected that she was only a year out of school. She supposed it was as good an excuse as any for having a hissy fit in the office.

She called Cody, reached his voicemail—of course!—and left a message explaining the problem and asking him to come down and fix it. Then she went back to work.

Her first inkling that something odd was happening was about five minutes later. Her office door opened out into the bullpen, but her desk faced the window with its panoramic view of the parking lot, so she heard what was going on rather than saw it. Usually there was a low murmur of sound as people exchanged information relating to their jobs. Occasionally, there was laughter and very rarely, when something out of the ordinary happened, there was an excited babble.

Like now.

Over the next couple of minutes the volume rose. Mystified, Faith went to her doorway. From her viewpoint all she could see was that the whole place seemed to have congregated around Angela's desk.

And they were giggling.

She had a bad feeling about this. Had Angela gotten bored and decided to access the net? Had she found a site that featured beef-cake photos? The local firemen did a calendar every year that Liz loved, because the firemen had such outrageously gorgeous bodies. Maybe they did a website too. And maybe Angela had found it...

Or maybe not.

One of the women crowding around the desk moved away, allowing Faith a clear view of the person sitting in Angela's chair. And it wasn't Angela.

It was a man. A man with dark hair, wearing a shirt that fit across his broad, muscular shoulders in a way that made a woman want to rub her hands along it. A man with dark hair, working on a computer. Was it possible? Had Cody Simpson actually descended from his secluded office to fix a lowly word processing clerk's computer?

The group shifted again and Faith's amazement grew as she saw that Angela was perched on the edge of her desk in a way that could only be called flirtatious. She was leaning toward Cody, watching him. From time to time she touched her dress, smoothing the fabric against her thighs. A little bemused at the difference a man could make, even in a timid soul like Angela, Faith observed the scene unabashedly.

Cody typed furiously on the keyboard. Dialogue boxes appeared and disappeared. He asked Angela a question. She pouted and shrugged. More dialogue boxes flashed on the screen and then he said, "I think that will fix it for awhile, Angela. Just be sure you don't..."

It had taken Cody all of ten minutes to fix the glitch. Faith glanced at her watch. It was twenty-eight minutes after four. Wow, thanks to Cody Simpson she really was going to get away on time. There was a spring to her step as she retreated to her desk to log off her computer and lock up.

In the bullpen the female giggles were joined by a deeper male voice. Faith frowned. Was Cody Simpson flirting with the clerks? She went back to her task. If her staff wanted to flirt with Cody and he with them it was none of her business. It was four-thirty, quitting time. They were no longer her responsibility, any of them...

"Good. You haven't left yet."

Faith was so deep into her mental meandering that she shrieked and jumped up, knocking her chair, which wheeled away leaving her teetering precariously on the edge of falling on her backside. Cody leapt forward, caught her by the arm and steadied her.

"Thanks," she said, a little breathlessly.

"Sorry about that." He spoiled the effect of the apology by frowning at her and adding, "I didn't think I moved that quietly."

Faith took a deep breath to steady herself. "I was going over what needed to be done and planning my day tomorrow. I tend to be pretty focused." No way was she going to admit she'd been thinking about him.

He nodded, accepting her explanation. Not surprising, since he was known to concentrate on a project so intensely that he might not emerge for hours on end.

"I found the problem in Angela's computer."

"Oh?" Another thing she did not intended to tell Cody was that she, like the rest of the women in the office, had been watching him work. He had a big enough ego as it was.

"It's a simple problem, operator generated."

She frowned at that. "So you're saying that Angela causes her problems by something she does?"

"You've got it. What's more, I think she does it intentionally."

Faith was so astounded her jaw dropped. She couldn't help it. "Angela? Angela who types correspondence for everyone in the office? Angela in the bullpen?"

He nodded.

Faith laughed. "Give it up, Cody! Angela is a timid little mouse who would never intentionally disrupt anything because she'd be too scared of making waves." Faith had an uneasy memory of

Angela propping up her doorframe, then later, leaning toward Cody, her hand on her thigh, her expression worshipful.

Cody had raised his brows. Perhaps he was visualizing the same behavior that Faith was. "Angela likes the attention she gets when her computer goes down. It breaks up the monotony, makes her day more interesting. Sue was tracking her requests for assistance. Before Sue's accident Angela was calling once a week, usually on a Friday, often just before lunch, but not always." He stopped when Faith sucked in her breath. "Ah, I've hit a nerve."

Now that he mentioned it, Angela would often say that her computer was down just before she took off for lunch. She even said it was terrific timing as it could be fixed while she was away from her desk. Sometimes she returned within her usual forty-five minutes, others she was a few minutes late. It wasn't a big issue when her workstation was occupied by Sue Green and she'd only be standing around looking useless anyway.

Faith remembered Angela's request just a half-an-hour before. *Can I go home early?* Anger began to replace shock. How long had Angela been playing her this way? True, when Sue was there the staff were encouraged to call her themselves, rather than go through Faith. That meant that Faith couldn't be expected to know of every problem that occurred. But still, it was her job to manage the clerical and secretarial employees. In Angela's case she had clearly failed.

"It's harmless stuff," Cody was saying. "I made a big deal of going into the code on her computer and messing around in it. She thinks that I've made it problem-proof so for a while there won't be any more disasters. She's pretty bright though. She'll figure it out soon enough."

"Great," Faith muttered. "At least I'm on to her now."

Cody rubbed his hand down her arm and Faith suddenly realized that he hadn't moved since he'd valiantly kept her from falling on her behind. Not only hadn't he moved, but he was standing so close that she could feel his body heat and smell the clean male scent of him. Her stomach knotted unexpectedly as her heartbeat sped up.

"I know your instinct is to pounce on the kid and send her packing," he said, "but I think that would be a mistake."

She looked up into his eyes. They were a warm, caring blue. For Angela? Or for Faith? "Why?"

Almost absently his hand slid down to hers and his thumb stroked small circles on the back of her hand. "I think she's being under-utilized. She probably needs the job so she's sticking it out, even though she's bored. Find her something more challenging and I believe she would make an excellent employee."

With Cody caressing her hand and smiling at her in a way that was entirely too enticing, Faith was ready to concede pretty much anything. She felt the same way she did when she'd had too much wine on an empty stomach. Giddy. Delighted with the world and everyone in it. Irresponsible. Above all she wanted those euphoric feelings to continue forever.

She pulled her hand away and stepped back. With feigned composure, she gathered her purse from her desk drawer. That done she headed for the door, a clear and final dismissal to Cody Simpson. "I'll monitor Angela for the next few weeks. Thanks for the heads up Cody." She paused at the opening to her office so he could precede her into the now quiet bullpen.

He waited for her as she locked her door, clearly intending to walk out of the office with her. He was standing very close, making Faith feel as if she was off balance, not quite in control. She didn't like the sensation. "It would have been nice if you and Sue had included me in the loop on Angela."

He shot her a guarded look. "How so?"

"You could have shared your suspicions." Faith heard the tension in her voice. She took a deep breath as she struggled for control. Losing her temper with Cody Simpson hadn't done her any good so far. "Had I known, I could have checked on her from my end. As it is, what you've just told me has come as a complete surprise."

"We had suspicions, with no evidence to support them!"

Faith could hear the frustration of the scientist in his voice. A hypothesis had to be made, data gathered, and a theory formed before action could be taken. That was the way he'd been trained and even in matters of personnel he wasn't prepared to abandon the process and go with his gut.

He was just like her father, grounded in a methodical world where everything had an explanation and nothing happened magically.

They reached the door to the outer office. After they exited Faith locked that door too. Then she stood with her back to it and surveyed Cody Simpson. "So why did you decide to say something now?"

He shoved his hands into the pockets of his jeans. "I discovered a pattern and once I'd found that, I analyzed it and drew a conclusion. It seemed to fit so I thought you ought to know about it. Like I said, I've dealt with my end of it. If you handle yours, I think Angela's computer problems will be a thing of the past."

He was standing in front of her, tall and strong and far too good-looking for a computer nerd. A promise hovered on the tip of her tongue. *Of course I will! Smile at me one more time and I'll agree to anything.* She slung her purse on her shoulder and said, "I'll think about it. Right now I don't feel too positive about Angela."

His eyes searched her face, almost intimately. "I can understand that." Then he grinned. "She's a total pain. Smart people often are."

Faith made a derogatory noise in her throat. Before she could stop herself the words slipped out. "You ought to know."

For a moment he looked incredulous, as if he couldn't believe she'd dare describe him that way, then he laughed. "Me?"

*Yes, you!* Faith wanted to reply. Instead she eased past him as she said, "I've got to get going. Thanks for coming down to troubleshoot this afternoon."

He nodded and said, "No problem."

Faith could feel his eyes on her until she'd pushed her way through the door out to the street. It was an unsettling feeling that put her on edge.

Damn the man!

# CHAPTER 8

Cody Simpson had a way of getting under Faith's skin. That last comment of his about Angela made her doubt herself and her ability to do her job to the top-notch standards she demanded of herself. Could he have been right about Angela? Was she being under-used in her current job? If Faith accepted that possibility, then why hadn't she noticed it? Why hadn't she provided Angela with something more challenging to test her abilities?

As she tossed and turned, trying without success to get to sleep, she finally admitted to herself that it wasn't how well she was doing her job that was bothering her, it was how she appeared in Cody Simpson's eyes that had her restless. She wanted to wow him and the only way she could think of doing that was to be the most efficient manager to have ever graced an office building.

But why should she want to wow him at all?

She couldn't be attracted to him—she wouldn't allow it. Sure he was great to look at, but she didn't have relationships, especially with men schooled in the sciences. No, it must be something about his refusal to be part of the team. He was the outsider and she wanted to show him what he was missing. Sure, that was it. Simple. Now go to sleep!

The next day her mother breezed into the office as Faith was eating lunch at her desk. Faith shrieked and jumped up to hug her. "Mom, you're back! You're here. You're safe!"

"Of course I am." As the hug ended Chloe stepped back to observe her daughter. "Darling," she said with her usual extravagance, "you look tired and worn out. Why are you sitting here munching when you ought to be at a nice restaurant taking a much needed break?"

"I'm backed up. I decided I'd work through my lunch so I could leave the office at a reasonable time."

Chloe sat down rather gingerly on the small seat that served as Faith's guest chair. "There are some benefits to living in the twenty-first century. Office furniture isn't one of them."

Making a decision, Faith packed up her lunch. Chloe had a way of drawing a crowd and Faith didn't think she could handle listening to her mother chatting about her trip to Washington when anyone might drop in. "It's a nice day outside..."

"So it is! It was raining when I left Washington."

Faith eyed her doorway warily. "When did you get back, Mom?"

"Last night." Chloe leaned forward and lowered her voice in a conspiratorial way. "It was fascinating, Faith. Much more civilized than I expected, but appallingly brutal as well." A look of contentment crossed Chloe's face. "It was an amazing experience. Imagine being part of the Civil War! Experiencing what the people of the time did, but knowing, as they do not, what the outcome will be. I was hard put not to—"

"Mom, it's such a beautiful day and I haven't finished eating my lunch. There's a park not too far away with a bench. Let's go there and sit. You can tell me all about your—trip—while I eat." And her stomach wouldn't be in a knot because she was terrified someone might hear Chloe's wacky-sounding conversation.

Chloe looked down at her fashionable suit and patted her newly styled blond hair. "A bench, you say."

"I'll bring paper towels for you to sit on. How does that sound?" Since Chloe dressed to suit the time period she was visiting, she liked to be thoroughly modern when she was in her own era. As soon as she returned she always paid a visit to her hairdresser, then went out and indulged herself by purchasing the most up-to-date, vivid clothes she could find. This time the outfit consisted of a vibrant red jacket, teamed with a brightly patterned skirt. The blouse she wore under the jacket was an eye-popping citron yellow.

"All right," Chloe said, rising regally. "I still think you ought to be eating in a restaurant. What do you have left in your bag?"

"A half-a-ham sandwich, some cottage cheese and an apple. Are you hungry?"

"Famished."

"There's a vending machine in the lobby. We can raid it on our way out."

The machine dispensed chips, cookies and pop. Faith and Chloe bought samples of each then proceeded to the park. They found a bench near a bed of roses and while they lazily shared their meal they watched the bees energetically hunt for pollen among the fragrant flowers.

"This is a very unhealthy lunch," Chloe said, munching on a barbeque chip then dusting her fingers on one of the paper towels provided by Faith. "As a mother I should forbid you to eat such foods." She consumed more chips. "I have to admit, though, that I love these things, junk food or not. I really miss them when I'm away."

"Mom—"

Chloe swigged some pop from the can, then said, "I talked to

Liz. She told me about the problems at NIT. Is Cody Simpson that sexy, dark-haired man we met at the elevator before I went away?"

"Yes. And don't say anything about my package, Mom. There's nothing between us beyond a lot of office-based conflict."

Chloe looked seriously at Faith for a minute, then she smiled. "It's a beginning."

"No, it's not! Listen, Mom, you don't understand. It doesn't matter if Cody Simpson likes me. Or more to the point, if I like him. I can't get involved with a guy from the real world. Especially a guy like him."

"What do you mean, 'like him'?"

Faith stared at the cottage cheese container she was holding. She had to swallow hard to keep self-indulgent tears at bay. "He comes from the same world Dad does. And Dad couldn't accept us. He left us as soon as he was sure I was a Beacon. He dumped us, Mom, because we're different. Because we're weird."

"He didn't leave you, Faith. He left me. Don't blame yourself for your father's and my divorce, honey. We did that between the two of us."

Faith stared down at her spoon without seeing it. "I haven't seen him in three years, Mom."

"He travels a lot..."

"He visits Liz all the time!"

Chloe sighed. "Just because your father has a closed mind does not mean this young man, Cody Simpson, will be the same way."

Faith smiled humorlessly. "The odds are pretty good."

"Nonsense!" Chloe said. "You can't judge a person on what someone else has done. Cody Simpson may be a generous, open, thoughtful individual who is entranced by your ability."

"I can't take that chance," Faith said quietly. She put cottage cheese in her mouth and chewed without tasting. "Mom, I know you won't understand, but...I want to stop being a Beacon."

Chloe stared at Faith, saying nothing, her expression unreadable. She ate a chip slowly, apparently savoring the taste and texture, then she said, "It's a God-given talent, Faith, honey. If you were not a Beacon, you wouldn't be the person you are."

Faith took ate more cottage cheese. "How do I do it, Mom?"

"Elizabeth would love to have the ability."

Faith heard disappointment in her mother's voice and responded to it with an aggression that surprised her. "I wish Liz was the one who was the Beacon! Then I wouldn't feel as if I was caught between two competing worlds."

"Ah," Chloe said. "We've come to the cause of your feelings, I think. You're in the wrong job, you know. You need to find something where you can make use of your talent, rather than having it lurking behind you like a burglar toting a gun."

"The way you do, you mean? Going back into the past to experience history, then writing about it when you come back to your own time?"

Not only was Chloe Hamilton a tenured professor at the university, but she was considered to be one of the foremost experts on American history in the country. And in that other world, the one of time travel, Chloe Hamilton was just as formidable, for she was both a Traveler and a Beacon.

There was a faint smile in Chloe's eyes as she nodded. "Something like that."

"Can't you understand? I don't want to change my job. I like my job! I want to keep my job! That's the problem. With Andrew popping in at least once a week I'm afraid he'll somehow find out where I work and show up there. Poof! Suddenly there is a guy with long hair and ruffled shirtsleeves standing in my office. What do I do then?"

"You don't worry about it," Chloe said. She eyed her daughter. "You're crossing your bridges before you come to them, Faith. Andrew doesn't know where you work and he won't unless you tell him. Right now he appears in your living room because it is located in what was once a copse of trees on his farm. It's easy for him to get to you, so he does. He's not likely to go hunting for your business location. Why should he, when he can see you on Friday evenings and bathe in a luxury that is sinfully self-indulgent in his own time?"

"You're missing the point, Mom."

"So explain it to me." She finished the last of her chips and crumpled up the bag. Faith offered her the half sandwich, which Chloe took with a greedy pleasure. Faith finished the cottage cheese then bit into her apple.

While she chewed she tried to put her feelings into words. It wasn't easy. "Mom, I find being a Beacon stressful. It interferes with my goals. You tell me I should open myself up to new experiences, that I need to allow myself to get close to a guy. How can I as long as I am a Beacon and I might have Uncle Andrew show up at any moment? If I am to have any kind of life, I need to stop being a Beacon. I want it to go away."

Chloe finished the sandwich and discarded the wrappings into her chip bag. She wiped her fingers as she said, "It won't—go away I mean. To be a Beacon is a privilege that few people have. It is programmed into you at birth; it's not a learned skill. You are a Beacon, Faith, just as your eyes are gray and your hair is blonde and you stand five-foot-nine inches tall. It's part of you."

"Mom—"

"Hello, Faith."

Faith's body jerked with tension and she looked up with terrified eyes. "Ah, hi Cody." What was he doing here? And, oh my heavens, how much had he heard?

Well, the first one was easy to figure out. His long body was clad in runners, shorts and a t-shirt. A portable media player was attached to a black armband that peeked out from under a short sleeve. Clearly Cody was out jogging. He pulled his earbuds out as he spoke and swung them gently back and forth.

Though it was interesting to discover how Cody kept that excellent body of his toned and fit, Faith refused to be distracted by his appearance. She had to find out how much of her conversation with her mother he had heard.

She was staring up at him, trying to read his expression, when her mother cleared her throat and said, "We met once before, but I don't think we were introduced. I'm Faith's mother, Chloe Hamilton. And you are?"

Cody's blue eyes slid from Faith to Chloe and he smiled.

Boy, did he smile. Cody Simpson's smile could melt the polar ice cap, not that Faith was affected by it, but she could see that her mother was. Chloe was dimpling and—dear heaven! Was she flirting with him?

Cody laughed and introduced himself, apparently perfectly happy to have a woman old enough to be his mother make eyes at him. Faith glared at Chloe. Where had she learned that head tilted thing and looking up through her lashes? She had evidently picked up some very bad habits during her visit to the 1860s.

Still smiling, Cody looked over at Faith. "Hey, your mom is great, Faith. You should bring her to the picnic tomorrow."

When pigs could fly.

"What picnic?" Chloe asked, all innocence.

"The company picnic, Mom. It's for NIT employees only."

"That's the official word," Cody said. "But I'm told lots of guys bring their wives and kids. It's on a Saturday, which is family time, not company time. Ava the Oppressor ought to realize that when she makes an event a command performance."

"Is Ava an oppressor?" Chloe asked, interested. "Faith's sister calls her the Tyrant Lizard, but I thought that was because Liz is studying evolutionary biology and links all kinds of inefficient behavior to extinct creatures like the dinosaurs. Faith never confirms or denies."

"She's just trying her best, Mom."

Cody laughed. "Ava the Tyrant Lizard. I'll have to keep that in mind." He shot a sideways look at Faith. "I think Faith is more tolerant than I am. I'm not happy with Ava at the moment. I don't think she's doing her job and, to be fair, she doesn't think I'm doing mine."

Heat flooded Faith's cheeks as he eyed her. She moved her head, denying her reaction. Cody smiled.

He turned back to Chloe. "Faith is caught in the middle, I'm afraid. It's not fair to her, but then there's plenty of things Ava does that aren't fair."

"This is very interesting," Chloe said, looking from Cody to her daughter. "It helps me understand some of the problems Faith and I were just discussing."

"Mother!" Faith said loudly.

Chloe grinned mischievously. "My poor daughter would have a fit if I told you what we were talking about, so I won't. I won't come to the picnic either, though I can guarantee Faith will. She always goes to NIT functions."

"Cody doesn't care about what you and I were talking about," Faith said, having finally gotten over the shock of meeting Cody Simpson here.

Cody's brows shot up and he said, "I think that was a very broad hint that I'm not wanted. It was a pleasure meeting you, Mrs. Hamilton."

"What a nice young man," Chloe said, as both women watched his muscular form jog down the pathway.

"He's a computer geek and he's driving me crazy," Faith said. "When Sue Green gets back from her medical leave, he'll be out of my life. Forever."

Chloe shot her a speculative look. "Think so?"

"Yes, and you're crossing bridges that aren't even there."

Chloe laughed and didn't pretend to misunderstand. "Maybe. Maybe not."

# CHAPTER 9

"Fabulous day, isn't it?" Ralph Warren gazed around the park where the annual NIT company picnic was taking place. Ava had exceeded expectations this year, finding a location that boasted plantings of annuals and perennials, all in bloom; graveled paths that twisted through groves of evergreen bushes and lofty trees; and charming walkways under vines of jasmine and honeysuckle. As well, there were open areas where a croquet game had been set up and volleyball and badminton nets erected. In the center of it all was the NIT command post, where the beverages were laid out and the food was prepared. The whole event had an air of upscale, casual fun. Ralph was clearly very satisfied with everything about the party, including the weather, which had cooperated with warm temperatures and a bright blue sky, peppered with white fluffy clouds.

Faith smiled at him. Ralph had every right to be pleased. Back in the days when she'd handled all the management details except sales and promotion, she'd been the one to put this event together, so she had a good idea of what the elegant charm was costing—more than it had in the past, that was for sure. But then NIT had changed and grown so much in the last year that image had become an important component in the annual event. Trust Ava to understand and capitalize on that.

"I spoke to Grant Balfour and Jason Wong earlier. They were about to play volleyball against Ava and Angela. They all seemed to be having a terrific time." Balfour and Wong were info tech executives from two of their new long-term contracts. It had been Ava's suggestion that top-level clients be added to the guest list, to bring them into the NIT family, so to speak. Ralph loved the idea.

Now he nodded, suddenly serious. "I'm delighted to hear that. I must say, Ava excels at ensuring that NIT puts on the right corporate image. I think today she's outdone herself, though. Perfect weather, a great location..." This time his sweeping gesture was meant to encompass the park they had rented for the afternoon. "Wonderful food and drink—have you had anything to eat yet?"

Faith held up her glass, which had once contained lemonade. "I've already munched on a hotdog, thank you, Ralph."

He looked horrified. "Not just a hotdog, Faith. A gourmet European sausage. Surely you noticed the difference?"

Faith smiled, not about to argue. "It was delicious. I enjoyed it very much."

Ralph nodded. "I did too. A great choice." His gaze strayed, swept the crowd. "You'll excuse me, Faith?"

"Sure," Faith said to Ralph's retreating back. She scanned the crowd, found a likely contact and started networking.

An hour later she had chatted with three members of the Board of Directors, two senior engineers, the vice-president of marketing and the chief financial officer. Each conversation had included the weather, the charming location, the fabulous food, and what a great company NIT was.

Tired of mixing, she wandered over to the awning where Ava and her helpers had set up the food and beverage tables. Ava wasn't around, but her secretary, along with Ralph's executive assistant and the CFO's secretary were keeping the area tidy. Faith refilled her lemonade then asked if she could spell anyone. She wasn't surprised when her offer was cheerfully refused. She looked at her watch and decided she'd stick it out for another half hour, then be off.

Sipping her lemonade she glanced around. The volleyball game was underway in a grassy area some distance from the refreshment table. She could go over and cheer the teams on, but she might get pressured to join the game. Though the people playing were laughing, they were sweating too and wearing shorts and t-shirts. Faith glanced down at her crisply pressed linen slacks and silk blouse. She didn't see volleyball in her future.

She caught sight of Ava near an ornamental pond, talking to a new employee. A moment later Ava was on the move, dragging the new staff member behind her. Ava caught sight of another solitary employee and steered in his direction. Once she reached her victim, she made introductions and left with a wave, having successfully achieved her goal. Faith chuckled to herself. Ava playing hostess was a formidable sight.

And a dangerous one. Now on the prowl, looking for someone else who wasn't mixing, Ava would be onto Faith at any moment if she didn't appear to be busy. Faith was still uneasily aware that Ava wanted to use the picnic for a little lesson in Cooperation 101 between Faith and Cody. Since that was something Faith would be happy to do without, she checked for someone to mix with. She caught sight of one of the project managers looking a little lost and headed over in his direction.

They chatted about—what else?—the good weather, the tasty hotdogs, and the effort that had gone into putting on the party.

The project manager was one of the new employees hired as a result of the successful contract bids. Faith couldn't remember his name right at the moment, but he was friendly and as desperate for someone to talk to as she was.

The conversation passed a good fifteen minutes before it petered out as another of the new managers appeared and the two men began to talk shop. Faith did a quick scan for Ava, but couldn't see her anywhere nearby. She breathed a sigh of relief and decided that in another quarter of an hour she could decently head off. She was considering how she could safely pass the final few minutes when she heard Ava Taylor's voice behind her.

"Hello, Faith. Having a good time?"

Silently cursing her bad luck, Faith turned. "Lovely, thank you, Ava. You've outdone yourself."

Ava smiled, a little smugly. In shorts and a t-shirt, wearing tiny tennis socks and pristine white runners, she looked fashionable, tanned, and healthy. "I have an excellent team. They did all the hard work. Have you had a chance to talk to Cody Simpson yet today?"

Feeling overdressed and at a disadvantage, Faith said, "I haven't, no." She'd seen him just before she'd gone to the refreshment table, though. He was wearing his standard jeans and a t-shirt and a lock of his thick black hair had fallen over his forehead in a way that was far too attractive. Faith hadn't deliberately avoided him, but then she hadn't tried to connect with him either.

"You must," Ava said. Before Faith could react, Ava grabbed her arm. "Come on, I saw him over by the rhododendrons."

"Ava, what are you doing?"

"Making sure that you and Cody Simpson deal with your differences," Ava said, striding purposefully across the grass. Faith was nearly trotting as she tried to keep up with her. "Communication is important in situations like yours," Ava was saying. They reached the rhododendron bed. Ava circled it with the concentration of a hound dog trying to catch a scent, but she came up empty. Cody had moved on.

Relieved, Faith said, "Well, thanks for trying, Ava. Cody must be somewhere around here. I'll keep an eye out for him."

Ava wasn't listening. "Ha! There he is. Over by the volleyball game." She headed off, Faith in tow.

Faith could see he was eating. He popped the last of a hamburger into his mouth, licked each of his fingers, then chewed in a leisurely way while he watched the game. As they neared he tipped his head back and tossed the dregs of whatever beverage remained in a paper cup down his throat. Faith swallowed. He looked fit and strong, and way too sexy for a computer geek.

"Cody!" Ava said.

He turned. His eyes were shaded by sunglasses, so Faith couldn't tell what he was thinking, but after a moment of stillness he strolled toward them.

"Cody, here's Faith. I realize you two don't know each other well, which can be a problem when you have to work closely together, so take this opportunity to chat. Talk about anything that interests you—but not about work!" She smiled at both of them, but the expression didn't reach her eyes. "That way you can discover something about each other and relate as individuals, rather than employees. I'll go now and leave you to it." She waved airily and moved off.

Cody watched Ava walk away. "That woman is quite terrifying."

Faith grimaced. She was dusting herself off, as if this could somehow get rid of the embarrassment she was feeling now. "She's not my favorite person at the moment."

Cody took off his dark glasses and smiled. "Don't like being dragged around like a reluctant kid?"

Faith finished dusting herself as she nodded. "She'd never understand, though."

He laughed. "You've got that right. Let's see, we could Ava-bash for the next fifteen minutes or so, or talk about something else, since we're supposed to be relating on a deeper level. What do you think?"

Mischievously Faith said, "I heard it was going to rain at five-oh-two. That's in forty-five minutes. Did you bring your umbrella?"

Cody didn't bother to glance at the blue sky, which didn't have a cloud in it. "Well, that's not a bad gambit to keep the conversational ball rolling without revealing much about yourself. How about something more in-depth?"

Faith's breath caught and she felt herself blushing. Revealing her personal life to Cody was not in her agenda—no matter what Ava wanted. The problem was, he was a perceptive man. She'd have to be careful as she steered him away from the information she didn't want him to know. "You don't believe in small talk about the weather?"

He shook his head and smiled into her eyes.

Unsettled, she resisted the urge to smile back and spill her entire life history to him. "Every conversation I've had today began with a comment about the weather."

His gaze drifted slowly down her body, then back up. "Useless chat isn't my style."

Faith blamed the heat burning through her on the afternoon sun, not that visual caress that had her imagining long sensual kisses with a guy she'd decided she had better stay away from. She took a deep breath and opted to meet him head on. Otherwise, they might end up flirting through the rest of the afternoon and—horrors!—connecting on what was definitely a personal level. "Cody, I don't think this is exactly what Ava had in mind."

Cody's shrewd gaze scanned her face. He laughed, not pretending that he didn't understand where she was coming from.

She liked that about him. Damn it, he was already getting too close and they'd only been talking for three minutes.

"I know it isn't," he said, his voice low and filled with—oh, heavens—a sensual amusement. "The thing is, I don't really care what kind of textbook mixing Ava's got us down for."

"Amen to that. Sometimes she creeps me out the way she talks." Faith considered him seriously. There was a warmth in his eyes that was truly unnerving. She heard herself say hastily, "Now, let's see. What can we talk about for a few minutes so we look like we're connecting that isn't, um, useless chat? How about this—you were jogging during lunch the other day. Do you do it often?"

Behind them the volleyball game was breaking up. Cody began to walk. Faith followed. Part of her wanted to refuse to move. The other part, the curious part, was happy to wander along with him.

Staring ahead, he said, "For the record, I don't fulfill anyone's expectations. I choose to do what interests me." He looked at her, his eyes hooded, his mouth turned up in just the sexiest hint of a smile. "And right now what interests me is talking to you, so I'll play nice and make small talk..." He paused for the space of a heartbeat, then another. When he resumed his voice was lower and rough with unmistakable promise. "But what I'd prefer to be doing is something else entirely."

Faith's skin felt as if it was crackling with heat. She wished she'd worn shorts as Ava had, short shorts with a bikini top that showed off her figure. "Cody..."

He put his sunglasses on again. "I jog every day, but not always during the lunch hour. There are times I don't remember to take a lunch break and if I get hungry in the middle of working on something I simply eat at my computer."

"Hence the fridge in your office."

"Hey, we're not supposed to be talking about work, remember?"

"Right." Faith blushed. She was the one who had insisted on doing the Ava-enforced networking. She needed to stick to the program. Before she could figure out another bland topic to discuss, Cody had chosen a new gambit.

"Your mother seems like a nice person."

Faith could feel herself freezing up. "She is."

He tilted his head. She couldn't read his eyes behind the dark glasses, but she sensed he was studying her. "You have a similar bone structure, which probably means that in twenty years you'll look much as your mother does now. Not a bad way to age, to my way of thinking."

It was such a stupid thing to say that Faith forgot to be tense and laughed at him. "Excuse me?"

He shrugged and smiled a little ruefully. "It was a compliment."

"Some compliment. I'll stick with the present, thank you very much. Don't try to morph me into the future."

There was that sexy hint of a reserved smile again. "Struck out there. I'll have to try again."

"What kind of books do you read?" Faith asked before he could bring up another, potentially dangerous, topic. "Computer manuals?"

"Tolstoy." They entered one of the paths, shaded by large trees, and bordered by mature bushes. He took off his sunglasses.

Faith choked back a laugh at his quick answer. "Really?"

"No, but it sounds good. What kind of books do you read?"

"Mystery novels."

"No kidding." He looked intrigued. "Funny, I would have put you down as more of an erotica type."

His eyes slid down her body again, slowly, with obvious enjoyment. Faith could feel her skin prickling. She raised her eyebrows in surprise. "Why?"

83

A smile twitched the corners of his lips. "Wishful thinking perhaps?"

Faith's heart leapt with pleasure. She told herself it was nothing more than a reaction, purely instinctive, to a good-looking male making a blatantly sexual move on her. She also told herself that it was not quite what Ava had had in mind when she put Faith and Cody together and told them to get to know one another. The thing was, did she really care what Ava wanted? "Cody, look, I…"

He held up his hand and smiled rather ruefully at her. "You don't have to say it. That comment was way out of line. I apologize."

"No, it's okay. It's just…I'm a bit surprised at the way our conversation has been going. I mean, we never do anything but argue." The bushes and trees that lined their path created an illusion of separation from the rest of the garden, providing an aura of privacy that wasn't quite real. "I didn't…well, you know, expect it." She closed her mouth tightly. She had to stop talking. She'd already made enough of a fool of herself, given that he'd been flirting with her since Ava had made herself scarce.

"We don't always have to argue. In fact, I was wondering if you would like to go out for dinner with me one evening?"

His invitation was so completely unexpected that Faith could only gape at him. "Like, um, on a date?"

His eyes lit up and he laughed. "Yeah, like a date."

"Well, I don't know…"

"Cody, Faith, hi!" Angela, the computer destroyer, bounced up, shattering the illusion of privacy. She was followed more sedately by Faith's assistant, June. "Isn't this a great party?"

That wasn't precisely how Faith would describe it, but she supposed it was as good a label as any. "Wonderful," she said.

Cody didn't appear to be at all disturbed by the invasion. "As company parties go, it's okay."

Angela flashed him a big smile. "Are you always a grouch, Cody?"

Faith's eyes opened wide and her mouth rounded in a silent exclamation of surprise.

Cody crumpled up the empty paper cup he was holding. "I'm only grumpy when I'm interrupted in the middle of something."

Angela looked from Cody to Faith, her expression surprised.

June tugged at Angela. "Let's go. Becky is starting to pack up the refreshments. She needs some help."

"We interrupted something?" Angela said, ignoring June and sounding absolutely astounded.

"Nothing special," Faith said easily. "We were just chatting."

"You were chatting. I was asking you out on a date," Cody said.

Heat burned Faith's cheeks in a wash of red. "Cody!"

"It's true, isn't it?" he demanded, unrepentant.

"Maybe, but do you really want to broadcast it to the world?"

"Way cool! An office romance!" Angela announced in a loud voice.

"Your secret's safe with us," June said. She grabbed Angela's arm to drag her away.

"Bye!" Angela said over her shoulder. "Have fun!"

"Well?" Cody demanded as June and Angela moved out of range. "How about it?"

How about it indeed?

For the sake of her job Faith figured she should say yes. It would be one evening, just a few hours of her time. Maybe she should take a chance and go. She would be fulfilling Ava's demand that she get to know Cody. Maybe a better understanding between them really would help their work relationship. So why not say yes to his invitation?

Mainly because those hot looks he kept sending her way were stirring things within her that hadn't come to life before. Cody Simpson was a computer scientist, a mathematician whose life was dedicated to finding a logical answer to every question. To Cody her Beacon ability would be both irrational and impossible. He wouldn't see it as a special, magical, gift found in very few people and closely guarded so that it could not be abused by those who might wish to change the past, and in turn, the present and future.

As she pondered his invitation she looked up at him. He raised his brows and smiled. His eyes were the vivid blue of the afternoon sky. His expression said that he really would like her to say yes, but he wasn't going to pressure her. Faith liked that. She liked the way that sexy little smile played about his lips, how that errant lock of hair fell on his forehead, and the look of the body-hugging t-shirt and jeans.

But she had to remember that his world was not her world. It took a very special man to trust a woman who was a Beacon. A man who was imaginative and flexible. One who was willing to accept all sorts of strange events. Her mother had married a civil engineer, a man whose life was dedicated to taking dreams and giving them an enduring reality. He should have been able to cope with the indefinable that was a Beacon's life, but he couldn't, and his family had suffered because of it.

Faith reminded herself that Cody Simpson worked in the applied sciences field, just as her father did. Though Cody made her heart beat harder and had her senses rioting, that wasn't enough to create a strong or lasting connection between their two worlds. "Cody, look…um, thank you for the invitation, but…you know, I don't think it's a good idea to mix, um, private life and, ah, work life. So, you know, right now I'll say, um, no."

He studied her for a few moments. Faith squirmed under his intense glance, shuffling her feet like an inexperienced teenager.

After a minute he smiled. "Timing," he said, "is everything and mine stinks. Clearly I need to reassess."

Disappointment washed over Faith. It wasn't until she was in her car heading home that she realized that Cody hadn't taken no for an answer. Like all good scientists, when he'd reached a road-block he'd just stepped back to take a hard look at it before he tried another method of dismantling it. Cody didn't see her refusal as an ending, but as a temporary barrier that could be swept away.

The thought that Cody might ask her out again sent a pleasurable tingle racing through Faith's body. While her mind might tell her that dating Cody Simpson was not a good idea, her body was urging her to go for it.

# CHAPTER 10

"The picnic was fun, wasn't it?" June handed Faith a printout of the staffing schedule for the summer vacation period. "Did you enjoy it?"

Faith scanned the printout, not really paying attention to June's small talk. "Sure, it was okay."

June laughed. "Don't let Ava hear you say that. She's been asking everyone if it was the greatest picnic they've ever gone to. She's not really into lukewarm praise."

That caught Faith's attention. "I can see where Ava is coming from. She and the executive secretaries did a terrific job." She tapped the paper. "This is excellent, June. Can you post it in the staff room?" She handed the paper back to June, expecting that she would take it and go back to her workstation.

Instead, June lingered. "I was a little surprised by some people."

Faith sat back in her chair. Evidently June wanted to unburden herself of something and she wasn't about to do it quickly. "That's the purpose of the picnic and the Christmas party. We're supposed to discover each other in a non-work setting. That way we'll become closer and work more effectively as a team." She stopped, grinned and added, "At least that's the theory."

June looked at the staffing schedule. "It's an interesting idea. Do you buy into it?"

Good question. Faith wasn't sure she did, but then again, sometimes it worked. She'd seen a different side of Cody Simpson on Saturday, and she'd liked what she'd seen. Did that mean they would be able to work together more effectively? She doubted it. "I discovered that some of our staff members are interesting people who I like very much."

"Like Cody Simpson?"

Faith hesitated, then said carefully, "I suppose."

"He's really good looking, isn't he?" June said, a rather dreamy expression on her face.

"I suppose," Faith said again, deliberately noncommittal.

"If he asked me to go out with him, I would," June said.

Faith suppressed a petty desire to snap, forcing herself to smile instead. "And I'd wish you good luck and a good time." Standing up, she escorted June to the open door of her office. "I didn't accept Cody's invitation, June, so if you are interested in him, go for it."

June muttered something incoherent that sounded like, "No, I wasn't...I just..." before Faith firmly shut the door behind her.

Inside her office, Faith leaned against the closed door. She shut her eyes and breathed deeply. June had been digging for information because Cody had made his request for a date very public. She was curious and in her way had been complimenting Faith on her good luck in attracting a great looking guy. That was all.

Okay, she admitted it. She'd overreacted. But why?

Probably because June had touched a sensitive spot.

With a small sigh, Faith straightened. Stupid, stupid, stupid! She was the one who had refused his invitation. She made the decision to stand apart and she had to live with it. She drew a shaky breath, blew it out, then inhaled again, more deeply this time, before she walked to her desk. It took a long time for her to get back to work, but she did.

She almost made it through the day without a computer glitch. It was three-thirty when one of the clerks—not Angela, this time—asked for help. Faith checked out the problem and discovered it wasn't a simple one based on operator error. Nor was it one she had an easy answer for. She would have to phone Cody.

She went back to her office, her mood suddenly light and playful. Although she was not willing to start a relationship with Cody she wanted to see him again. Maybe Ava was right—getting to know a person would make working together easier. As she dialed Cody's number she imagined the sound of his voice as he answered the phone, visualized him tucking the receiver between his shoulder and his cheek so he could continue to work on his keyboard, thought about what she'd say to him.

The phone rang. Once, twice, a third time. At the fourth ring his voicemail activated. "This is Cody Simpson. I'm not at my desk right now. Please leave a message..."

Completely deflated, and absurdly disappointed, she gave her name and stated the problem. She hung up with a distinct click. What did she expect? The man never answered his phone.

After sending him a follow-up e-mail with more details, she went back to work, but when the office cleared at 4:30 and she'd had no response from Cody she decided she would take a stab at fixing the problem. She didn't want to start the next day with a non-working computer. She was still there at five o'clock when Ava wandered by, her purse over her shoulder and a coat hung over one arm.

"Faith, what are you doing?" Ava's expression was as disapproving as her tone.

Faith silently cursed her bad luck. "Trying to fix this computer before I go home."

"I thought you'd realized that the computers were Cody Simpson's responsibility?" Although Ava must be heading out, she had planted herself firmly beside Faith's chair and had apparently set down roots.

"I did. I do," Faith said. She stared at the screen. She'd just spent another half hour getting nowhere. Ava might be annoying and unreasonable, but this time she could be right. Computers were Cody's specialty, so sorting out this glitch was his job.

Ava pulled a chair from one of the other desks. "This wasteful behavior has got to stop, Faith. You're a valuable member of our team, but you are not using your time effectively trying to do work you know nothing about."

Good point, Faith thought. If you tossed in the added stress levels, you had a really good argument. Still, she had one better. "Someone had to repair the computer, Ava. Cody wasn't at his desk and hasn't picked up the voicemail I left."

"But you haven't fixed it. What if you made the problem worse? You should have waited for Cody to come down."

Ava's words stung, but there was absolutely nothing Faith could say to defend herself. "Ava, I—"

"I understand Cody asked you to go out with him at the picnic."

Faith shot Ava a cautious look. "Where did you hear that?"

"You refused."

"That's up to me."

Ava put her hand on the back of Faith's. "If the invitation was issued as the beginning of a personal relationship, the decision would, of course, be yours. However, this was a business invitation, wasn't it, Faith?"

Faith looked at Ava's hand where it rested on hers. The gesture should have been comforting, just as Ava's gentle tone should have been. Neither was. "Look, Ava—"

"What harm is there in going out with him?"

Ava sounded so reasonable. How could Faith explain that

dinner with Cody Simpson was much more likely to be personal than business related? Ava saw what she wanted, heard what she expected. "Ava, there's no harm in my refusing to go out with him. I just don't…"

"Don't is a negative word," Ava removed her hand so she could wave her forefinger at Faith. "If you think more positively the issues will resolve themselves."

Faith had a vision of Cody looking down at her, those blue eyes of his warm with amusement. Her insides melted at the memory. This was all so unfair! She wanted to go out with Cody. If she'd been a normal woman she'd have jumped at the chance to spend time with him.

The problem was, she wasn't a normal woman. She was a Beacon. Dates were out of the question. Frustration made her snap, "Great. Tell Cody that. In the meantime, I'm going to head home and leave this problem for him to solve tomorrow."

Ava stood when Faith did. Instead of leaving she followed Faith to her office. Her annoyance was clear in her voice as she continued to press her point. "Think about what I've said, Faith. Accept his invitation."

Faith logged off her computer and locked her desk. "As to that, Ava, I can't. He asked and I refused." She threw her purse over her shoulder and headed for the door.

"Then you must ask him out," Ava said, hovering beside Faith and getting in her way.

Her hand on the light switch, Faith stared at Ava. "You want me to invite him out?"

Ava nodded.

The main door to the suite slammed. Both women froze.

Ava frowned. "The cleaners come every other day. This is not one of their scheduled nights."

Quiet footsteps sounded in the bullpen. Faith's heart pounded a fast, heavy beat. Gathering up her courage, she walked out of her office to accost whoever had entered after hours. Ava stayed in her doorway, near her phone, offering support and little else.

The footsteps neared. A large male form appeared out of the gloom of the interior office lit by little other than the reflected glow from the windows in Faith's open office.

Faith's heart slammed into overdrive. "Who is it?"

The shadowy form coalesced into a good-looking male in jeans and a t-shirt. "I just picked up your e-mail. Which unit has the problem?"

Faith felt her knees go weak with relief. "That one," she said a little shakily. She pointed out the one she'd been working on a few minutes before.

Cody frowned. "What's up?"

A moment ago he'd sounded all business, but now his voice offered the promise of protection and the warmth of concern. Though Faith had been thinking of ways of carving him up into little pieces a mere half hour before, now she found herself softening as she made haste to reassure him. "It's late. I didn't know there was anyone else left in the building."

Relaxing, he smiled that sexy little half-smile that darkened the blue of his eyes and made every look a caress. "Neither did I. Usually I'm on my own by this time." Footsteps dragged his gaze from Faith's. His eyes iced as he looked over her shoulder. "Hello, Ava."

"You gave us quite a start, Cody." The expression on Ava's face was decidedly unfriendly.

Faith was reminded of her sister's description of the two of them being tyrannosaurs doing battle and she had to resist a very strong urge to scuttle back to the safety of her office.

The feeling only intensified as Ava hitched her purse higher on her shoulder and shifted the coat more comfortably on her arm. "Remember what we were talking about, Faith. I'd like a report in the morning." She nodded to both of them, then said good night and marched away, her head tilted in a defiant manner.

Cody watched her for a minute before he sat down at the ailing computer. "That woman constantly amazes me." He shook his head. "Okay, remind me what went wrong and any details you can think of."

As Faith filled him in on the problem he set to work. She perched on the chair Ava had recently vacated and watched him. She liked the way his thick dark lashes framed those vivid blue eyes, the quiet intensity with which he worked. Her gaze traveled lower. His fingers were blunt, the nails pared short. They moved over the keyboard with the ease of a pianist. She could imagine those hands on her skin, stroking her. The caress would be gentle, but sure, just as his touch on the keyboard was sure. A prickle of heat burned across her skin and she had to look away.

"Okay, I think I've got it," Cody said.

He leaned back and stretched. It had taken him ten minutes to solve the problem. Maybe Ava was right. Waiting for Cody to help was a more effective use of the company's time, even if he didn't show up until three hours later.

As he logged off, he said, "Call me tomorrow if there are any more problems."

Faith looked at him dubiously. "What's your schedule look like?"

He shrugged. "The usual." Amusement gleamed in his eyes. "Are you trying to tell me diplomatically that you don't believe that I'll be around to troubleshoot?"

She laughed. "Now that you mention it…"

He rubbed his chin. "Unfortunately, you're right. I only check my messages from time to time." He looked at her, then apparently came to a decision. "If you need me and I'm not in my office, try two-oh-seven. That's where I hang out when I need quiet."

"Two-oh-seven." Two-oh-seven was located on the inside of

the building and had no windows. Originally, it had been used as a storage space, then, as NIT grew, it had become a small workspace area for casual staff. Come to think of it, she hadn't heard of anyone putting a temp in that room in a while. Cody must have taken over the workspace for his own use. She realized that he was giving her the key to his privacy and that he trusted her not to abuse it. "Cody, about the picnic…"

He leaned back in the chair. "Changed your mind?"

"Well, you see…" She wanted to say yes, but she knew, for her peace of mind, she should say no. Then there was the pressure Ava had put on her tonight. She didn't want to say yes to a date with Cody because Ava had told her she must. She wanted to say yes because he was a thoroughly attractive man. Which was why she had to say no.

His gaze caught her. It burned into her, hopeful, encouraging. Good sense told her she should retreat and say, no she hadn't changed her mind. The trouble was, when he smiled at her like that, she couldn't do it. "Yeah, I have."

"Good." He caught her hand and held it between his. His thumb caressed her palm, sending shivers down her spine. "I'll pick you up at seven on Friday."

Faith almost said sure, fine, any time. She knew she was in deep trouble when a man's touch was enough to make her forget who she was. Seven was when Uncle Andrew usually showed up. That was just what she needed, to have Uncle Andrew materialize in front of Cody. "No! Friday doesn't work for me. How about Thursday at seven?"

Cody flashed her a wicked smile. "All the better. Okay, it's a date."

THURSDAY CAME with a flutter of nerves and pleasurable anticipation. Faith wasn't sure what she expected from the evening. She'd been playing out possibilities in her mind ever since Monday and her ideas fluctuated wildly between co-workers talking politely about work to a flirtatious conversation that led to sexually charged kisses on her doorstep. She figured Ava would definitely go for the polite co-worker scenario and, while part of her liked the security of that image, another part, the part that was turned on by Cody Simpson, much preferred the evening that ended in a hot, passionate kiss.

She was running late on Thursday afternoon, but she figured she had enough time to shower and change and still be ready before Cody reached her doorstep. Heavens knew why he wanted to pick her up at home, instead of meeting her somewhere after work. Or better yet, working late and going somewhere straight from the office. However, since he was picking her up, she also had to straighten the living room so she could ask him in when he arrived.

Glancing at her watch as she raced in the door she noted that it was five-forty-five. Still time to manage all the things she had to do and be ready on time. She dumped her purse on the table in the hall, slipped out of her shoes and ran into the living room. She was organizing the week's newspapers into a pile when a male voice said, "It's about time! Where the devil have you been?"

Faith screamed and jumped. The papers went flying, then floated majestically down to land strewn across the living room floor. Her hand clamped to her mouth, she turned.

She knew whom she'd see. "Andrew, what are you doing here? It's only Thursday."

Andrew stood with his hands on his hips, temper flaring in his eyes. "George Strand is to come from Boston town for the week's end so tomorrow evening Mary Elizabeth will have to dance attendance upon her papa, instead of walking out with me. If I am to see her this week it will have to be tonight."

Faith looked at the scattered newspapers in some despair. "Yeah, well, okay." As she began to gather up the sections realization dawned. "You want to use my shower!"

"Aye, that I do."

"Andrew, you can't! I have a date tonight. I need to use the shower."

His gray eyes narrowed. "A date? With a man?"

"Of course with a man and he's coming to get me at seven." She dumped the papers into a magazine basket. "That's not much time, so go away."

"I will not!"

"What? You have to!"

"I do not."

Frustrated and very, very worried that he was going to mess up her evening with Cody, Faith said, "For the love of Pete, Andrew, I have a date! Go away!"

Andrew shrugged and headed for the stairs. "I'll be quick, lass, see if I'm not."

Groaning, Faith scuttled after him. "Andrew, don't you dare go up those stairs! I want you to go home. Now!"

"That I will not do, lass." He took the stairs two at a time with Faith hurrying after him.

"I'll leave!" she shrieked, desperate. "I'll walk out of this house and go to my mother's." Though Chloe's house was only a short distance from Faith's, it was far enough that Andrew would be in deep trouble if Faith did go there. For if Faith stepped out of the house, leaving Andrew behind, he would disappear back into the past, in whatever state of dress—or undress—he happened to be wearing.

At the top of the staircase he turned slowly. "You would not do that to me, Faith."

Faith admitted to herself that he was right, but she raised her chin and said, "Try me."

Andrew gritted his teeth. "Fifteen minutes is all I need. Fifteen minutes!"

"You've never showered and shaved in less than an hour," Faith retorted, following him to the bathroom door.

"That's because I always stop for a visit with you! Fifteen minutes, Faith. That's all I ask."

He was looking woebegone now, his expression so like that of a hopeful puppy that Faith almost laughed. She managed to keep her expression disapproving though, as she said, "Okay. I'll finish sorting out the living room and get my outfit ready. But when I knock on the door, Andrew, the bathroom is mine. Understood?"

He shut the door at the same time as he said, "Aye!"

Faith headed down to the living room to the sound of running water and Andrew singing.

It was twenty after six when Andrew sauntered into her bedroom, a towel around his hips. "What did you do with my clothes, then lass?"

"I put them in the spare bedroom," Faith said. She'd changed out of the slacks and tailored shirt she'd worn to work and was clad in a dressing gown. "Andrew, don't take forever to dress. I don't want you here when Cody arrives."

Andrew leaned against the doorjamb making it impossible for Faith to leave her room without brushing past him. "Is that the name of the fellow you're walking out with tonight?"

"It is," Faith said, somewhat impatiently.

Andrew crossed his arms over his chest. "What's he like then?"

"He's taller than you are and he packs a lethal left hook." Andrew's brows climbed up toward his dark hair. "Andrew, I don't have time to chat. Not tonight. Come back tomorrow and we can compare dates."

"I might just do that, Faith my girl," he said. But he straightened and cleared out of the doorway. Faith dove past him, heading for the shower.

Twenty minutes later she was putting on her makeup when there was a tap on the bathroom door. "Faith, I'll be going now. You'd best hurry, though. Your young man is waiting for you in the front parlor."

Oh, no! Shock held her immobile. She stared into the mirror, seeing a wild-eyed young woman with pale skin and long blond hair framing her face and spilling over her shoulders. As her eyes grappled with an image she couldn't comprehend, her mind scurried around like a trapped and very frightened rabbit.

Cody Simpson was here, in the living room? Cody had met Andrew? She began to move. If Cody was in the living room he would see Andrew disappear as he stepped back into the past. "Andrew, wait!" she shrieked.

There was no answer. She flung on her robe and charged out the door. Only to find Andrew lounging against the banister, silently laughing so hard he was holding his sides.

She stopped in her tracks. "Cody's not here, is he?"

Andrew took a deep breath and collected himself. Still he didn't attempt to talk. He simply nodded agreement.

He was dressed in his best clothes, all ready for his date with Mary Elizabeth, while Faith was still in her dressing gown, her makeup half-done, her nerves fried, all because of him. Faith made a growling sound in her throat and flew at him. Andrew, his face still alight with mischief, dove down the stairs and into the living room. Faith was close behind him, yelling that she would make him pay for this. He reached his magical spot and—poof!—he was gone.

Faith stood for a moment, panting, then the clock on the mantle bonged the quarter hour and she realized with horror that Cody would be here in fifteen minutes and she wasn't dressed, her hair wasn't brushed, and her makeup needed finishing. She raced back up to the bathroom.

She had completed her makeup and flung on a green knit dress that accented her dark blond hair when the doorbell rang at precisely seven o'clock. Faith groaned. She still needed to add stockings and do something with her hair.

She ran down the stairs and jerked open the door. And stared.

Now she knew why Cody had insisted that he pick her up, rather than have them leave from the office. He was dressed in a suit. A gray suit that fit his long, lean body very nicely indeed. Beneath the tailored jacket was a white shirt and a tie. A tie? If she wasn't looking at it right now, she'd never have imagined that Cody Simpson would own a tie, let alone wear one. A tie. Who'd believe it?

"Hi," he said, his gaze sweeping the length of her.

Faith swallowed. "Where are my manners? Cody, come on in." She took a quick, nervous look at the living room. "Into the kitchen. I'm running a bit late. Make yourself at home. I won't be more than a minute or two."

# CHAPTER 11

She walked with a definite swing to her step. He liked that about her, the way she moved, the way she handled her body. As Cody followed Faith across the hall to the kitchen he watched the sweep of her long blond hair as it cascaded over her shoulders and halfway down her back. He shouldn't be thinking about running his fingers through that thick golden mass—it was way too soon in the relationship for that—but he couldn't resist letting his imagination run riot. It was probably the most wicked he'd be all evening.

She left him in the kitchen to look after himself as she rushed off to finish her prep for the evening. That surprised him. Faith Hamilton had a fearsome reputation at NIT for her organizational skills. If you wanted a problem sorted out, if you were looking to get something pulled together from nothing in no time at all, you went to Faith. He'd assumed she'd be waiting for him when he arrived tonight, perfectly groomed with not a hair out of place. He certainly hadn't anticipated a flustered woman eyeing him sideways as if she wasn't sure what to expect next.

He pondered this behavior as he investigated her fridge to see if she had stashed a bottle of beer inside as compensation for abandoned dates while she hid away in the bathroom prettying herself up.

There was no beer, but he did find a bottle of designer water. He decided that would have to do, but when he went searching for a glass, he discovered a bottle of merlot beside some wineglasses. Now this was more like it. He put the water back in the fridge.

Very orderly, he thought, as he took down a glass and the bottle of wine. It tallied with his idea of Faith Hamilton. But it didn't fit the charming bundle of nerves who was now in the bathroom primping.

He leaned against the counter as he sipped the wine, speculating. Her kitchen was neat, the counters clean, the table clear. Again, the sort of thing he would expect of her.

Faith's kitchen was nothing like the disaster area that was his kitchen. His kitchen was cluttered, the table piled high with—stuff. He liked his kitchen. It faced west and got a generous share of afternoon sun. Because of the light, because he liked light, he did a lot of his work at his kitchen table. The result was that it was covered with papers, books, pens, pencils, paper clips, a computer he was repairing, and anything else that caught his interest.

His laptop sat at one end and when he needed the table for a meal, on those odd occasions when he actually ate in, he closed down the laptop and used the small clear space it left behind for his plate. When he finished eating he returned the computer to the spot. As an effective use of limited space he felt it was a system that worked remarkably well.

This big kitchen, with not an article out of place, was a resounding statement about the woman who lived here. It said she was tidy and organized and liked it that way. It asked—no demanded!—to know why he even thought dating her would be a good idea.

He drank some more merlot.

Since the day when she'd come up to his office he'd been thinking about Faith Hamilton. Strike that. He'd been more than thinking of her. He'd been fantasizing about her curvy body and those beautiful gray-green eyes of hers. He'd teased her into losing her temper and watched those eyes flash with a passion that had nothing to do with work. Faith Hamilton might like to have everything done correctly, but he'd proven she had limits and she could be pushed to them and past them with remarkable ease.

As if his thoughts of her had brought her to him in the flesh, Faith bounded into the kitchen, her gray-green eyes wide and anxious. She'd added shoes, sensible ones with low heels, and she'd twisted her hair up into some sort of knot in the back, much to his disappointment. She peered around the room carefully, looking at him and around him. "Is everything okay? Nothing to worry about?"

Cody glanced around the tidy room. What was there to worry about in a room that was so neat and scrubbed that he couldn't see any need to clean it again for the next year and a half? Still Faith seemed to be so concerned he decided to tease her a bit to see what she would do. He pointed to a corner near the sink. "There's a spider web over by the window."

He expected her to shriek and demand to be rescued from the danger of the spider the way his ex-wife used to. Or to haul out the broom and have a go at eliminating the spider web right now, before they left for the evening.

Instead she shrugged. "It's an old house. I get lots of spiders."

Now Cody was intrigued. As he watched her take a deep breath to calm her agitation, he wondered with considerable satisfaction if being with him had shaken her so much that she was showing another side to her personality. He rather hoped that was what was happening.

He downed the merlot in the glass and set it on the counter. "I raided your cupboards," he said, waving at the bottle and the now empty glass.

A smile lit up Faith's lovely heart-shaped face. "I'm glad you did. Sorry I ran out on you like that. I planned to be ready by seven but..." She didn't bother to state the obvious. Instead her smile turned enticing and she held out her hand. "I'm ready now. Shall we go?"

The prospect of catching her hand in his was enough to get Cody moving. He levered himself away from the counter and took what she offered. Her hand was warm in his, the skin smooth and supple.

As soon as his fingers closed around hers, she tugged, hard.

"Good, we're off. Don't worry about the lights. I always leave them on. I like to come home to a brightly lit house." She dragged him through the hall, pausing briefly to peer into the living room, before she grabbed her purse from the hall table.

As she looked into the living room Cody looked too, but he could see nothing beyond a perfectly ordinary room. He wondered if the newspapers dumped casually into a basket were the reason for her apparent concern. If so, curvy body or not, they were doomed. Any woman who cared so much about keeping her space that tidy was off his Christmas list.

When they were out the door and in the car she sagged visibly. "Are you okay?" he asked, somewhat alarmed.

She took a deep breath and smiled, although it seemed to him that it took considerable effort for her to relax. "Yeah. I'm sorry. I got a little flustered when I wasn't ready on time."

He made some polite comment, but that really worried him. A woman who got upset because she was late was too tense for him. He was always late. Heck, some days he hardly knew where he was, let alone what time it was. In order to make it to Faith's house on time tonight he had set the alarm on his watch to ring every

104

half hour from five o'clock on. He had been on edge and jumpy all afternoon. Running by the clock was just not his style.

He put the car in reverse, turning to check as he backed out of the drive. "I thought we could go to Mel's place." On the street he glanced at Faith. She was staring down at her watch, for heaven's sake.

She looked up, frowning. "Mel's? I don't think I've ever heard of it before."

It was Cody's turn to frown. Mel's place was one of the most popular restaurants in Boston. She must have heard of it.

"It's in Beacon Hill, in an old house…"

"La Renaissance? Mel's place is La Renaissance?"

"Yeah." Cody concentrated on driving. The evening was not going as he'd predicted. He worked in variables and probabilities. When the data didn't produce the kind of results he expected, he needed to back away from the problem and ponder it until he figured out where he went wrong. Clearly he didn't have time to do that now, but he was definitely going to have to reassess once he'd dropped Faith at her home tonight.

"So who's Mel?" Faith asked, considerable amusement in her voice.

Mel Stewart had become a good friend. He was a brilliant chef, a creative genius with food. "He owns the restaurant," Cody said. It dawned on him that he knew that, but he shouldn't expect Faith to. He added hastily, "To me Mel Stewart is La Renaissance and I forget that other people don't see it that way." They stopped at a light and he took the opportunity to look over at her.

Faith smiled that wide generous smile of hers and said, "Well, I can't complain about being taken out to La Renaissance. Thank you, Cody."

Her comment shot a burst of warmth through him. He didn't analyze it, he just went with the pleasure it brought him. He decided this was going to be a terrific evening after all. He was going to enjoy himself, even if Faith did have the tidiest house he'd seen since he moved out on his own.

CODY SIMPSON WAS NOT A JERK.

Faith ruefully admitted that to herself about a half-an-hour after they'd arrived at La Renaissance. He had a beautiful smile that made her tingle right down to the tips of her toes. His use of it had put her so at ease that she'd shoved Uncle Andrew's visit and Ava Taylor's ultimatum into a back recess in her mind. She was here with a very sexy guy and that was all she wanted to think about.

Mel Stewart stopped by their table to chat. La Renaissance took up the ground floor of a wonderful old brick building on Charles Street. The owner's front-of-the-house visits were something the restaurant was known for, but the esteem with which Mel Stewart, the creative chef, held Cody Simpson, the practical computer scientist, was obvious. "How do you know Mel?" she asked when she and Cody were once more alone at their table.

Cody was cutting into his appetizer, a chunk of Ahi tuna served with compote of red peppers and corn that had been artistically mounded beside it. A sprig of oregano adorned the top and two slender pieces of crisp bread completed the display. "I like food and I don't cook much," he said, before he popped some tuna and compote into his mouth.

"Well, the food here is certainly wonderful." Faith had a bowl of creamy soup in front of her, a combination of carrot and squash that was heavenly.

"That's what I thought too," Cody said. He picked up his glass and considered the wine, a white that blended perfectly with both the fish and the soup. "So I came here a lot. Mel visited my table to chat the way he does and pretty soon he noticed that I'd become a regular. So instead of chatting about the weather, we got to talking about each other."

It sounded so simple. "And that's the way the friendship started."

Cody took a sip and nodded. "Then one day Mel was complaining that he needed to control costs and the system he was using wasn't giving him the data he needed. I was between jobs so I offered to write him a more efficient program." He stopped and shrugged, then ate some more tuna.

"And so you did." She smiled at him. He grinned back a little ruefully.

"Yeah, as much as I could. You should see Mel's kitchen. It seems chaotic if you don't know anything about running a restaurant kitchen, but it's pretty organized—at least that's what Mel tells me. It looks like a disaster area to me. Mel claims my program has helped immensely." Cody laughed. "I have to take his word for it."

Faith looked around the restaurant. The décor was spare and simple, with clean modern lines that utilized chrome, white linen and glass. The modern design provided an elegant contrast to the gracious proportions of the heritage construction. The servers moved through the three large rooms that made up the restaurant with a quiet efficiency. "It's hard to believe that behind closed doors the kitchen is so totally different from the eating area."

Cody laughed. "Yeah, you'd have no idea looking around here, would you?" He shot her a questioning look. "It's sort of like people. You get an idea of someone and then they go and do something totally unexpected."

Faith's heart skipped a beat. "Unexpected?"

"Sure. You know, the mild mannered guy who suddenly throws a rock through his neighbor's window. Or the woman who lives in the suburbs bringing up the kids, but was once an exotic dancer."

Faith choked back a laugh. "There are a lot of those?"

"Absolutely," he said. "So tell me about yourself, Faith. Do you have a dark underside that remains hidden from the rest of us?"

For a moment she couldn't breathe. Forcing herself to be calm, she dipped her spoon into the soup. "What you see is what you get," she said, keeping her eyes on the bowl.

"Well, that looks pretty good to me," he said.

Faith glanced up quickly. His eyes were warm and there was a caress in them that almost covered the question that lurked beneath the friendly expression.

Somehow she had to get rid of that question. Cody Simpson was an attractive guy, but she was here because Ava Taylor had pressured her into accepting a date. She had to remember that and remember too, that no one at work must know about her special ability.

How did she deal with a question that couldn't be asked and shouldn't be answered? With a response that said nothing, but seemed to tell all. "I have to confess, Cody, that I spend way too much time at work."

He grimaced. "Me too."

She nodded in a companionable way, two workaholics commiserating. "So when I get home I usually do my chores then read for a while or watch TV. Not long ago my sister wanted to go out to a club for the evening, but I just didn't have the energy. She thinks I'm a total loss." She smiled then waited, sipping her soup, pretending to be perfectly calm.

Cody nodded. "Sounds reasonable to me. I'd rather clean toilets than go solo to a club." He stopped abruptly, a sudden, guilty look on his face.

Faith laughed. "Is that your version of a deep, dark secret, then? That you aren't a party animal?"

The server came to clear their plates, replacing used cutlery with fresh and refilling their wineglasses. He was silent as the man moved unobtrusively around the table. When he had gone Cody said, "Actually, I have to confess that I hate housekeeping and I'm lousy at it."

"Get a cleaning service," Faith said. "That's what I do." Their entrees arrived with a flourish along with Mel to explain the special nuances of each dish. When Faith tasted her braised lamb shank she sighed with pleasure. "This is wonderful!"

Mel beamed. "You are too kind!" He turned to Cody. "My friend, keep this one around. She has taste as well as beauty."

Faith could feel the blush rush into her cheeks. She would have stammered something incoherent, but Cody smiled at her, then winked. Relief flooded through her. Mel might be flowery and continental in his manner, but Cody wasn't taking him seriously and she didn't have to either.

Mel departed to make pleasant conversation at another table. Cody zoned in on the comment she'd made just as their meals arrived. "You have a cleaning service for your house?"

"You bet. There's a team of three. I don't make much of a mess, so I only have them in once a month. They vacuum, dust, do the bathrooms, all the heavy stuff. I keep the place tidy and do the dishes and the ironing, that sort of thing."

He fiddled with the steak on his plate. "You have a big yard. Do you have a landscaping service too?"

"Of course." Faith laughed at the amazement on his face. "Hey, I'm much better at organizing people than I am at doing all the little bits and pieces of life. I figured out long ago that if I found the right person to do a job, the results would be much better than if I tried to do it myself." Cody's amazement had given way to a frown. That didn't make sense to Faith. Her cheerful confidence slipped a notch. What if he was the kind of guy who figured that there was something faintly sinful about a woman who is not the primary cleaner of the household?

Then he wasn't for her. She lifted her chin. "I've found that what works in the office also works at home."

The frown disappeared and that sexy, half-smile quirked up the edge of his mouth. Despite herself, Faith responded to that look. Butterflies took flight in her stomach and a tiny, but unmistakable shiver of anticipation swept through her. She took a sip of wine, hoping it would calm her, but his eyes followed her as she brought the glass to her lips. Instead of cooling her response, his gaze added fire. The tingle became a full body flush.

"You have no idea how empowering I find this conversation," he said, still watching her intently as she lowered the glass.

"Oh?" As comebacks went, this was pretty weak, but it was about all Faith was capable of at that moment.

He nodded. His little smile grew wider. "I'm not the tidiest male in the world."

"And that relates to my using a cleaning service in what way?"

"It makes you less intimidating."

Faith stared at him. "Intimidating? Me?"

He laughed, his eyes warm. "You have a fearsome reputation, lady."

Putting her hands on either side of her plate, she leaned forward. "Let me get this straight. You find me intimidating." He nodded, amusement in his eyes and a rueful curl to his lips. "And that is because...?"

The quirk broadened into a grin and he laughed outright. "I told you. I'm not a tidy person. I file by pile, so my house—particularly my kitchen—is cluttered."

Understanding dawned. "And my kitchen is the exact opposite."

He nodded. The amusement was still warm in his eyes.

Faith basked in that warmth as she thought for a minute. There were things going on here that she had to get a handle on. She said cautiously, "Your office wasn't full of piles."

He shrugged, serious now. "Work is different. Most of my archive material is backed up onto a separate hard drive and I don't bother to keep paper files. Sue Green does. If she thinks we need a paper track, she prints the document out and puts it in a filing cabinet somewhere." His rueful grin flashed again. "Since she's been off I've been using her office as a stacking place. If something comes in on paper I just dump it on her desk."

Faith stared at him in amazement. "Wow. I had no idea. Cody, do you want some help dealing with the everyday stuff?"

He rubbed his hand over his chin. "I hadn't thought of it. I am supposed to be doing Sue's job, after all."

"No one..." Ava Taylor's name hung between them, there but unspoken, "expects you do the clerical parts of Sue's job. Angela is a quick worker and I like to keep her busy, particularly now that I know she's been creating her computer problems out of boredom. I'll talk to her tomorrow."

"See what I mean?"

He was smiling at her in that warm, amused way that made her tingle from head to toe. "What?"

"You are one formidable lady, Faith Hamilton."

# CHAPTER 12

Faith was still tingling when she danced into the office on Friday morning. Her date with Cody had been a delight. Her mood was so good she'd put on a favorite summer dress, a splash of blues and yellows that reached mid-thigh and hugged her hips. Everything had cooperated for her this morning. The day had woken with a blaze of sunshine, her drive in had been a breeze—minus its usual moments of traffic madness—and she'd found a prime parking spot in the crowded NIT lot.

She dumped her purse into her desk drawer, then got down to business. After she'd arranged for Angela to file the stack of materials Cody had been collecting, she checked her e-mail and dealt with the various replies. She was deep into a review of budget figures for the quarter, when June came by with the news that she couldn't access certain files on the network.

Faith sat back, stretched, and said, "Have you called Cody Simpson?"

June nodded. "I left a voicemail."

Faith considered that. Cody might be at his desk, but even if he was, he didn't pay much attention to messages. There was also a good chance that he was hiding away in his secret place, working on one of his projects. She stood up. "I'll take a look. If it's a little thing I can easily sort out we won't have to wait on Cody."

It wasn't. Faith spent fifteen minutes assessing the situation, then glanced at her watch. "Okay, it's eleven o'clock. Let's give Cody until noon to get down here. If he hasn't shown up by then, I'll call him and ask him to come down as soon as possible. Yesterday, if he can."

At noon June poked her head in the door. "He didn't come."

That meant she was going to have to call Cody herself. She thought about the little bit of a dress that made her feel and look good and considered taking a trip up to his second floor lair, but decided to stick with voice and e-mail. When he came down she'd have a chance to see him. "Okay, I'll organize this, June. Let me know when Cody arrives."

Of course his voicemail was on, so Faith left a message and sent him an urgent e-mail. Assuming he'd call right back after the way they'd meshed last night, she stayed at her desk and worked through lunch. An hour flew by, but Cody hadn't come down.

That put a damper on Faith's buoyant good mood, but only a small one. Sooner or later Cody was going to show up and then she'd have a chance to talk to him. Humming a little tune, she called him again, then added an e-mail for good measure, and went back to work.

June was back again a while later—over an hour later!—to say her network link was still down. Faith considered her options. Between them, she and June had contacted Cody several times. If he ever picked up his phone or checked his e-mail he'd be awash with requests to come down to the main offices to fix June's malfunctioning computer. Adding another one to the total would be like pouring a glass of water into a lake—unnoticeable.

What this needed was the personal touch. She'd go up to the

second floor and seek out Cody in his secret hiding place, room two-oh-seven. She let June know her plan, then hummed as she climbed the stairs and followed the hallway around corners into the depths of the building.

When she reached two-oh-seven Cody wasn't there. Nor was he in his corner office with the big windows. Faith's mood plummeted. Where in heavens was he? She glanced at her watch. It was nearly two-thirty. He couldn't be at lunch. No one ate lunch this late in the afternoon. Maybe he was in the washroom. She waited five minutes. Frustration grew. When he didn't show up, she gritted her teeth and checked the men's washroom by knocking on the door, then pushing it open and asking if there was anyone in there.

There wasn't. Or at least, there wasn't anyone who was willing to admit his presence. With frustration rapidly ballooning into annoyance, Faith again checked his office, two-oh-seven, and even Sue Green's office. When she had no luck finding Cody, she returned to the main suite.

Somewhere between the second floor and the first, annoyance settled into a stubborn determination that June's computer was going to be fixed today and that Cody was going to do it. Buried deep within that determination was a sense of betrayal. Last night Cody had made her believe that he understood why she had to contact him to make the repairs on her department's computers, that he was willing to work with her to ensure that what needed to be done would be done. He had told her about two-oh-seven hadn't he? Wasn't that evidence of his new cooperative attitude?

Evidently not. The moment Faith reached her office she e-mailed, then phoned Cody. She did a follow-up five minutes later, then five minutes after that. With each unanswered call her stress levels rose, along with her temper.

The clock was hovering between three-thirty and three-forty-five when June tapped on Faith's door and announced that Cody was fixing her computer. Faith breathed a sigh of relief. After wrestling her temper under tight control she went out to June's desk.

Cody's attention was riveted to the computer. He was dressed as he normally was, in jeans that hugged his lean hips and a t-shirt that made the most of his shoulders and strong arms. As he worked a lock of dark hair fell over his forehead, creating a look that was relaxed and decidedly sexy. Some of Faith's tension eased, but not all of it. She'd needed his help hours ago and his slow response to her urgent messages had caused her and her staff problems that need not have happened.

As if he'd felt her presence, he looked up. His expression shifted to one that was decidedly hostile. "We need to talk."

"Yes, we do," Faith replied. She didn't like his tone, or the grim look on his face. "My office when you're done." She deliberately turned and walked away without waiting for his response. She figured if they were going to have a battle over this, she needed to do everything she could to get the upper hand.

She was halfway to her office when she felt a hand close around her arm. Surprised, she looked up to see Cody. Then suddenly he was leading her to her office, she wasn't heading there on her own. Her temper started to steam again. It reached a full boil when he hauled her into her own office and shut her door behind them.

"Did you fix June's problem?" she asked. The effort to keep her tone coolly controlled when she wanted to shriek at him set her temper sizzling even more.

Standing with his back to the closed door, he observed her thoughtfully, his hands in his pockets. His apparent calm was in sharp contrast to her annoyance.

He advanced into the room, stopping just in front of her. "Yes. It was nothing major."

"Great. I have a staff member who couldn't do her job all day because of a simple little problem."

Something akin to humor danced in his eyes. "You should have come up to two-oh-seven."

His response freed her seething temper. "I did. You weren't there. You weren't in your office either. You weren't even in the bathroom! Cody, it took five hours and phone calls every few minutes to get a response from you! I thought we went out last night so we could get better acquainted and make sure this kind of miscommunication wouldn't happen anymore."

A frown snapped his brows together. "Is that why you went out with me? To create a better working relationship between us?"

"No! That's not it…" Flustered, Faith's voice dwindled to a stop. "Yes, it is. After I turned down your invitation at the picnic Ava put pressure on me to accept it."

"So you dated me because you had to?" He sounded more baffled than outraged.

Faith wished she'd never opened her mouth. "Yes."

He took one quick step that brought him within inches of her. "That's too bad," he said, "because it's not why I went out with you. As far as I'm concerned last night was a date, with everything that goes along with it."

She pressed her lips together. "Yeah? Then why didn't you kiss me when you dropped me at my house?"

His eyes narrowed. "My mistake." He caught her waist and drew her hard against him. "I'll just fix that now."

His free hand caught her head, holding it steady as he slowly, oh so slowly, lowered his lips to hers.

Though Faith put her hands against his shoulders and pushed, he was too strong for her. "What are you doing, Cody? Stop this right—"

He paid no attention, swallowing her words as his mouth closed over hers. Faith stood stiffly, determined not to respond, but there was nothing distasteful about the kiss, except for the fact that it was happening in her office. His mouth was warm on hers, inquiring and gentle, a first date kiss that asked rather than demanded.

And it didn't last nearly long enough.

Her eyes were closed when Cody released her mouth. She opened them to find him staring down at her, looking all together very pleased with himself.

"Let's get something straight, shall we?" he said.

He was still holding her, one hand around her waist and one cradling her head. "And what would that be?" she heard herself ask in a languid voice.

"I'm not dating you because Ava Taylor thinks it's a good idea. I'm dating you because I like you—though I'm not entirely sure why."

Faith gave his shoulders another push. This time he released her. She straightened her dress. "Try not to be too lavish with your compliments, okay?"

He laughed. "Maybe it's because just when I think you're completely uptight, you do something off-the-wall. Or it could be because I want to tear your gorgeous hair out of that prim little bun you wear all the time." He reached out to fiddle with her hair.

Horrified, Faith slapped his hand away. If he pulled out her knot she'd never get it back in place. Then the whole office would know that something other than an argument had been going on in her office. "Cody! You can't do that here!"

"Why not? I just kissed you here."

"That's true, but...Look, it's my office, okay? And it's during working hours. I can't...I shouldn't..."

"You look so cute when you're flustered," he murmured. "I feel like kissing you again, just to shake you up even more."

"Cody!"

He laughed. "Instead I'll ask you to go out with me tomorrow night."

Faith didn't even stop to think. "Okay."

"I'll pick you up."

"Okay."

He laughed and ran his knuckles down her cheek. "Wear jeans and comfortable shoes."

And then he was gone.

FAITH TOUCHED her fingers to her lips, lips that still tingled from his touch. A shiver of awareness crawled through her, along with a wish that he was still here so he could recreate the kiss one more time.

His restraint had surprised her. They were both angry and he'd kissed her out of—what? Annoyance because she'd admitted that she'd only gone to dinner with him because of Ava?

No, not annoyance. Faith visualized his face, saw again the determination there and that elusive something else. What was it?

As she imagined the kiss again, she enjoyed the tingle of pleasure even thinking about his touch created, and she understood very well what Cody had been feeling when he'd decided to kiss her. She understood because it was what she was feeling at this very moment. Desire. He had wanted to taste her and his anger today had slipped whatever restraints he'd put on himself the previous night. He'd wanted and he'd taken. It was that simple.

It was amazingly powerful.

Even now, when Cody had been gone a full five minutes, Faith still couldn't stop thinking about him or the way he had kissed her. Or the fact that they were going out again tomorrow night and this time it was for man-woman reasons, not sensible business associates reasons. That meant another kiss, maybe many other kisses from Cody.

She grinned at nothing in particular. She could handle that. Heck, she was even looking forward to it.

Her telephone rang. She stared at it for a moment, completely disoriented. The ringing stopped as voicemail picked up the call. She realized that her light was blinking and that one or more messages had been left since she and Cody had kissed…here in her office…during business hours…

She sank down into her chair, resting her head in her hands. Dear heavens what was she thinking of?

She had just been kissed by another NIT employee, in her office. Okay, her door was closed so the staff couldn't see them. That was good. That it had been done at all was bad.

She'd agreed to go on a date with said employee. That was good. She liked him and she wanted to get to know him better. He said he wanted a relationship with her. A man-woman relationship, not a 'let's work well together' relationship. That was…good, maybe. It was certainly a complication.

Then there was Uncle Andrew. He was another complication. A big one. Said employee didn't know about Uncle Andrew. She groaned. If her relationship with Cody had just been a work association, there would be no reason for Andrew's name to even come up. But in a man-woman relationship? Wouldn't Cody expect to know her odder characteristics, like her ability to draw people through time?

The possibility that Uncle Andrew might accidentally meet Cody Simpson made her sweat just thinking about it. Somehow she was going to have to convince Andrew to stay away, at least for the next little while.

Andrew was supposed to be coming by tonight so they could compare dates. She'd talk to him then and convince him that he should do as she asked.

What if he refused? Andrew liked to be clean. To do that he used her bathroom. He could be quite stubborn at times, particularly when something impacted directly on his comforts.

She'd better have back up.

Ignoring the flashing light that indicated waiting voicemail, she called her sister.

# CHAPTER 13

"*H*e can't come anymore." At her sister's horrified look, Faith hastily amended her statement. "At least, not while I'm dating Cody."

"How are you going to stop him?"

Faith chewed the inside of her lip. "I don't know. Mom says that there's no way to stop the beacon. She told me that if Andrew wants to come and he can find me, he will come."

"So, you'll have to make arrangements that suit both of you." Elizabeth opened Faith's fridge door. "Don't you have any milk? How am I supposed to make Alfredo sauce without milk?"

"I ran out this morning. What suits Andrew is my bathroom, accessible to him whenever he wants it. We're not going to be able to work out any compromises." Faith watched Elizabeth as she rummaged around in the fridge, her back bent, her behind wiggling as she danced to some internal beat. "Look, there's tomato sauce in the cupboard. We can use that on the pasta."

"No good. I want Alfredo. You've got the parmesan. Is there cream?"

"I never buy cream. You know that."

"A girl can hope. Okay…" She pretended to roll up her sleeves, although they were enjoying a mid-June warm spell that had pushed the temperature into the eighties so she was wearing a skimpy tank top that showed off both her shoulders and her abdomen. "I'll do modified Alfredo. Liz Hamilton's own cream-based sauce with cheese. Now, what can I find in here? Is there plain yogurt? Cottage cheese? Honest to Pete, Faith. Don't you keep anything useful in your fridge?"

"Of course I do—normally. I've been distracted this week," Faith said with considerable dignity.

"Oh, right. Cody Simpson. From the sounds of the guy he'd distract me too. Ah-ha!" Liz pounced on a pot of sour cream, opened it up and sniffed to determine if it was still good. "Ummm, I can work with this. Okay, we're in business. Oh, look, you have bacon! We'll make it a creamy bacon and parmesan sauce." She dumped the food items on the counter and rolled up her sleeves. "Out of the way! I am cooking!"

"Uncle Andrew has also been on my mind," Faith sat down at the kitchen table, feeling rather gloomy. "Liz, what if Cody and Andrew meet?"

Liz dumped a half a pound of bacon into the skillet, then scooped butter into a pan. As it was melting she pulled out the canister that contained flour. She shook some into the bubbling butter, then whisked it into a roux. As she added sour cream thinned with water, she said, "Well, they'll either like each other or they won't." She mixed the cream into the flour, careful to keep lumps from forming.

"Liz!"

Satisfied that the sauce was heating nicely, Elizabeth left it to thicken as she turned her attention to adding pasta to the boiling water. "Faith, Andrew can take care of himself. And—" She broke off as she fussed with the bacon, which was just beginning to sizzle.

"And?"

"Do you want to do a salad, Faith? I saw lettuce and tomatoes in your fridge."

Faith stood up. "Yes, I'll do a salad, but you're not answering my question. You were going to add something. What was it?"

The bacon popped. Elizabeth turned down the heat then faced her sister. "Do you really want to get involved with a guy who won't accept your special abilities?"

"Who says I'm getting 'involved' with Cody Simpson?"

"You do." The bacon spat and Elizabeth turned back to the stove.

Staring into the fridge, searching for lettuce and tomatoes, Faith sighed. "You're right. I do want to get involved with Cody. But…I'm not ready to reveal I'm a Beacon. I want to wait, to see how the relationship goes, before I unload one of my weirder characteristics on him. Is that so bad?"

"Nah," said Liz, flipping the bacon. "Pass me the parmesan, would you?" Faith pulled out the pot of grated cheese, which she handed to her sister.

Liz watched the pan as she whisked the cheese into the sauce. "Talk to Andrew, Faith. You two have been friends since you were teenagers. Ask him to back off for awhile." She looked over at Faith and her expression softened. "He'll understand."

"He's courting Mary Elizabeth." Faith washed lettuce, then tore the leaves into pieces she dumped into a pottery bowl. "This is it. He's found—although he may not realize it yet—the love of his life. He'll want to impress her. He'll want to use the bathroom."

"So let him use the bathroom. Just ask him to use it earlier in the evening, like around five o'clock, after you're back from work and before Cody shows up."

Faith sliced up tomato. "Could work."

"Okay, we're done," Liz said. "If the salad is ready, Faith, rinse the pasta while I put the sauce into a bowl."

Together they laid the table. Faith thoughtfully set a third place for Andrew, then she opened a bottle of wine and poured three glasses.

Liz was ladling sauce into a bowl when Andrew arrived without fanfare, sauntering into the kitchen with the ease of one who assumes he is welcome. She smiled and indicated the full glass of wine. "Hi, Andrew. We've already started, so help yourself."

Faith glowered at him.

Andrew picked up the glass. "My thanks, Miss Elizabeth." He glanced at Faith. "Is there something wrong, Faith, my girl? Did your evening with your young man go wrong, then?"

"No." Faith brought the salad bowl over to the table. She thumped it down in front of Andrew, who was standing with one hand on a chair back, sipping his wine. "I like him, Andrew."

He looked from the bowl to Faith, a cautious expression on his face. "Well, that would be perfectly fine. Would it not?"

Liz brought serving bowls of pasta and sauce over to the table. "It is and it isn't, Andrew."

Andrew was frowning now. "You speak in riddles, both of you. Pray say what you must plainly so that I may understand."

Liz patted him on the shoulder. "I love the way you talk when you're upset, Andrew. Have a seat. Dinner is served."

Looking grim, Andrew sat down at the table. Liz sat beside him, while Faith settled opposite. Food was passed, wineglasses refilled. "Let us be frank—"

"Let's," Faith said. She had to swallow hard to ensure she had enough nerve to get the words out. "Andrew, you have to stop visiting me. For the next few weeks anyway."

She caught him just at the moment when he'd filled his mouth with salad. His eyes narrowed as he crunched the lettuce without any sign of enjoyment. "Why?"

There was no gentle way to phrase this. Faith picked up her wineglass and saw that her hand was trembling. She put the goblet down with a thump. "I don't want people to know that I'm a Beacon."

Andrew stared at her through those cautious, narrowed eyes. "You live in an enlightened age. It cannot be that you fear for your safety if the world should come to know of your skill."

"No."

"Then it must be some particular person who is the cause of this sudden decision. Is it the man you spent last evening with?"

Faith fiddled with her pasta, pushing the noodles around on her plate with as much concentration as if she was counting her lifesavings. Finally she looked up. "Yes."

Andrew picked up his wineglass then leaned back in his chair. Raising the glass, he observed Faith over it. "I believe you feel the same way about this man—what is his name?"

"Cody."

"Of course. The same way about this Cody as I do about Mary Elizabeth."

"I don't know. How do you feel about Mary Elizabeth?"

Andrew smiled. "She intrigues me. I desire to understand her, to know what she thinks, to spend my time with her." He paused to sip again, then captured Faith's gaze with his own over the rim of the glass. "Does that describe your feelings for this Cody?"

Faith pushed her plate away. "Andrew, I'm not sure what I feel for Cody. All I know is that I want to be with him so I can learn more about him. I can't do that while I'm worried that you might suddenly appear out of nowhere."

He stared at her for an endless time, then he looked down at his plate. He lowered the wineglass to the table, fiddling with it to make sure it was in the correct position. "I had not realized my visits to you were a burden, Mistress Hamilton. I will come to you no more, then."

"Andrew!" Liz reached out to him, pleading silently. "If you stop visiting there is no way Faith can contact you when she changes her mind."

"And when would that be? When she has no more use for this Cody fellow?"

"That's unfair, Andrew! I didn't say forever. I just said for a while. Until I get to know Cody well enough to figure out if he'll understand the Beacon. If he'll accept that I'm different."

"What you are asking is insulting to our friendship." There was anger in Andrew's voice, carefully restrained, but there nonetheless.

"I'm asking for a compromise," Faith said, feeling a bit angry herself. "Friends compromise. They accept each other's differences."

"And yet, you do not expect this Cody to accept you."

Faith wanted to protest, but she felt a despairing knot in her stomach. Andrew wouldn't listen.

He stood and pushed his chair back from the table. "I will miss you both," he said as he bowed, very formally, and with finality.

Liz whirled on her sister. "Faith, do something. Say something. Stop this!"

The knot in Faith's stomach tightened. She didn't know how to keep Andrew from doing exactly what she'd hoped he'd do.

Andrew smiled sadly. "Miss Elizabeth, can you not see? She is ashamed."

"There's no reason for Faith to be ashamed of you, Andrew!"

"It is not me, she is ashamed of, Miss Elizabeth," he said gently. "It is herself."

"I DON'T KNOW why I'm here, Faith." Elizabeth sat on Faith's bed, watching as her sister dragged a brush through her hair.

"You're here," Faith said, tossing her head to add a little element of muss to the hair she'd just brushed into sleek submission, "in case Andrew shows up."

"He won't come."

"Ha!" Faith stared in the mirror. Behind her own image she could see Liz's head and shoulders, hovering there, reminding her of the immensity of what she'd done. Liz believed Andrew would never return to this time period. Liz was wrong. She had to be wrong. Andrew would show up, if not today then another day. She had not sent him away forever. She wasn't going to feel guilty about that and she certainly wasn't going to accept his parting shot that she was ashamed of what she was.

"I should leave before Cody gets here."

If anything, Liz was more upset by Andrew's banishment than Faith was. Faith tossed the brush on the bureau and went over to sit beside her sister. "Liz, Andrew will be back tonight or another night to wash his hair or get his clothes dry cleaned or because another cow calved and he's a mess. You don't have to worry about him. Trust me on this. I know the guy. He likes our century. He'll be back, no matter what he said."

"He doesn't come forward just for the cleaning facilities, Faith!" Liz said fiercely. "Don't you get it? He's family! He comes because he loves us and he knows that whatever happens we'll be there for him." She crossed her arms over her breasts and glowered at Faith. "Or at least he used to know that. Now I'm not so sure."

"You're making way more of this than there is."

Liz bounced to her feet. "Am I? If I was the one who was a Beacon would you cut me out of your life because you'd met a guy who wouldn't believe or accept what I did?"

"Liz, you're my sister!" The doorbell rang. "Shoot, there's Cody now." She put her hands on Elizabeth's shoulders and gave them a quick squeeze. "We can talk about this later, if you want, but I think we're arguing over nothing. Andrew will be back."

Liz shook her head. Faith fled the room and raced down the stairs to grab the door, leaving her sister to follow more slowly.

She greeted Cody with a big, cheerful smile she wasn't really feeling. He looked great. Like Faith, he was casually dressed, but she loved the way his jeans hugged his slim hips. A lock of his dark hair fell over his forehead, adding a disheveled charm to the warm smile of appreciation in his eyes and on his lips.

"Ready?"

Faith nodded, then she remembered Liz. As annoyed as she was with her sister, she couldn't walk out without saying good-bye. "Liz, we're off! Let yourself out when you're done. We can talk later."

Liz leaned against the banister, crossing one leg in front of the other in a casual stance. "You can bet on that."

Before Faith could close the door, Cody smiled over her shoulder and said, "Hi, I'm Cody."

Liz pushed away from the banister and ran lightly down the worn treads. Reaching the door she looked at Faith then back to Cody. "Apologies for Faith. Introducing family isn't one of her stronger skills." She held out her hand. "I'm Faith's sister, Liz. Nice to meet you, Cody."

Strangling her sister would be too easy a death. "Liz!"

Liz showed her teeth in a wolfish smile. "Can't leave Cody with the impression that family isn't important to you."

Faith shot her a lethal look. "We have to go." She took Cody's hand then turned her back on her sister.

"Nice meeting you, Cody," Liz said.

Stiff with fury, Faith tugged at Cody's hand as she crossed the porch and headed down the stairs. Liz was being a total jerk. Sure she had a grievance, but there was no reason to take it outside the family. What if Cody started asking questions she couldn't answer, all because of Liz's snark?

"You guys have a good time tonight," Liz called. The front door closed with an annoyed clunk. Faith relaxed.

Once in the car Cody laughed and said, "I don't have much experience in this, but I think you and your sister bicker really well."

Dragged out of her brooding, Faith smiled at him. "You don't have any siblings, Cody?"

He shook his head. "The only child of workaholic parents." He changed the subject quickly. "So, are you ready for an evening of Mountain Madness?"

Faith laughed. She pushed away the memory of Liz's words and the expression in Andrew's eyes. Tonight she was going to have fun, if it killed her.

THE MOUNTAIN MADNESS MUSIC FESTIVAL was one of Cody's favorite events. Held annually in a small town in the Berkshire Mountains, the festival took place over three nights, with the big night being Saturday. Because the event featured alternative music mixed with upcoming bands, you never knew what you were going to get.

"I asked Mel to pack us a picnic supper that we could eat while we were waiting for the concert to begin," he said with a quick smile in her direction. "They usually start late, but you never know. You've got to be prepared for anything at Mountain Madness."

"You certainly do," Faith said, laughing. "Including the weather. A couple of years ago I went with my mom and sister. There was a monumental rainstorm. The stage was covered, so the musicians were okay, but we were soaked. We came home looking and feeling like we'd spent the evening swimming in our clothes, not at a concert."

He negotiated the exit to the Interstate. "You could have left early."

She made a good-natured, rude sound. "No way! So we got a little wet. It was a warm evening."

A part of him relaxed. Faith was so organized at work, so composed and controlled, that he had to know if that was all there was to her. Was she the kind of woman who would be flexible enough to enjoy an evening spent in the outdoors with mosquitoes, black flies, and thousands of people?

He admitted to himself that he'd chosen tonight and this event deliberately. He wanted to see how Faith responded to the beat of the music, if she could lose herself in the sound. Above all he needed to know if she could adapt to the planned chaos that was the Mountain Madness Music Festival.

Faith had passed the first hurdle—she was excited about going. That lifted Cody's spirits and gave him hope for the rest of the evening, and beyond. His ex-wife would never go to Mountain Madness. She'd said, more than once, that mud and music that sounded like angry cats or loud bands that relied on energy, not talent, were not her thing. She preferred a piano bar and the intimacy of a small, select audience. Those kinds of evenings had bored Cody silly, particularly when they included kissing up to your boss or his wife. Gillian, his ex, never seemed to mind though.

"I'm glad you suggested I wear jeans tonight," Faith said, breaking into thoughts that were darkening nastily.

His mood lifted at the sound of her voice. "Yeah. I didn't think you'd want to wear heels if we were going to be tromping through a field."

She laughed again and he sneaked a glance her way. Her long blond hair spilled over the faded blue jean jacket she wore over a scooped neck knit shirt. His gaze drifted lower, noting with approval the black jeans that hugged her hips and legs. She looked very different from the uptight, put-together office manager he saw during the day.

It took them an hour to reach their destination and another twenty minutes to walk from the enormous parking lot that had been carved out of a farmer's field to the hillside where the stage had been set up. Most of the distance was uphill. Cody carried the picnic basket in one hand while Faith tucked her hand into the other in a spontaneous action that had Cody's heart lurching with pleasure.

As they found a place close to the stage, dusk was on the way. They settled into their spot, Cody laying a blanket over the cool ground, Faith unpacking the picnic basket.

They ate while a band consisting of an electric violin, guitar, organ, and a torch singer performed, then swayed along with another group featuring an energetic drummer. As the evening went on the rhythms intensified as the musicians responded to the enthusiasm of the crowd. Cody watched with delight as Faith came out of herself, singing along, clapping and hooting. Her enthusiasm intoxicated him far more than the wine they'd had with dinner. He wanted her—in his arms, in his life—wild and passionate, uptight and businesslike.

He caught her hand, turning it so he could kiss the throbbing vein at her wrist. Her eyes opened wide with surprise. The music flowed around them, exotic and rhythmic. Her lips parted. He took advantage of the moment to bend his head and cover her mouth with his.

Faith stood still. Her eyes slid closed as, tentatively, she responded to his touch. His heart stopped then slammed into overdrive. He let go of her wrist so he could catch her around the waist and pull her close. Then he kissed her with all the feelings that had been growing in him through the evening. Her body quivered, then eased closer.

Elation grabbed him when she stroked his lips with the tip of her tongue. He opened his mouth to deepen the kiss. Her body melted into his, relying on him to keep her steady. He was throbbing now, desire licking through him. He touched her tongue with his, reveling in the stab of pleasure that resulted. Faith made a breathy sound in her throat that wasn't quite a groan, but more a purr of pure pleasure.

The mood of the music changed and along with it the rhythm of their kiss. The singer was a woman, her voice dark and sensual, but the sound was in the background now, no longer the focus of their evening together. With their mouths still hungrily tasting, Cody was lost in desire for Faith. He wanted to lower her down to the blanket that protected their little patch of ground and make love to her right there. But he couldn't—wouldn't—do that. If he was going to make love to her it would be in a place where they could be private, where they could savor the feelings they were rousing in each other.

He lifted his head and took a deep breath. Unable to keep himself from touching her, he stroked her hair away from her face as he said, "You're so beautiful."

Faith blushed. "Wow, Cody. Where did you ever learn to kiss like that?"

He laughed and kissed her again, this time grazing with little nibbling kisses along the sensitive skin on her neck.

"Oh man," Faith said as he pushed her jacket and top off her shoulder. She made that little purring sound again as she turned her head so their lips would meet.

This time when they kissed Cody allowed himself to slip his hand under her top. Her skin was smooth and warm, an enticement to explore further.

Faith groaned. She pulled her mouth away from his. "Cody, what you are doing to me." She moistened her lips.

He couldn't resist. He touched where her tongue had been with his.

She whimpered. "Oh my."

"I want to make love to you."

She went still. "Cody, I—"

He put a finger over her mouth. "Not here. Later. When we get home."

"I'm not sure. This is only the second time we've been out together."

"Don't say no." He kissed her fiercely, hungrily, his mouth hard on hers, showing her his passion, demanding hers in return. She gave it to him, her tongue clashing with his, her body moving sensuously against him. He was on fire, lost in her, lost in his own desire.

He had to come up for air. Faith put her head on his shoulder. She was trembling, her body still soft and warm against his. The woman singer finished her set. The crowd cheered and clapped.

The lights came up. The concert was over.

"Well?" he said.

# CHAPTER 14

*F*aith could still hear the music in her head when she took Cody's hand as she climbed out of the car. She danced a little as they walked to her door. The evening had been wonderful and it was about to get even better.

They were on her front porch now and she knew Cody was going to kiss her again. She still hadn't consciously acknowledged that she was going to invite him in, but she knew, deep in her heart, that she would. Normally she wouldn't even think about making love on the second date, but with Cody everything was different. Quicker, more intense. All that was keeping her from allowing desire to overcome caution was commitment. Commitment to the new path she had chosen. Commitment to the real world and the man who was so much a part of it. She was alone with Cody, her bedroom within easy reach. They could let the kiss take them to where they both wanted to go.

A week ago—two nights ago!—she had been a Beacon, afraid of inviting her real world friends to her home. Afraid because she couldn't be sure that Uncle Andrew wouldn't walk in at any time.

She was still a Beacon, and always would be one, but now she had an opportunity to see what life was like without the specter of Andrew's sudden appearance to hold her back.

She could begin tonight. She could ask Cody in. She could let him make love to her on her own bed, in her own room, without being fearful Andrew would interrupt them. Although, to be fair, she would never have expected Andrew to show up at three-thirty in the morning.

Her body tingled with anticipation. She could ask Cody in. She wanted to ask him in. Did she dare?

Cody's mouth was on hers, shutting off rational thought. His lips were warm, dry, and evocative as he gave her little nibbling kisses that made her nerve endings tingle. She moved her head, tilting it so she could enjoy his touch more, then put her hands on his shoulders to hold herself upright. She could feel the evidence of his response hard against her. He wanted her as much as she wanted him.

"My key," she mumbled against his mouth, still drowning in his kisses. "It's here. In my jacket, I think. What did I do with it?" She let his shoulder go so she could reach in her pocket. Her fingers fumbled inside, finding nothing, even though the keychain had to be there. She wasn't functioning very well at the moment. His kisses were too seductive and she wanted him too much. "Cody, you'll have to give me a second here. I can't think."

"I don't want you to think," he said, taking the opportunity to nibble the throbbing artery in her neck.

Faith groaned. "Cody, stop! For a minute. Only a minute. Just till I get my key."

"Promise?" He kissed his way up and along her jawline back to her mouth.

This time the kiss was long, intense and deep. Faith surrendered to it, allowed her body to flame with desire. She forgot she was supposed to be hunting for her door key.

He released her mouth. Lifted his head. "Okay. Take a break. Find your key." He kept her close to him. One hand slid up under her shirt to stroke her body. It lingered at her breast, caressing, teasing. Her nipple came alive, shot sensation through her body, added heat to the firestorm inside her.

Faith drew a shaky breath. If this was taking a break, she wasn't going to make it. Her fingers trembled as she searched in her pocket. She touched something hard, with sharp edges, but her mind had apparently become incapable of rational thought and she couldn't identify the object. She closed her fingers over it and pulled it out.

Then laughed with delight. "My key!"

The moment for commitment was very close. With key in hand she could open the door. Then she would have to decide whether to invite him in or say good-night.

She wrapped her arms around his neck and looked up at him, an invitation in her eyes. He responded, his mouth coming down on hers. His tongue teased her lips, and she opened to him. He probed deeply and she responded, wanting more. The need to be with him, to invite him in and give herself to him, was strong. Did she dare?

Yes. The kiss blazed between them, providing pleasure, offering a promise. When it had burned low enough for Faith to break away she said, in a voice that was sultry with anticipation, "I don't know if I'm going to be able to manipulate the door. Would you like to do the honors?"

"My pleasure," he said, his voice as husky as hers. But he didn't move. He kissed her again and built up the flame that had forged her commitment to this moment.

Faith sighed and moved against him. Her breasts were rubbing over his hard chest, her already sensitized nipples pulsing with arousal. She wanted him, oh my how she wanted him. Nothing mattered right now but Cody and her desire for him. Nothing. He drove her crazy, but he was the most unexpected, the most fun man she'd ever met. "Take me inside."

He reached up, snagged the key chain that dangled off one finger and reached past her for the door. He fumbled a bit as he turned the key, throwing the deadbolt, but his grip was firm as he lifted the latch and shoved, hard.

A relic of nineteenth century construction, the door was big and heavy, but over the years the hinges had been kept well oiled. Cody's push, full of pent up energy, contained more force than he needed. The door swept open, hit the doorstop with a thump, then bounced back before it stopped.

"Wow," Faith said, and giggled.

Cody looked a little surprised for a moment, but it didn't take him long to recover. He eased Faith into the dark hall. With her back against the wall he pinned her with his body. "Are you sure about this?"

"Yes." She reached up to stroke his cheek. "Stay the night."

"Oh yeah," he said. He caught her lower lip with his teeth and sucked.

Faith melted. "Upstairs. Now!"

He laughed. Then stilled. "What was that?"

Faith escaped from the sensual fog he'd created, but slowly. "What are you talking about?"

Cody straightened, then stepped away from her, tension in every muscle of his gorgeous body.

Frowning, Faith stared at him. "What's the matter?"

"A sound, coming from there." He pointed.

To the living room.

Faith's heart shuddered. Horror enveloped her.

Uncle Andrew had already broken his promise.

Improbable as it seemed, he'd lain in wait until he'd seen her beacon, then he'd come forward to interrupt her evening. Just to prove he could.

Or maybe he wanted to continue their argument. That would be a more charitable assumption. After all, he'd always respected her privacy in the past. The Friday evening visit was a compromise they'd worked out at the beginning. She'd been in high school then, a gangly girl with little or no social life. Andrew's regular visits had begun after her father had left, when they were all raw with the pain of his abandonment. Chloe had made Andrew welcome, treated him as part of the family. It had seemed right to see him every week, to talk over her experiences, to hear about his.

They all knew he could come forward any time he could find Faith's beacon, but he'd always respected her space. Still, there was no denying that it was three-thirty in the morning and he was here. That in itself was an intrusion.

So what was she going to do about it? "Cody, it's okay. This is an old house. It creaks and groans all the time."

His body language didn't change. "That wasn't a house sound I heard. It was someone moving around. There it is again!"

He was right. The sound was definitely the kind made by a person trying to be quiet but not quite succeeding.

Oh, damn and double damn. Now what was she going to do?

Cody looked around the hall. It didn't contain a lot. There was a cupboard for coats and shoes and the antique half-table on which she had placed a bronze tray she used to catch the mail, but little else. He zoomed in on the metal plate, the only moveable object in the area. "It's not much," he muttered, scooping up the mail and dumping it on the table, "but it will have to do." He hefted his weapon.

Faith stared at him, aghast. He was planning to do battle to protect her. Though the sentiment was lovely—the thought that he would fight for her warmed her right to her toes—it was totally unnecessary.

Furthermore, she was quite sure Uncle Andrew would not bother to pause for discussion or questions when Cody leapt into the living room brandishing a bronze tray. If attacked Andrew would retaliate. There would be a scuffle.

The thought of two big males fighting for survival in the confined space of her living room had visions of broken tables, shattered crystal, and torn curtains blazing in her mind. She grabbed his arm. "Cody, wait!"

Her voice rang out, loud in the heavy silence. As the sound died off, there was a moment when nothing happened. She and Cody stood frozen, waiting, testing the potential for utter disaster. In the living room, the quiet sounds of someone moving about had stilled. Uncle Andrew was taking stock of the situation.

Maybe, if she was lucky, he'd take the hint that she was with someone and go back to his own time.

He didn't. He switched on a light in the living room.

Cody shook Faith loose and lunged, clearly intent on doing damage. Faith screamed, "No, Cody! Don't!" and followed him as he charged into the living room.

Just inside the opening he stopped short. Faith landed hard against his back. Though his body still quivered with the preparation for battle, she could feel the tension easing out of him. She peeked over his shoulder, knowing what she would see. Wishing she would not.

"Oh, my heavens!" Liz said. Her face was puffy with sleep, though her eyes were wild with fright. "I've interrupted you. I'm so sorry!"

"Liz?" Faith said, coming around Cody to stand in front of her sister. "What are you doing here?"

"After you and Cody left I sat down for a minute to think. I must have fallen asleep." She rubbed a hand across her face. "What time is it, anyway?"

Cody glanced at his watch. "It's almost four."

"In the morning?" Liz squeaked.

Cody nodded. He turned to Faith. Putting his hands on her

shoulders he said gently, "It's too late for your sister to go home on her own so I'm going to take off." When Faith opened her mouth to protest, he silenced her with a kiss that left her wanting, but told her clearly that he was not about to change his mind. Moments later the door closed after him.

Liz flopped down on the couch were she'd so recently been snoozing.

"Why did you stay?" Faith remained where she stood, her hands bunched into fists.

Liz rubbed her face again. "I didn't plan to. Like I said, after you and Cody left I sat for a while thinking about things. It got dark and I was tired—and unhappy! I guess everything caught up with me."

Faith sighed and sat down beside her sister. "I was going to go to bed with him."

"I kind of figured that. Sorry."

Faith patted her on the knee. "It's okay. I thought you were Uncle Andrew, you know."

"Yeah. When I realized it was you and Cody, I thought you'd jump to that conclusion. Just because Andrew has never shown up in the middle of the night and has always respected your need for private times, I knew you'd figure he was far more likely to be here than your sister, who was in the house when you left."

"Stop it, Liz! I know your opinion."

"Who embarrassed you tonight, Faith? Your eighteenth century ancestor or your twenty-first century sister?"

"I get the point," Faith said curtly.

Liz nodded, then stood up. "Okay. Can I crash on your spare bed? Cody's right. I don't want to have to go home tonight."

"Sure." As she headed out of the room, Faith said, "Liz. What am I going to do? I'm in lust for a guy I work with who comes from the same kind of background Dad does. I like him, a lot, but I don't even know if we have anything that will last beyond a few nights of hot sex. What if I'm tearing my life apart for a guy I'll lose eventually, anyway?"

In the doorway Liz paused. "You're not tearing your life apart because of Cody, Faith. Andrew was right. You're doing this for yourself, because you can't accept that you are different. Instead of celebrating that special part of you, you want to destroy it. Think hard, Faith. This isn't about Cody. It's about you."

AT NINE O'CLOCK on Monday morning Faith settled at her desk with a hot, strong coffee, and logged into her computer. She'd spent Sunday trying to come to grips with her issues, but got nowhere. That had led to a restless night and not enough sleep. She stared at the screen as the computer went through the initialization process. She was so tired she was enjoying watching the various messages flash across the pretty blue backdrop.

A few sustaining jolts of coffee cut through the fog. She opened her e-mail, downloaded a dozen messages and focused on the most important. The first one she opened was from Cody. "Call me when you get in," it said.

A warmth spread through her as she read the words. She picked up the phone and dialed his number, but got his voicemail. Of course. What else was new? "Hi," she said into the machine. "I'm in. Call me when you can." She heard her voice as she spoke. It was low and husky, sounding sexy even to her ears. What was Cody going to think?

Hopefully, exactly what her voice was telling him.

As she hung up the phone she closed her eyes very briefly. Memories of Saturday night made her smile and sway a little in her chair as music blared in her brain. The music festival had been fun—and not just because Cody had sent her flying with his kisses.

He was unexpected and spontaneous. Being with him made her feel—what?

Happy.

She shivered. She shouldn't feel that way with Cody. She couldn't. He was a computer scientist. He dealt in algorithms and binary codes. In Cody's world everything was rational, reasonable and calculable.

Faith was a Beacon. In her world things happened through emotion, visualization and desire. Though there might be a scientific reason for her Beacon ability, it was buried pretty deep. What Faith did was magical, unexplainable even to her. How could the scientist in Cody Simpson cope with a talent like Faith's? If he ever found out, he would run away so fast she wouldn't have time to catch her breath.

She stared gloomily at the computer screen. Her life was a mess. She'd pretty much forced Uncle Andrew to abandon a friendship that spanned ten years and more. She was obsessing over a guy she expected to dump her if he ever got to know her well enough to build a relationship worth having and her sister was mad at her. She needed help. Big time.

"Hi there."

Faith's heart leapt and her spirits soared at the sound of his voice. It was as if a lamp had been turned on to light a dark afternoon. "Cody! I left you a message."

"I know. I just picked it up." He'd been leaning against the doorjamb. Now he entered her office. She stood up and discovered that he was very, very close.

She lifted her head. Her lips parted.

He smiled and his eyes narrowed. His head moved, bending closer. "I called you yesterday."

"I wanted to see you," she whispered. What she really meant was that she wanted to kiss him. Right now. Here in her office. Oh heavens!

"Come out with me tonight," he said.

Her body throbbed. Yes! Yes! Yes! pounded through her veins. Go out with him tonight, retire to his apartment—not hers since there was always the possibility Andrew would show up once he got over his annoyance—and satisfy the need that was clawing at her. "Cody..."

His mouth hovered over hers. Dropped a light kiss. Retreated before she could demand more. "Please."

She was trembling with pent up desire. "Cody, I want to, but..."

He kissed her again, another light fleeting caress that she tried to capture but couldn't. "But what?"

She took a step back, physically and mentally. Yesterday she had sat in her kitchen and stared at the phone as it rang, not once, but twice and then a third time. Stared at it and knew that the person calling was Cody. She'd been afraid to answer, afraid of the choice she'd almost made. She'd thought about what Uncle Andrew had said, about Liz and her anger, and she'd asked herself if going to bed with Cody was the answer. If they made love she'd be giving herself to him. She'd be committing to him. Surely that kind of commitment needed something stronger than the hot flame of desire to sustain it.

She looked at Cody. He was watching her with that sexy half-smile on his mouth, a question in his eyes. She cursed herself for what she was about to say. "I want to get to know you better. There are things...we need discover about each other."

He stared at her for what was probably only a few seconds. For Faith it was a lifetime. Her heart slammed against her ribs, racing with fear and hope until he smiled. "Fair enough. Have lunch with me today. And tomorrow and Wednesday and every other day you can."

"Lunch," she said. Her voice was little more than a whisper.

He smiled, caught her chin in his hand and stroked her skin. "Yeah, lunch. Nice and safe. No opportunity for us to let the physical overwhelm the intellectual. I can't promise I'll wait forever, but for now, I'm happy to explore the many different parts of Faith Hamilton."

He understood. Between the lazy, sensual stroke of his thumb and the stimulating caress of concern, she felt as if she was melting. She wanted him to take that smiling mouth and place it where his thumb was, then work his way along her jaw to her lips. As he kissed her, she would lean her body close to his and rub against him until they were both hot with desire.

He drew his thumb across her lips, then turned away.

And froze.

"Hello, Ava," he said. He positioned himself so that his body was in front of Faith, giving her the time to pull herself together.

"Cody!" Ava said. "I see you and Faith are talking. Did I just hear you say you would be having lunch together?"

Faith almost groaned. How long had Ava been standing in her doorway, listening to their conversation? Too long probably.

"Faith will be having lunch with me, yes. You're welcome to join us."

No! Faith shrieked in her mind. "Yes, Ava, do join us," she said, coming out from behind Cody and smiling as if she wasn't worried about a thing.

Ava waved her hand. "Thank you both, but I've got an appointment at one o'clock that I will need to prepare for. You enjoy yourselves."

Cody smiled at her, a wolfish grin that was more dangerous than amused. "We will."

Ava glanced at her watch. "Faith, would you drop into my office as soon as you have a moment? There's no rush. I just came by to talk to you about Angela. I need your input on how she's handling her new duties."

"Sure, Ava."

Cody said, "Why don't I leave now?" He smiled at Faith. "Twelve okay?"

She nodded. There was a lump in her throat as she watched him go. Dressed in his usual body-hugging jeans and t-shirt he really was a pleasure to look at.

She came back to earth to find Ava watching her in a probing way that was very disconcerting. She raised her brows. "What's up?"

Ava didn't respond directly. She wandered over to Faith's computer, viewed the screen for a minute, then turned back to her. "You know why Cody Simpson was hired, don't you?"

Faith shrugged. "To create software for our new clients."

"He was hired," Ava said, her tone edgy, almost grim, "because he is brilliant. Management and our Board want to keep him within the company. They do not want to see him leave because of personal differences."

Then why was Ava indulging in a power struggle with him? "Personal differences. You mean, like bad vibes between staff members?"

Ava nodded. "Or relationships gone wrong."

The comment hit Faith like a shot to the solar plexus. Ava the tyrannosaur was on the hunt. "Are you talking about Cody and me?"

Ava considered her through narrowed eyes. "I recommended that you get to know Cody Simpson so the two of you could work together in a more productive way. I did not think that anything more would come of it." She smiled briefly. "And I am sure nothing will. Just keep in mind that you and Cody are co-workers, that's all, and everything will be fine."

# CHAPTER 15

She had lunch with Cody. That day and the next, and into the week after. They normally went to The Sandwich Hut and although they usually began sitting alone at a table, by the time their lunch break was over other NIT employees had joined them. Cody, previously elusive and seen only at official company events like the picnic, had the fascination of an eight-day wonder. Everyone seemed to value the opportunity to get to know him in a non-corporate setting.

While Faith would rather have spent time alone with Cody, she had enough secrets to keep in her life. Sneaking around during office hours was more than she was prepared to handle, and would just confirm Ava Taylor's suspicions. So she made the best of the time by making sure that everyone they dined with realized that Cody had his own job to do, as well as Sue Green's. She also coaxed Cody into talking about his work, in layman's terms. The result was that people came away with a much better appreciation of the pressures he was under and his position within the organization.

The lunches helped Faith understand Cody as well. Watching him flash that irresistible smile of his at June as if he had no idea of just how potent it was, or discuss programming with Angela—at her level, not his—showed Faith a side of him that she would have discovered eventually, though perhaps not so effectively, on her own. Cody, blissfully unaware that Ava saw his romantic relationship with Faith as a threat to the NIT organization, was perfectly happy to be seen lunching with Faith and seemed to enjoy their 'dates'.

People began coming to Faith and thanking her for drawing Cody into the mainstream of company life. She accepted those compliments with a rueful smile, but when Ava showed up on the Wednesday afternoon of the second week, to congratulate her on doing what was best for her career and the corporate good, Faith had had enough. That night she packed a picnic lunch and when Cody picked her up the next day, a little late as usual, she told him they were driving to a park away from the office.

He shot her an amused look as she started the car. "Tired of sharing me with the rest of the world?"

She laughed as she steered the car out of the lot. "You could say that." Then she sobered. "I'm getting to know you, Cody, but as a co-worker not—" Lover hovered on her lips. She wanted to say the word, but this wasn't the right time. "Not anything else. And that's what we are supposed to be doing when we meet at lunch. Finding out about Cody and Faith so that we don't let our hormones get the better of our brains."

"So that's why we're going to a park where we can hide behind a tree and neck where no one can see us?"

A rueful smile twitched Faith's lips. "That's why we're going to an urban park where we can sit on a bench out in the open and eat the delicious lunch I've prepared. Then we'll feed the birds while we talk about ourselves." She added severely, "There's no necking involved."

"Too bad."

She heard the laughter in his voice and sighed a little. "Yeah, I know. I kind of liked the necking behind the tree idea too." Out of the corner of her eye she saw him flex his long legs. The jeans he habitually wore to work tightened around his thighs. She wondered if there were any parks in the area that boasted large trees—nix that—large, leafy, overgrown bushes they could hide under, behind, or in, and make that necking-behind-the-tree scenario come true. "Be strong," she muttered to herself.

Cody laughed out loud and reached over to stroke a finger along the sensitive skin on her neck. It was a good thing they had reached their destination. Driving was definitely turning dangerous.

She parked on the street that bordered one side of the park. The park was handkerchief-size and painfully open. There was grass, a couple of benches and a fountain in the center. Brick buildings that housed shops and offices huddled against the sidewalks that edged the streets surrounding the tiny green space. Cody contemplated the location for a time, before he remarked, "The park by the office has three trees and bushes planted all over the place. It also has a flowerbed that's already in bloom."

"That's true," Faith opened her door. "It's also crawling with NIT employees at this time of day." As she slid out of the car she tossed over her shoulder, "Here we can be alone because no one from NIT ever comes here."

She was already at the trunk when he emerged from the car. She kept him busy—and his hands to himself—by giving him the picnic basket to carry. They headed over to one of the benches placed along the edge of the open area. The sun was shining brightly, so they chose the bench that faced away from the light. As they settled, Faith had Cody place the basket between them.

"Is this for security?" he asked as Faith leaned back, stretching out her legs.

She shot him an innocent look. "We can both get at the food without unpacking it all. Makes it much simpler, don't you think?"

"It is security," he said gloomily, but there was a twinkle in his eyes. "I know an excuse when I hear one."

Faith opened the lids on plastic containers. "There's a green salad, potato salad, cold meat, some olives and pickles, and a half a loaf of crusty bread." She handed him a plate. "Help yourself."

For a while they were busy eating. Cody complimented her on her potato salad and on the dressing she'd made for the green salad. Faith thanked him and told him it was a family recipe. That started them talking about food, cooking, and eating out.

Faith took a bite out of the sandwich she'd made with the crusty bread and cold meat. "You know, you've talked about La Renaissance and creating a new database system for Mel, but you've never explained why you were between jobs."

Cody put aside his now empty plate and stretched out his legs. He took a sip from a bottle of designer water, then eyed the label thoughtfully. "I told you that I dropped out of university for awhile after first year."

He glanced over at Faith. She nodded and said, "Yeah. On Monday. You also told June and Greg Blalock from Sales."

Cody took another swig and said, "I kept it simple because June and Greg were around. I don't like people probing too deeply into my personal life."

"I can understand that," Faith said. There was more meaning in that comment than Cody could possibly know.

He examined the label on the bottled water with considerable intensity. "I quit because I failed most of my first year courses."

Faith stared at him. "You, Cody? Everyone says you're brilliant. And I happen to know that you have a Ph.D. You don't get one of those for failing."

Briefly a smile quirked the corner of his mouth. "Everyone said I was brilliant in high school too. They had great plans for me. I was good at problem solving, so they figured I ought to be a doctor. I could diagnose patients and save humanity."

The rueful amusement in his voice touched Faith's heart. Beneath it she heard the confusion felt by the boy for whom learning had always come easy. "Who were 'they'?"

"The school counselors, the university pre-med faculty. My parents were swept along by the prestige of having a doctor in the family. Heck, I got swept up in it too." He straightened and looked over at her, then smiled. "I flunked out because I didn't want to be there. I didn't like biology or chemistry, though I could do them. Halfway through the second semester I just stopped making an effort. It wasn't a conscious decision. I had skipped grades in school and graduated when I was fifteen, so I was the youngest kid in all my classes. I didn't like what I was doing and everyone I knew was hitting the books, struggling to get through. I allowed myself to fail. It was the best thing I could have done."

"I'll bet your parents didn't see it that way."

He laughed. "They were pretty good about it. They were upset, but they believed in me. I got a job in a start-up tech company, working in their computer department. I loved it, even though I was given all the most basic jobs to do. I worked there for two years and by the end of that time I reported to a manager, but I had done every job in the department and could have run the division better than the guy with the official title. Hell, half the time the guy came to me for answers, though he never credited me for my input. At that point I realized that while I might have the knowl-edge and ability, the guys with the string of degrees after their names would always be the ones telling me what to do."

"So you decided to go back to university."

"Yeah. When I was eighteen I reapplied and managed to talk my way into a computer science program on a part-time basis. I really got into it. I had my undergrad in four years, my masters in two and the Ph.D in three."

"You must have spent a lot of time cracking the books. I guess you didn't have much of a social life."

There was a charged silence. Faith searched her memory for the reason, but couldn't come up with anything that would cause Cody to stare with such fierce intensity at a woman walking a dog along the sidewalk opposite the park. She took a small bite of her sandwich and waited.

Finally he said, "In a way I had too much social life."

"O...kay." She spaced the word into two separate syllables so that it was almost a question. Something had gone wrong in Cody's life, something that had left scars, but all she could come up with was that he'd been part of the drug scene. That didn't exactly fit with the kind of accomplishments he'd made, so it must be something else, but what? Faith took another bite of her sandwich and waited. His silence was killing her, but she forced herself to be still and to let him pick his time.

He put the bottle to his mouth and took a swig of water. After a moment he shifted so that he was facing her. "I got married between my third and fourth years, Faith." He paused for a heartbeat, and another. "I celebrated my graduation by getting divorced." He hurried on before she could speak. "I was twenty when we got married and she was twenty-one. She was beautiful and sexy and she wanted to be with me. She particularly liked going to parties organized by my co-workers. She fit in well and everyone thought she was great. I was flattered."

Faith finished her sandwich and swallowed. "No offence, Cody, but she sounds like a trophy wife."

His mouth quirked up to one side in a smile heavily laced with self-contempt, then he laughed humorlessly. "You've got it backwards. I was the trophy husband. She had great plans for me once I'd graduated. She had visions of me moving on to a big multinational and becoming a vice president so she could be an executive's wife. She was furious when I told her I was taking my masters degree and staying right where I was."

"Did she divorce you?"

"Yup. It was a big blow to my ego at the time, but I later decided it was one of those things that was for the best."

Faith understood Cody well enough by now to know that title and position weren't important to him. "Your ex must have been pretty self-centered to have believed you would change your style because she thought it would be a good idea."

He laughed, again without a lot of humor. "She was one of those people who liked to organize everything and everyone. She'd plan out my day and arrange my schedule. At first I thought it was amazingly generous of her, because she had a full load of courses and as much to do as I did. Later I came to realize she was controlling me. That's when I started questioning everything she did. By then it was too late, though. We were already married."

Faith sighed, having some understanding of what he was going through. "I've never had a serious relationship that ended in a painful breakup, but my parents' divorce was pretty bitter." She reached across the picnic basket, placing her hand over the back of his. "If it means anything, I think she was a big dummy for trying to change who you are."

He turned his hand so he could clasp hers. "You mean you don't care that it takes me hours to get down to fix your computer problems?"

She laughed. "Yes, I care! That's work, Cody. I have to be organized in my job and I expect the people I work with to be equally efficient. At home, though. At home is different. People are what they are and they deserve the freedom of living their lives the way they want to. And that includes career and lifestyle choices."

He stared down at their entwined fingers, then looked up and flashed her that wicked, heart-breaking smile of his. "I wish you'd been around when I was an undergrad. You'd have saved me from making a big mistake."

"I'm here now," she said softly.

He leaned toward her, his gaze intent. Faith guessed that he wanted to kiss her, but the picnic basket was between them and there were people wandering across the park, along the sidewalks. He cleared his throat and instead lifted her hand to his mouth and kissed her knuckles.

The caress burned through Faith, igniting a firestorm of feeling. No matter how open the park, how public every action was, it would be easy to forget everything and let the moment get out of hand. She had to do something to get them both talking again, now, before her body took over from her brain.

Desperately she went back to where the conversation had been before they'd detoured onto the rough road of broken relationships. "So did you meet Mel when you were at university?"

He didn't answer immediately. Instead he turned her hand and took his time kissing the throbbing vein on the underside of her wrist. Faith almost groaned.

Finally he carefully put her hand on her lap and said, "I was working on my Ph.D. The high tech company where I was employed had grown, but there wasn't a whole lot of cash. Salaries were low and they paid out bonuses in the form of equity. The company was bought out by a heavy-weight player in the industry, so my shares were suddenly worth a whole bunch of money. After the buyout I had to sign a non-compete clause that said I wouldn't work for another company in the same industry again for three years. That was fine with me. I had enough money to live well and still focus on completing the degree. I'm not much of a cook and I liked Mel's food, so I spent a lot of time at La Renaissance." He smiled. "You know the rest."

"I don't really. I know you did the project for Mel and that you've been employed by NIT for the past six months. But I don't understand why you're working for us, if you have enough money to live independently and do projects like the one you did for Mel."

He spread his hands out, palms upward. "Faith, I don't know if you'll understand, but…NIT offered me creative freedom, as well as a financial package that I couldn't turn down."

She considered that, watching him. "I'd heard the money part. I didn't know creative freedom was so important."

He laughed. "It's my key. The multinational asked me to stay on after the takeover. I did for a while, but they expected me to wear a suit and keep regular hours even if I'd worked for forty-eight straight on the weekend. It was as if I was punching a clock." He paused. "I felt the same way I did that first year in university pre-med. I hated it. So I quit, even though I didn't know where I'd work again. I had the non-compete clause, so I couldn't go into the same field. The work I did for Mel showed me there were other uses for my skills, but I still didn't know how to market them. Or even if anyone other than a small operation like Mel's would be interested in a…freak…like me. When my Ph.D supervisor suggested NIT contact me, it was a validation of everything I'd done with my life. "

Faith stared at him in disbelief. "You see yourself as a freak?"

He smiled ruefully and shrugged. "As different anyway. I don't fit into neat categories, Faith. I work without stopping when the urge is upon me, I'm a clock watcher's nightmare, and I like to follow my own path." He reached out, stroked her cheek. "Do you think you can tolerate that about me?"

His words echoed in her heart. He would understand, she thought joyfully. He wouldn't condemn her for being a Beacon. She was certain of it. Liz was right. She needed to tell him. "Cody, do you think you'd like to come over and meet my family on Saturday night?"

# CHAPTER 16

"*D*ad's in town."

"What?" Faith blinked at her sister who was standing framed in the front doorway. She opened the door wider. "No, he's not. He's working on that mega-project in China."

Liz flew into the house, urgency in her expression and movement. The fabric of her flowing skirt swirled about her ankles, like the froth of an incoming wave. "Wrong! Dad's here! He called me yesterday as soon as his plane got in." She shoved a bowl filled with salad greens at Faith. "He wanted to have dinner with me tonight."

Faith's fingers curled around the bowl as Liz gulped and brushed past her. She kicked the door closed and followed her sister. "But you're here."

Liz stopped in the middle of the perfectly proportioned hall and turned to Faith. Her eyes pleaded for understanding. "Yeah. And Dad will be too. Faith, I am so sorry!"

Faith opened her mouth then closed it again without uttering a sound. This could not be happening. Not tonight. Finally she said thinly, "You invited Dad to my dinner party for Cody?"

Liz nodded unhappily. "He is family."

Only the distress in her sister's eyes kept Faith from snapping an angry reply. Liz had been their father's favorite and he in turn had always known how to coax her into doing whatever he wanted. "You know why I've invited Cody tonight?"

Liz nodded. Her expression said she was miserably aware that she'd gone way beyond sisterly limits this time.

"Mom's in the kitchen," Faith said helplessly. "They weren't even civil to each other the last time we all got together."

They stared at each other. "Oh, Faith! Oh, hell, I wish I hadn't done this!" Liz said again. She sounded as if she was on the verge of tears. "He called and I said I was coming over here tonight and he said, 'I haven't seen Faith in years—'"

"Three years," Faith said, a hint of bitterness in her voice. "His choice, not mine."

Elizabeth nodded miserably. "And then he said 'We argued the last time I saw her—'"

"He told me I would never succeed in the real world because I was a Beacon. I remember that night vividly. I was starting at NIT the next day. It was a real boost to my confidence."

Liz shrugged helplessly. "He wants to make amends."

Faith stared at her sister. She didn't know why Daniel Hamilton wanted to come to her family dinner tonight, but she sincerely doubted that it was because he wanted to straighten out his relationship with his eldest daughter. She couldn't say that aloud, however. She wouldn't ruin the relationship Liz had with their father, just because it was different from hers. "Maybe he does. Look, Mom's in the kitchen. We'd best tell her what's up." They headed across the hall. "Does Dad know Mom is going to be here?"

Liz brightened and nodded. "I told him he had to be good or else he couldn't come. He said he would."

"I'll bet," Faith muttered. They reached the kitchen. Dressed in a crimson silk blouse, tailored white trousers, and a bibbed apron to protect her outfit, Chloe Hamilton was at the counter stirring batter in an old-fashioned stoneware mixing bowl. She looked around when her daughters entered. "Strawberry shortcake for dessert. Do you think Cody will like it, Faith?"

"Sure. Mom…" She couldn't finish. She put the salad bowl on the table and looked at Elizabeth. "It's your news. You tell her."

Liz said, "Ummmm, Mom."

Chloe stopped stirring and narrowed her eyes. She looked from one daughter to the other. "Something is wrong. What is it?"

Liz cleared her throat, fiddled with her hair, and finally said in a rush, "Dad's coming tonight."

"I see." Chloe returned to her stirring. "Is that all? I thought something dreadful had happened."

Liz and Faith looked at each other. Faith supposed her expression was as baffled as her sister's was. "So you're okay with seeing Dad?"

Chloe poured the batter into cake pans. "It's a good thing this recipe serves six. With your father's sweet tooth, he's bound to want at least two servings." When she finished she set the bowl down and turned to face her daughters. As she thoughtfully wiped her fingers on the apron, she said, "Your father and I have had our differences…"

That was putting it mildly, Faith thought.

"But we're adults and we can deal with it."

Chloe's comment set off warning bells in Faith's head. Though her mother was reasonable and calm away from her father, meetings between her parents tended to be filled with hostility. The sinking sensation in the pit of her stomach deepened. This was not going to work. "Liz, can you call Dad and tell him that I'll see him another time? He can come over tomorrow. Or we can meet somewhere for dinner."

The doorbell rang. Faith groaned.

Liz moistened her lips. "I think we're too late."

"It might be Cody," Faith said. She glanced at her watch. She'd invited Cody to arrive a good forty-five minutes after her family had assembled. There were still thirty minutes to go. Since Cody resisted schedules he might just be early tonight, rather than late. She could hope.

Hope fled as she opened the door to find her father standing there. There was a bottle of wine in his hands. He held it out like a peace offering. "Hi," he said.

She stared at him. Dressed in a golf shirt and beige slacks, he looked chunkier than the last time she'd seen him. His dark hair had wings of gray at the temples and there were lines on his face she hadn't noticed before. He was still much the same as she remembered him from her childhood, though. That narrow face and the nose with a bit of a hook to it, set off by a mouth with lips that were thin and kept tightly closed, even in repose, and a chin with a determined jut. Throughout her childhood this was the man she had wanted to please more than anyone in her world, and he was the man who had rejected her because she was different. Because she was a Beacon.

And now he was here at her house with some goofy idea of reconciliation on the same night she'd invited the new man in her life to meet her family. The night when she planned to tell him that she drew people from the past into the present. That she was a Beacon.

"Hi." She stared at her father. Did she open the door wider to allow him to come in? Or did she turn him away? She had not invited him. She didn't want him here, but he was her father. He was family.

Daniel Hamilton was not a man who relished losing control. He did as he had always done in Faith's life. He took command and made the decision. He thrust the bottle of wine into Faith's hands and stepped forward. Automatically, she retreated and before she knew it he was inside the house.

Faith looked at the wine and then at her father, who had halted his charge in the middle of the hall. "Thanks," she said. Holding the bottle in one hand, away from her body, she closed the door behind her father.

Daniel contemplated her with that cool, assessing stare that had always made Faith squirm inwardly. Finally he said, "You look well, Faith."

The comment, as mild as it had been, was an approval. A warmth spread through her. "Thanks, Dad. How are you?"

"I'm fine, thank you."

With that small social ritual done, they stared at each other. The uneasy silence highlighted the enormous emotional gap that loomed between them. As the little burst of pleasure in being with her father fizzled and died, Faith realized it had been nothing more than a holdover from a teenage fantasy. *Daddy loves you. Daddy thinks you're the greatest. You can wrap Daddy around your little finger like all the other girls do.* None of it was true. The reality was that this man might be her biological father, but his emotional connection to her existed only in her own mind.

"You know Mom's here."

He nodded. "Elizabeth warned me you'd invited her."

Warned. Faith didn't think there could be a better description of her troubled family dynamics. They didn't gather together in spontaneous, joyous pleasure, they warned each other they were coming.

"By the way, is Elizabeth here yet?"

"In the kitchen with Mom. That's where we're gathering, so you might as well come through."

As she walked with her father across the hall to the kitchen she thought about the evening to come. She had invited Cody tonight because she liked him, a lot, and she was ready to move their relationship back to that hot, passionate level they'd reached the night he'd taken her to Mountain Madness.

But she couldn't do it until she'd bared her soul. Until she'd told him she was a Beacon.

And that was the problem.

Her mother and Liz knew she was serious about Cody, that she hoped he would accept her for who she was, that she needed to take the ultimate risk and tell him that she was not just an ordinary young woman with a business degree trying to make a career. They understood that she could not live a lie, pretending she was like everyone else, keeping her ability a secret, and still commit to the kind of intense, passionate relationship she wanted to have with Cody.

They knew how much she desired to fit in, how deeply she feared rejection because of her ability. How much more intensely she wished she'd never told Andrew to stop visiting and how desperately she wanted him to ignore her demand.

They were behind her, supporting her, whatever happened. When the time came for Faith to take that risk, to tell Cody what she was, they would give her space, but they'd be there to help her if he rejected her, to cuddle her when she cried, to bitch with her about how stupid Cody was, to tear apart his character until they were all satisfied that Faith had had a miraculous escape from an arrogant male jerk. And if Cody accepted her ability, they'd be there to celebrate and welcome him into their tight little circle.

Daniel, on the other hand, saw her as a dangerous weirdo. If asked, he'd tell Cody to run away from Faith as fast as he could, without looking back.

She knew she couldn't do it. Not tonight. She couldn't tell Cody what she was, not with her father sitting in the same room, his disapproval a black thundercloud above them.

In the kitchen Chloe was slicing strawberries. Liz was sitting at the table, looking guilty. Chloe glanced briefly at her ex-husband when he entered the room, then refocused on her preparations. "Hello, Daniel."

"Chloe," he said. He went over to Liz and wrapped her in a bear hug. "How's my girl?"

Liz squealed and laughed, her expression miraculously changed at the sight of her father. Faith's stomach knotted. Emotion clogged the back of her throat. "Dad, did Liz tell you why I invited everyone over tonight?"

Daniel Hamilton turned away from his favorite daughter, his normal daughter. "She mentioned something about a family get-together."

Oh man, he didn't know! This was getting worse and worse. She moistened her lips. "I've invited a friend from work—" The doorbell rang. Faith froze. This had to be Cody. She glanced at her watch. He was a full fifteen minutes early. She looked desperately at her mother and sister. "You explain to him!" and went to answer the door.

It was Cody. He was standing with his hands in the pockets of gray trousers that he'd matched with a dark blue shirt. There was an apologetic expression on his face. "I'm early," he said, sounding quite surprised by that. "I didn't think, that is, I hoped you wouldn't mind."

He's nervous, she thought. She beamed at him. Warmth flowed through her, easing a little of the tension generated by her father's arrival. "No, I don't mind." She opened the door wider. "Come on in."

He looked relieved. She led him into the living room. There, in the middle of the room, the place where Uncle Andrew usually appeared, she stopped. Cody was frowning, reading the tension in her body language, but not understanding where it was coming from. Why would he? Helplessly, Faith raised her hands. "Cody, I'm sorry but..."

He took a step toward her. She held him off with one hand, palm forward. "Tonight is going to be a disaster."

Standing poised, he scanned her face. He was so close that her senses took flight and she imagined how it would feel if he covered her lips with his, fantasized about the hot sex she'd planned for the hours after the Big Admission. "I don't understand," he said.

"My father is here!" The words came out as a wail. Horrified, she put her hand over her mouth. Staring into his concerned gaze, she told herself to get a grip. Drawing a deep, shuddering breath, she dropped her hand as she tried to do just that. "Liz mentioned she was coming over and he decided he would too. I didn't invite him!"

Cody caught her hands and held them, his grasp warm and strong. "Your parents are divorced, aren't they?"

Faith stared up into his wonderful blue eyes and nodded.

"And you expect them to have a spat at some point during the evening, don't you?"

She sniffed, then nodded again.

He smiled. Gathering both of her hands together in one of his, he used his free hand to gently cup her cheek. "Okay, I'm warned."

She leaned into his hand, like a cat rubbing against a beloved human companion. "Cody, my dad and I don't get along." She looked up into his eyes. They were dark with an emotion that she thought might be tenderness. That shocked her, but it warmed her too. "He doesn't approve of me. I...I'm not sure what he's likely to do tonight. What kinds of things he might say."

He tugged her gently, drawing her against him. "You think he might do the heavy father bit?"

Faith shuddered. If only it was that simple. "He might. He might just be worse. I'm not sure. That's the problem."

Cody slipped his fingers under her chin and tipped her face up, then he kissed her. His mouth lingered over hers, teasing, tasting—

taking. Faith leaned into that kiss, wanting more, knowing she wasn't going to get it, at least not right now.

"Whatever happens, we'll weather it," he said.

Faith hoped so, but the cautious, doubting part of her couldn't quite believe it.

HOSTILITIES OPENED ALMOST IMMEDIATELY.

Faith had created a spicy *Chicken Etouffée* served with rice, roasted vegetables, and a salad, knowing Cody would enjoy the exotic flavors in the main dish. Her mother and sister wouldn't complain either—they were used to her love of hot foods. Daniel was another matter.

As the serving bowls were passed around the table Daniel frowned at the rice. "What's this? No potatoes?"

Liz laughed. "Mashed or baked, Dad?"

"Mashed," Daniel passed the bowl of rice to Chloe whose mouth was pursed with annoyance.

"I suppose you expect gravy too," she said, accepting the bowl and spooning rice onto her plate.

"It would be nice," Daniel said, inspecting the *Etouffée* platter. After a moment, he carefully speared a small chicken breast. "I suppose this is coated in something I won't like?" he said as he scrapped off the sauce and spices.

In the middle of pouring the wine, Faith paused to stare aghast at her father. She'd hoped they would at least have raised a glass before he began his litany of criticism.

"Gravy isn't going to come," Chloe announced. "Nor are potatoes. You need to join the twenty-first century, Daniel." She looked pointedly at his plate, a portrait of a picky eater's tastes, with its lone chicken breast and a minimalist helping of vegetables. "You need to open your mind to new experiences."

The bottle of chardonnay in Faith's hand began to shake.

"You want me to open up to new experiences? I just got back from China. While I was there I lived as the people lived. I ate goose feet and turtle eggs and heaven knows what else. I had rice for breakfast, along with a gruel made out of pumpkins. Now I'm home I want normal food, like potatoes and plain, roasted chicken!"

Faith managed to finish pouring the wine. "Everyone okay with white?" she said, handing out the glasses.

Deep into it, Chloe nodded, accepted a glass and plowed on. She was staring narrow-eyed at her ex, clearly intent on doing battle. "If you need normalcy so much, why don't you stay here in America, instead of accepting postings halfway across the world?"

Daniel wasn't about to allow his former spouse to grab the initiative in the disapproval category. "When it comes to travel, Chloe, you've got me beat. You log more distance than I'll ever do." He pointed a finger at her as he spoke, "And when you return don't you have a little ritual you always do? What was it now? Something about an expensive new outfit and a trip to the salon?"

Chloe blushed. "There's no need to be patronizing, Daniel."

"Dad, can't you leave it?" Liz said, her eyes pleading.

Daniel frowned at her, as if he didn't quite understand what was upsetting her, then he shrugged. "Of course, Elizabeth." He looked around the table. "Cody, my daughter told me you work for the same company Faith does. What exactly do you do?"

*My daughter.* Liz, not Faith. Maybe Daniel hadn't intended to hurt Faith with his comment, but he had. After all this time, despite knowing that her father had always preferred Liz over her, Faith still longed for her father's affection.

Cody stared at Daniel for a minute, then he turned to Faith and smiled that beautiful, sensual smile that warmed her heart. Her breath caught as he took her hand. It was more than a gesture, it was a symbolic and very deliberate act. When he answered Daniel a moment later his message was clear. He and Faith were linked.

A speculative look lit Daniel's eyes, but he didn't comment. The next half hour passed in a conversation that focused safely on computers, mathematics, and NIT projects. Food was eaten and as Daniel became more interested in his discussion with Cody he absently added rice, a chicken leg and even a little of the *Etouffée* sauce to his plate. The bottle of wine emptied. Faith fetched another. Cody smiled his special smile at her as she poured and she enjoyed a surge of optimism that the night wouldn't be the complete disaster she had feared.

Their talk flowed from NIT projects to Daniel's engineering ones. Faith picked at her food, holding optimism at bay, waiting for her father to say something that would drive a wedge between her and Cody. Nothing happened.

By eight o'clock she was able to suggest they have the dessert her mother had prepared. She began to clear the table. Ominously her father offered to help her.

Her heart stopped. "Dad, it's okay. Don't worry about it."

"No," he said genially, stacking his completely clear plate on top of Liz's, then reaching for Chloe's. "I insist. I've been out of town so much working on construction projects in the third world that I don't get to see my little girl enough. This will give me an opportunity to catch up."

On the surface that sounded reasonable. Except that they all knew he visited Liz regularly no matter what contracts he was working on—so catching up with his "little girl" was just an excuse for him to lecture her in the kitchen. Faith knew how her father felt about her dating normal guys. Her heart did a nosedive down to her toes. He wanted to remind her about her differences, to tell her to stay away from regular boys, just the way he had when she reached puberty and became a Beacon. *They'll laugh at you, Faith.*

*They'll call you a freak. You can never tell anyone —anyone!—what you are. Do you understand?*

She risked a glance at Cody. He was looking at Daniel. There was an amused expression on his face, but his eyes were watchful. He caught Faith staring at him and shot her one of those sexy half-smiles of his. Her heart did a little jump. She smiled back then headed for the kitchen. Better get the one-on-one with her father over with.

"That's a very nice young man," Daniel said when they reached the kitchen.

"He is," Faith opened the dishwasher. She pulled out the rack and began to fill it, taking the dishes her father held out to her.

"I like Cody." Daniel frowned. "Does he know?"

"No," Faith said shortly.

Cody strolled into the kitchen, a load of dishes in his hands. "Do I know what?"

Horror washed over Faith. Would her father take this opportunity to blurt out her secret? Despair, swiftly followed by resignation, washed over her. If he did, Daniel would describe her special ability in a negative way and she would watch Cody's face change from affection to contempt.

This was not how she wanted to tell him that she was a Beacon. She wanted to sit next to him and explain quietly that she had inherited a family trait that might make her seem different, even strange, but was nothing to be concerned about. She wanted to tell him in a joyous way, not a disapproving one, exactly who she was.

Certain that her father was once again about to abandon her, she hunted up desert forks in the cutlery drawer.

"About Chloe's strawberry shortcake. I always have two helpings." Daniel patted his stomach. "I shouldn't, but it's marvelous. That dessert is probably the thing I miss most about being married to her." He headed for the fridge and the shortcake.

Cody plunked his load of dishes onto the counter and said quietly, "What was that all about?"

"My father's peculiar sense of humor, I guess," Faith muttered in a low voice. In a more normal tone she said, "Thanks, Cody. Would you mind taking the coffee cups into the dining room for me?"

They ate the strawberry shortcake, with Daniel indulging in seconds as promised, and drank coffee, until Daniel stifled a yawn. "I haven't adjusted to the time change yet and it's catching up with me. Thank you for dinner, Faith. It was good to see you."

"Thanks for coming Dad. I'll walk you to the door."

On the porch, Daniel paused. "I know you don't care for my advice, Faith, but I hope you'll take it this time." There was a hint of compassion in his expression as he studied her. "Cody is an intelligent man with a flexible mind, but you'd be well advised not to become any more involved with him."

Faith swallowed hard. "Why?"

"Because of what you are, of course."

"Dad—"

He caught her shoulders in what may have been intended as a comforting grasp. "You're a pretty girl, Faith. A bright one, too, but this trait that you and your mother share..." He shook his head. "It's too weird for any man to accept. It broke up my marriage with Chloe and it hurt us both. Why open yourself up to that kind of grief?"

Hot tears clogged Faith's throat and filled her eyes. She fought them down. Despite everything, in her heart she wanted her father's approval of herself, of her growing feelings for Cody, even though in her mind she knew it would never come.

"Night, Dad," she said, without answering him. He turned away as she closed the door. Faith rubbed her forehead and sighed.

She found the others in the kitchen. Chloe was just finishing up the hand washing and Elizabeth was putting away the pots that

Cody had dried. Chloe was telling Cody her recent discoveries about the Civil War, which she cheerfully put down to some in-depth research she'd been doing. Cody made interested sounds and Liz winked at Faith, who wasn't sure whether to laugh or be terrified.

Despite her father's recommendation, she was going to tell Cody about herself. This business of living on the edge was too much for her. "Would you like to go into the living room, Cody? Mom, do you mind if I steal Cody away?"

"Off you go," Chloe said, wiping the counter. "Liz and I can finish up here."

Cody hung the damp tea towel on the handle of the stove door, then turned. Now, facing the three women, he was the only one whose back was not toward the kitchen doorway. His brows rose. "Hello. Who are you?"

# CHAPTER 17

For a moment Faith couldn't move. She heard a familiar voice say, "I'm Andrew. And who would you be? Ahhh, the boyfriend."

Elation fought with horror. Initially elation won. She whirled around, laughter bubbling from her lips. "Andrew! What are you doing here?"

He grinned at her, as best he could. There was a cut on his upper lip and swelling on his lower that suggested he'd been in a fight, recently. "I need a bolt hole."

Faith risked a look at Cody. He was studying Andrew through eyes bright with curiosity.

Faith couldn't blame him for wondering what was going on. Andrew was a mess. Locks of hair had escaped from the tail he wore tied at the back of his neck and twigs were caught in the dark strands. One of the ruffles on his fine linen shirt had been torn. There was mud on the leg of his velvet breeches and a hole gaped in the stocking below. Faith's delight at seeing him again eased into concern. "What happened to you?"

"Mary Elizabeth's father."

"Oh," said the Hamilton women in unison.

"Who's Mary Elizabeth?" Cody asked. "And why are you dressed that way, Andrew?"

"Mary Elizabeth is Andrew's girlfriend," Faith said. She deliberately ignored Cody's other question. Answering it would open doors she planned to take Cody through, but not like this, with Uncle Andrew and everyone else in the family listening in.

Andrew brushed some dirt from his breeches, then mournfully eyed the gaping hole in his stocking. "I am not usually such a sloven." He sat down at the kitchen table and put his chin in his hands. The bedraggled ruffles at his wrists flopped toward his elbows. "Mary Elizabeth's father does not approve of my intentions toward his daughter. Or of me, for that matter," he added sadly. "Our politics put us so far apart that there is a vast gulf between us."

Chloe sat down beside Andrew and patted him on the back. "You will win out, Andrew. You must be strong for everything to fall into place."

He was immediately alert. There was an almost crafty gleam in his eyes. "Are you promising me the government will change? Or that I will wed Mary Elizabeth?"

Chloe shook her head, pursing her lips and pretending to be annoyed. "Andrew! You know I cannot tell you what will happen."

"Oh, man," Faith said. Much as she wanted to talk to Andrew, to find out exactly what had brought him tonight, Cody was listening to this exchange with a fascination that was downright dangerous. She grabbed his arm with a half-formed idea that she'd be wise to tow him out of the kitchen.

Andrew said, "At this moment, I care not. Mary Elizabeth is furious at her father. Aye, and so too is her mother. I will wait here until the wretched man has gone back to Boston town. Then I will return to continue my courtship of Mary Elizabeth."

Totally aghast, Faith abandoned her idea of a strategic withdrawal. She had to deal with this now. She glared at Andrew. "I knew this would happen. I knew it! Didn't I tell you that the last time you came?"

"Aye, you did. But—"

Her hand was still clutching Cody's arm, and now, under a full head of steam, Faith propped her other hand on her hip. "Didn't you promise to stay away? Didn't you?"

Andrew stared at her steadily, maintaining a wary calm at odds with her stressed-out fury. "Aye, I did. But—"

"No buts, Andrew!" Letting go of Cody, she turned to Liz. "Did you hear him? Did you hear him say he was going to stay here?"

"Okay," Liz said. "So I was wrong."

"Wrong about what?" Cody asked.

Faith froze in place. Wide-eyed, she turned to Cody, wanting to tell him what was going on, but not sure how to do it, or even if it was a good idea to let him get involved.

To her surprise he smiled, a little ruefully, and drew his finger across her lips in a feather-light touch. "I get it. It's a family issue. I'll take off and give you the privacy to sort it out."

"No!" The vehemence of her response surprised Faith, even more than it surprised her watching family. She couldn't tell Cody that she was a Beacon, not in the middle of this emotional mess, but she could include him in this crisis. He didn't have to know that Andrew was a man who had been born two centuries earlier to add his input to help solve the problem. All he had to know was that Andrew was in trouble, needed a bolt hole and had decided her house was where he would find it.

She caught his hand. Holding it between both of hers, she said, "Stay, Cody, please."

Cody's eyes probed her face, looking for reasons for her request, trying to find the answer to her question.

Chloe said smoothly into the charged atmosphere, "Yes, please

171

don't go, Cody. I'm sure Andrew would welcome the presence of another male." She shot Andrew a quelling look. "Even a man from outside the family."

Faith almost groaned. If anything, her statement appeared to make Cody even more intrigued than before.

Andrew shot Chloe a mischievous look, before he thoughtfully inspected Cody. Cocking one eyebrow he said coolly, "He looks a fine fellow, indeed, Mistress Chloe. I would be pleased to add to my invitation to yours."

It was Cody's turn to raise his brows as Andrew ended his flowery speech. They rose even higher when Andrew stood to execute a short, but undeniable, bow. "Are you an actor?"

Liz laughed. Faith said, "He certainly tells enough untruths to be called one. Andrew, we talked about this the other night. You can't come here just because things are going wrong at...at home. And you certainly can't stay with me!"

"I must," Andrew said. "'Twill only be for the space of a sen'night."

This was getting worse and worse. Faith stepped away from Cody so she could advance on Andrew. "You can't."

"Sen'night?" Cody said. "I don't know that term."

Liz said helpfully, "It means a week in Andrew's jargon."

"See what you've started," Faith said, desperately afraid and absolutely furious as a result.

Andrew backed away until his behind met the edge of the table. There he stopped, holding up his hands, palms forward. "Surely you will not deny me sanctuary, Faith?"

"Andrew, you know what this means!"

"Aye," he said again. "But I cannot go home, at least not right now."

Chloe said calmly, "You cannot deny him sanctuary, Faith. When one of the family is in trouble, the others do what they can to help. It is why it all began. It is why we are as we are."

Faith glared at Andrew, who was nodding portentously at Chloe's words. She wanted to shake him like a terrier with a rat, then boot him back to 1772, but she knew her mother was right. Family lore had it that an early ancestor trapped in the hell of the Salem Witch Trials had discovered the beacon. Fearing she too would be charged and condemned, and desperate to escape, she had run into the woods, braving the dangers of the untamed North American continent rather than facing the probability of a quick conviction and a terrible death. Cold, hungry, exhausted, she was said to have followed a light in the woods—and found herself in a prosperous farm over one hundred years in the future.

"Okay. So you stay. Now we have to figure out what to do with you."

Looking much relieved, Andrew said, "Aye."

Faith was anything but. To stay in her time, Andrew had to be with her. That meant no private meals with Cody. No possibility of private evenings, of lovemaking, of being normal.

Chloe said, "Why don't we all sit down at the table and sort this out. Andrew, you look like you could use a cup of coffee. Anyone else want one?"

Coffee wasn't exactly what Faith would have preferred at that moment, but she figured she needed to keep her wits about her, so she put in a request for a cup. Cody followed suit. Liz opted for water. Then they all settled in at the big oak table and eyeballed each other.

Since it was her house and Andrew was her problem, Faith took the lead. "For Cody's benefit, I'm going to summarize the problems we're facing with Uncle Andrew's visit. Cody, Andrew suffers from an anxiety disorder that makes it impossible for him to remain alone in a house."

Cody raised his brows at this as he scrutinized Uncle Andrew. Andrew, looking extremely self-confident, smiled. The curious, intelligent expression that terrified Faith, crept into Cody's eyes.

She hurried on. "Ideally, when Andrew visits I take time off. But this is such short notice I can't, so we have to figure out what to do with him."

"Faith, you make him sound like that ugly old vase Great Aunt Mary gave you on your twenty-first birthday," Liz said. "Didn't you finally stash it down in the basement?"

"Great Aunt Mary?" Andrew said with interest. "And when was she?"

Cody leaned forward. "*When* was she? Not *who* is she? Or *where* is she?"

Andrew shot Cody a challenging grin. "Aye. When is the word I chose." He turned to Liz, a hopeful gleam in his eye. "Is she any relation to my Mary Elizabeth, then?"

Cody looked from Andrew, to Liz, then Chloe, then finally to Faith. "Marys and Elizabeths seem to run in your family."

They all stared at him, aghast. Except Andrew, who laughed. "I do believe you have found the key to my dilemma, Cody, my friend. I thank you." He turned to Faith, suddenly decisive. "Mary Elizabeth's father will expect me to seek her out before Friday next. That I will not do. But I must return to my own time soon thereafter, for Mary Elizabeth will be waiting for me and anxious to know why I did not come for her."

"No, Andrew, you can't stay till next Saturday. It just isn't possible. You can come into the office with me and hang around for a couple of days, but a week! No way."

"If I return too soon her father will be expecting me," Andrew pointed out with irritating logic. "What is the purpose of sanctuary if I cannot remain long enough to evade the danger that awaits me?"

"Why don't you call in sick, Faith?" Liz said. Her tone suggested she thought it was a long shot, but worth tossing out as an option.

"I can't do that." Faith played with her coffee cup, drawing circles on the table that evolved into figure eights, then into egg-shapes and finally triangles.

"It was easier in the old days," Chloe said. "People simply said you were visiting from afar and you were expected to go everywhere with them. In fact, you were asked to come join in and were welcomed. Our world is very different nowadays."

Faith stole a look at Cody. He was sitting back in his seat, listening intently as her family talked in what must sound like riddles to him. She would have to explain everything to him soon, but first she had to figure out how to deal with Uncle Andrew's visit. His week-long visit. "If you come to the NIT offices and hang around all day you'll have to have a purpose," she said, thinking aloud. "I suppose I could give you a job. You could do some filing or something."

"Filing?" Andrew said.

Cody stood up and went over to the counter. As he poured himself more coffee he said to Faith, "Are you backed up in that area? Do you need to bring in someone to deal with clerical overload?"

"No," she said, regretfully.

"Then Ava the Oppressor will never buy it. She'll ask questions. I don't think that's what we want."

His use of 'we' warmed her to her toes, adding brightness to the glow of the electric lighting. Still, she sighed. "You're right. So what kind of excuse can I use to explain Andrew's presence? He doesn't have a lot of office-type skills."

Cody leaned against the counter. As he sipped his coffee he aimed a thoughtful, narrow-eyed stare at Andrew. "There is one area in which we've had chronic problems over the last little while."

Faith frowned at him as she tried to figure out what he was referring to. In the past few weeks there had been no major issues, except Angela's computer problems. But they were solved now that she had more interesting responsibilities. True, there was the occasional glitch in one computer or another but...

The computers. Was Cody thinking of having Andrew work on the NIT computers? Was that possible?

Of course it was possible. Cody had no idea that Andrew didn't even know what a computer was, let alone how to operate one.

"Cody. It wouldn't work."

"What wouldn't work?" Liz asked.

Cody moved his considering stare from Andrew to Faith. "Why not?"

"Because when I say Andrew doesn't have any office skills, I mean none." She moved her hands in a slicing motion. "Zero. Zilch."

"Then I'll teach him." Cody's coffee mug landed on the counter with a clunk.

"Teach me what?" Andrew demanded.

Cody ignored him. He came over to the table. Pulling his chair beside Faith's, he took her hands in a warm clasp. "The only way Ava will accept Andrew without probing too deeply is if he has a believable reason for being at NIT. Can you think of anything else that will work?"

Faith stared into his eyes. Their incredible blue was warm and he was smiling the sexy half-smile that made her want to melt right into him. "No, but Cody, you have no idea how difficult a task you've given yourself."

He shrugged. "I don't mind. I'll work through it."

"Oh wow!" Liz said. She turned wide-eyed to her mother. "Cody is going to teach Andrew how to use a computer!"

They both laughed.

## CHAPTER 18

The next day Faith, Andrew and Cody gathered in the kitchen before they got started with the lessons. Faith had made coffee. She hauled three mugs from the cupboard and set them in a row. "Thank you for coming over today, Cody."

As he leaned against the sink, he watched her pour coffee into the three thick, stoneware mugs. The formal note to her statement alarmed him. It seemed so impersonal, as if they'd gone backward, not forward, since the arrival of her Uncle Andrew. "Not a problem."

"Well, it is," Faith said. "Andrew is clueless about computers. I tried to give him some basics this morning, so you're not starting from scratch, but they're..." Holding the coffee beaker high, she paused, searching for a word. "They're alien to him." She topped up the last of the mugs and set the beaker back on the hotplate.

The three mugs all had different decorations on them. One was the official NIT giveaway, with the company name and logo. He'd avoid that one. Another was adorned with some kind of flowers he thought might be violets. He figured that one would probably be

Faith's choice. The third had an image of the Statue of Liberty and the words, 'America's Symbol of Freedom' below. Cody figured that would be his.

"You make me sound incompetent, Faith," Andrew said. He'd been sitting at the table when Cody arrived. Now he stood up in a restless way and came over to collect a cup. He moved each so he could examine the decoration carefully. As he twisted the Statue of Liberty mug a look of horror washed over Faith's features. She snapped up the cup, putting her hand over the decoration, and sipped.

Cody reached for the NIT mug, leaving the flowers for Andrew.

Faith said, "You're not incompetent, Andrew. I didn't mean that. But you have no experience with computers, no frame of reference. We're expecting you to learn in one day everything we've been taught over years."

Andrew turned his mug, viewing it from all sides, before he picked it up. Then he lifted it high, looked at the bottom. He put the mug back on the counter. "No saucer?"

"No," Faith said shortly. "I save the good china cups and saucers for dinner guests and people who drop by for a short visit. When you're staying a week, you get the twenty-first century everyday stuff."

"I see," said Andrew. "Is there cream?"

Faith handed him the waxed carton. Andrew took it with a bemused expression on his face. Like the mug, he turned it this way and that, inspecting it carefully.

Trying to figure out how to create the spout to pour out the cream.

As soon as that thought flickered in his mind, Cody dismissed it. Everyone knew how to open the pour spout on a waxed milk or cream carton. Everyone. Even Uncle Andrew.

Faith took the carton from him and, with an impatient look,

flipped open the spout. She handed it back to Andrew, whose expression indicated fascinated delight.

Maybe not. Andrew wasn't the only one who was fascinated.

Andrew carefully poured cream into his mug, added sugar from the sugar bowl on the counter and stirred. Then he raised the mug with a little flourish and sipped.

Andrew had cleaned himself up and looked almost normal, Cody thought as he leaned against the sink, drinking his coffee and pondering the strangeness that was Uncle Andrew. He was still wearing his long hair tied back into a tail with a black velvet ribbon. In Cody's opinion the style was eccentric, but as the odd things that surrounded Andrew went, it was pretty tame. Particularly since Andrew was now dressed much as Cody was, in a t-shirt and jeans.

Both the t-shirt and the jeans looked new. The jeans were faded, but the fabric was still crisp, so they were probably the pre-washed type. The shirt was black, with the word 'Boston' and a bright green shamrock on the front. The shirts were available all over town and were sold to tourists at a variety of prices, none of them very expensive. Cody wondered if Andrew had been involved in the selection of clothes, or if it was one of the Hamilton ladies—Faith, her sister Liz, or perhaps her mother—who had done the shopping. He hoped it was Liz or Chloe. He didn't like the idea of Faith shopping for another man, even if he was a relative.

The stray thought rocked him back on his heels and was definitely one he was going to have to take out and examine in some depth, but not now. He looked over at Faith, focusing on her. She looked great today. She'd pulled her long blond hair into a ponytail that hung past her shoulders and swished back and forth as she moved. Her top had a boat neck that exposed the graceful line of shoulder, collarbone and neck. The fabric was a green that set off her eyes and seemed to make her skin glow. It also hugged her body, emphasizing the fact that she wasn't wearing a bra.

She looked up, caught him watching her, and smiled. Cody's heart did a little flip, then began to jump around as if it was doing a triumphant dance. He told himself to calm down, then couldn't breathe when she went over to the fridge to put away the carton of cream.

To get to the fridge she had to pass through a puddle of light from the window above the sink. Since he was leaning against the sink, the light was behind him and he had a great view of the way it streamed through the cotton fabric of her skirt, making the material translucent. For an instant, while she was bathed in the light, he could see the long length of her legs. Oh, yeah! His heart rate kicked into overdrive.

She'd dressed for him today, he was absolutely certain of it. No matter how difficult his self-appointed task of teaching Andrew the basics of the computer was, he could manage, because Faith was showing him in this simple, practical way that she wanted to please him.

They took their coffee into a small room that opened off the wide front hall. Located close to the kitchen, but behind the living room, the room was clearly Faith's all-purpose activity room. Besides her computer and the desk it sat on, there was a sewing machine on a small table, a larger table that was evidently a work surface, bookcases, a sofa, and a stereo. Unlike her organized, not-a-thing-out-of-place kitchen, this room was cluttered and it welcomed Cody as he followed Faith and Andrew inside.

"Okay, Andrew, remember to keep your coffee away from the keyboard," Faith said, nodding her approval as Andrew followed instructions and carefully placed his mug to one side of the desk, well out of accident range. "Now, turn on the computer and log in."

Cody stood behind and to one side of Andrew so he could

watch the man's face as he went through the process. That way he could judge how comfortable Andrew felt in dealing with the basics. The familiar whir of the hard drive activating soothed Cody, drawing him into the task at hand. The start up screen flashed. He noted with approval that Faith had put proper security protocols in place to keep her files safe.

The log-on dialogue box opened. She'd also set up a special log-on for Andrew. Cody watched with amazement as Andrew hunted for the letter 'a'.

"No," Faith said. "It has to be a capital. You make it that way by pressing 'shift' at the same time as you press the 'a' key."

Cody looked over Andrew's head at Faith. "He can't type?"

Her expression guilty, Faith shook her head.

This threw an unexpected wrinkle into Cody's plans. By the time they were Andrew's age everybody knew how to type these days. Well, evidently not everyone. "Where did you go to school, Andrew?"

Andrew had mastered the capital 'A' and found the rest of the letters of his name. He tabbed to the password field and pecked out the numbers one-seven-seven-two. The screen flashed into life.

The year 1772? Nah, couldn't be.

"I did not go to a school," Andrew said, a satisfied expression on his face as a beach scene with an aquamarine sea settled on the screen. "I had a tutor who taught me my letters and numbers." He glanced at Faith. "Do you want me to open some programs?"

"Sure," she said. "It'll be good practice for you."

Andrew nodded and set to work. One after another the standard office software came to life. Andrew looked pleased with himself. "I was also taught to draw and paint with watercolors, and to play the piano forte..."

Faith said sharply, "Let's focus on the task at hand, okay Andrew?"

Interesting and double interesting. Whatever was going on with Uncle Andrew had Faith worried. Cody grabbed the straight-backed chair tucked against the table that held the sewing machine and brought it over to the computer desk. Setting it beside Andrew's chair, he turned it backward, then straddled it so he could prop his crossed arms on top of the back.

If Faith was worried about Andrew saying something inappropriate to him today, she must be on tenterhooks about what would happen when she took Andrew to NIT. He was going to spend the rest of the day doing his best to ensure Andrew was as ready as he could make him for his entry into the computer age.

AT ELEVEN-FIFTEEN THAT NIGHT, Faith called a halt. She was weary and Andrew was glassy-eyed, but struggling manfully to keep up with Cody who appeared ready to continue for hours yet. His stamina was amazing, but then she knew that when he was in the middle of a project he often worked through the night, so she wasn't surprised.

Andrew had managed to hold his own during Cody's intense afternoon training course. When they broke for the roast beef dinner Faith had prepared, he'd talked in an animated way about computers and what he'd learned. He'd even agreed enthusiastically to Cody's suggestion that they return to the task after dinner. His energy had lasted until ten o'clock when he started to flag. Faith wasn't surprised. In the eighteenth century, when houses were lit by oil lamps or candlelight, people normally went to bed after the sun set and woke when the sun came back up. By ten Andrew was already up past his bedtime.

Faith left Andrew logging off the computer as she accompanied Cody to the door. With a quick look backward to make sure Andrew was still in her all-purpose room, she followed Cody out onto the front porch. She closed the door firmly behind her, then looked up. That sexy little half-smile curled the edges of Cody's mouth. Her insides quivered in a pleasurable way. She smiled and said softly, "Thank you."

That surprised a laugh out of him. "I now have a much better appreciation of why your sister and mom were so amused by my offer to teach Andrew about computers."

Faith nodded. "Cody, will he...I mean, will Ava be able to figure out how little he really knows?"

"If she sees him typing, she will." Faith bit her lip and he added hastily, "He's not totally hopeless." He grinned. "Those piano forte lessons obviously taught him manual dexterity, but the most used letters in the alphabet are on the left side of the keyboard, so it's hard for a beginner to pick up speed. Make him keep practicing and he should be okay."

Was there a question in his voice under the amusement over the 'piano forte'? Probably. It was risky to let Cody continue sorting through the bits of information that were accumulating around Andrew, because her distant ancestor was a puzzle and Cody was good at putting the pieces together to solve puzzles. But she wasn't totally sure yet that Cody wouldn't be frightened off if she told him that Andrew was visiting from the year 1772. "All of this must seem very strange to you."

He stroked his fingertip along her jawline to her chin, which he tipped up so she was staring into his eyes. "You're right, it does. But I like Andrew. I think he's a decent guy. Except—"

"Except?" Faith searched his face for clues. There were none.

She felt his shrug as well as saw it. "He's hiding something."

She closed her eyes for a brief moment, her thoughts in turmoil.

"Hey," Cody said, running his thumb across her lips. "Come back to me."

She opened her eyes, even though she was afraid of what he'd say next.

"I suppose he's got Mary Elizabeth pregnant."

If Cody hadn't been holding her chin with his fingertips, Faith knew she would have been standing there staring at him, her jaw hanging open. "Ummm, ahhhh…"

"It's okay." He lowered his head to brush a brief, teasing kiss over her lips. "He should go home and handle it, though. It's not fair to Mary Elizabeth and he's going to have to deal with her father when they're married. He may as well start now."

Faith breathed a mental sigh of relief. She could manage this. "I totally agree, but try convincing Andrew."

Cody smiled that sexy half-smile again. "We've got a week to work on him. He'll come round."

This time when he kissed her, Faith molded her body to his, as seduced by Cody's linking of himself to her family as by the taste and touch of him.

*Do I want you, Cody Simpson,* she thought? *Oh yeah. In more ways than one.*

# CHAPTER 19

*A*ndrew was up with the sun. The sound of his shower dragged Faith out of a deep sleep. She yawned and focused blearily on her bedside clock. Another hour before her alarm was due to go off. She groaned. Snuggling deeper under the covers she prepared to go back to sleep.

The shower stopped. The old house eased into its normal warm quiet.

Andrew began to sing. He had quite a good voice, a rich baritone, well-trained, with excellent projection. Faith listened lazily, half-asleep, half-awake. Part of her figured she wasn't going to get back to sleep, so she ought to get up now. The other part was enjoying doing nothing except sing along to the song Andrew was belting out as he did whatever he was doing in the bathroom. She knew the words and the melody, of course, because the song was one of her favorites—a rock song originally recorded in the eighties, then re-recorded recently as part of a movie soundtrack. She thought Andrew's version was even better than the original—

She sat bolt upright. Then scrambled out of bed and hit the floor running.

"Andrew!" She pounded on the bathroom door, breaking into the joyous sounds coming from the other side.

He opened the door, raising his brows as he took in the t-shirt that was all she used to sleep in. Under his gaze she blushed a little. The shirt was extra-long, but it still only reached mid-thigh. "What are you singing?"

He was holding a toothbrush, which he pointed at her. "A song from your computer. I do not know the name. Cody and I found it yesterday and played it. The singer has a limited range, but the melodic line is pleasant, although it does lack complexity."

"You can't sing the song, Andrew. You can't know it. You can't take it back with you. You have to forget it."

Andrew listened politely. "I know. But while I am here I can sing what I want. I can wear what I want. I can learn what I want." He waved the toothbrush. "Now, Madam, you have interrupted me in my ablutions. If you will excuse me?" He bowed his head and shoulders politely, then shut the door.

Faith stared at the door, slowly realizing that having Andrew in the twenty-first century for a protracted visit was not going to be restful.

They set off for NIT a half-an-hour earlier than Faith usually did, so of course the traffic patterns were all different. Faith had expected fewer cars. What she found was that there were more. As they waited in a left turn lane, watching the green turn to red for the second time, she decided this would be a good opportunity to let Andrew know what he could and he couldn't do at NIT. "When we get to the office, Andrew, you have to remember to stay close to me."

"Of course," he said. He put his hands on the window beside him, inspecting the edges with his fingertips.

"People will wonder who you are."

"A perfectly reasonable reaction." He was jerking his fingers down now, rubbing them along the glass.

Faith frowned, but plowed on. "You'll tell them you're an intern."

"We discussed this with Cody yesterday." He'd given up on the glass and was running his index finger along the edge of the frame.

"Yeah, well, I'm just going over it again. We can't have any slip-ups." The light turned green again. Faith gunned it so she could stay close to the car in front and successfully get through the intersection before the light turned again.

Andrew thumped the glass in a gesture filled with impatience, then he reached down, grabbed the door handle and released the latch. The door beside him swung open as Faith accelerated into her turn.

She screamed. "What are you doing? SHUT THE DOOR!"

It was a good thing Andrew was wearing a seat belt, because he leaned precariously, half-in, half-out as he reached for the heavy door, which was now swinging madly. With a shout of triumph he caught the handle. Pulling against momentum and velocity, he dragged the door back to the car, then slammed it shut.

Faith's heart was racing. Somehow she'd made the turn safely and was now on Massachusetts Avenue, the main artery she'd follow for most of her drive to NIT. She felt as if someone had just wadded her up and put her through the spin cycle of a washing machine. Andrew, on the other hand, appeared to be enjoying himself. His eyes gleamed and his whole body quivered in excitement.

"What on earth did you do that for?"

He rubbed his chin. "I wished to test the air temperature outside this vehicle. I also wished to listen to the sounds made by the others around us. When I could not find a way to lower the window beside me I decided to open the door instead."

"You could have been killed," Faith snapped.

"I would doubt that." He tugged at the shoulder belt. "This harness you are required to wear is remarkably sturdy. I was in no danger."

"Maybe you weren't," Faith muttered. Her voice rose. "But the cars around us were, because I was rattled enough that I could have driven into any one of them."

"My deepest apologies," Andrew said. He didn't look apologetic, though. He looked energized. He looked like he was having fun.

Faith eased to a stop again as they reached another light. "Listen, Andrew, you've got to be careful. Ask me before you act. For instance, the window is run by the electrical system. It opens by flicking that switch on the side of your door."

Andrew looked a little dubious, but he cautiously put his finger on the tiny lever and pushed. The window slid open with a mechanical hiss. Andrew's expression slipped into delight.

After that the window went up and down with monotonous regularity until Faith could stand it no more. "Okay. You've done the window thing. Now, listen. We're about fifteen minutes from NIT. When we get there I'll show you around, figure out where I'm going to put you, introduce you to people. Then I'll have to get to work and you'll have to look busy. Understand?"

Andrew raised the window. He nodded. "What have you done with all of the trees? And the fields."

"We cut the trees down and built houses and shops and office buildings on the fields. Andrew, are you listening to me?" The light changed. Traffic moved slowly forward.

He nodded. "I must appear busy." He turned in his seat so he could look directly at her and leaned against the passenger door.

"Good," Faith said, maneuvering through the intersection. On the other side was a long stretch without lights. Traffic began to move more quickly. "Now, about the computers. I know you're supposed to be an expert, but—" She glanced over at him. And almost had a heart attack. "Andrew! You can't do that!"

"Now what have I done?" he demanded indignantly, sitting up.

"You can't lean against the door. It might fly open. You could get hurt."

"It is latched quite securely."

"You're not supposed to lean against car doors. It isn't safe. Any kid knows that."

"I am not a child," Andrew said, on his dignity.

"I know," Faith said, but she was coming to think that when it came to the twenty-first century, a five-year-old was better equipped to handle everyday life than Andrew was.

ANDREW WAS a big hit in the bullpen. Not surprising, Faith reflected. Though not tall, his stocky body was roped with lean muscle toned not at the gym, but in everyday activity. He walked or rode a horse to reach a destination; he milked cows, chased chickens, and did God knows what else to his animals; though he had hired-help to manage his acreage, he walked behind a plow pulled by oxen to turn the earth in his fields, and he weeded a garden that was as large as the lot on which the average house was built. As long as Faith had known him, Andrew had been a man with a very fine physical presence. Dressed in the formal clothes of his own times, dripping with velvet, lace, and fine linen, he was imposing. Clad in the casual, form-fitting knits and tight denims of the twenty-first century he was second-look sexy and enough to make any sane woman salivate.

Which Angela and June, and all the others in the bullpen certainly did.

Andrew loved it, of course. He turned his old-fashioned charm on each of the women in turn and before long he had them laughing and giddy.

On Monday morning. At nine o'clock.

Faith towed him off to her office over the protests of her staff on the excuse that she had to go over his responsibilities with him.

The light was blinking on her phone, indicating she had one or more voicemail messages waiting. She unlocked her bottom drawer and dropped her purse inside. Andrew observed this with considerable interest.

"I have to work," she said, relocking the drawer. "So I need you to make yourself appear busy for the next little while. Think you can do that?"

"Why," he said, pointing to the desk, "do you feel a need to secure your belongings when you are in the privacy of your own study?"

"I always do," Faith said, sitting down and not really paying attention to him. She picked up the phone and punched in the voicemail code.

Andrew ambled over to a filing cabinet. He tugged at one closed drawer. It was locked. "Do you not trust those who work for you? Even on matters that relate to the organization?"

Faith tucked the phone against her shoulder, made a note, deleted one voicemail, went on to the next. "What was that?"

Andrew shrugged and sent her a dismissive wave. Faith accepted it with a nod, deleted another voicemail and logged on to her computer while she listened to the next voicemail. Andrew wandered around the room, checking things out. He flipped through file folders, lifted hanging racks to see what was behind them, opened drawers where he could, pricked his finger on a message nail. The contents of Faith's desk organizer—paper clips, elastics, ballpoint pens, highlighters, and tacks for her cork board —kept his attention all through Faith's voicemails and even into a few of the e-mails that had accumulated since Friday.

She hadn't quite finished her e-mails when her telephone rang. The call was from a client who wanted to discuss their latest billing so she took it. Out of the corner of her eye she noticed Andrew was at the window, searching the edges of the glass the way he had in the car. She spared a moment to reflect with relief that he couldn't open a door this time and almost fall out, then she focused on the problem at hand.

Faith's window consisted of two six-foot square panes, framed by black metal. These didn't open, but between them and the four-foot high walls that rose from the floor were two narrow rectangular windows that did. These were hinged to open outward with a gentle push and, like the non-functioning windows, they were framed in thin black aluminum.

A modern design, these windows were not the old-fashioned sash construction that moved up and down Andrew was used to. By the time Faith finished her conversation Andrew had found the handle that worked the window and thrust it open. As she put down the phone she took a good look at what he was doing.

He had his head stuck out the window and was in the process of pushing his shoulders out along with it.

"Andrew."

Focused on the task at hand, he didn't respond. Or that was what Faith told herself. Maybe he just didn't want to hear another lecture on what he could not do.

The open window provided a narrow opening between the sill, the frame and the angled windowpane. There wasn't a lot of room for a body to exit, particularly a muscular, big-boned one like Andrew's. "Andrew. What are you doing? You're going to get stuck."

The door to Faith's office opened.

For one panicked moment Faith thought Ava Taylor was about to come in. Her heart skipped a beat, then started again at a gallop.

She wasn't ready to face Ava. Andrew needed more coaching. Ava was never going to believe Andrew was an intern.

It wasn't Ava who entered, though, it was Cody. He smiled when he saw her, that sexy half-smile that made her think of his lips on hers, his hands stroking her body, the press and promise of his hips against hers.

Andrew said cheerfully, "The window opens outward, not up the way it should."

Cody ripped his gaze away from Faith's. One look at Andrew hanging half-in, half-out of the window, doing his best to wriggle into a better position to view the workings of the hinges, had Cody closing the door behind him. He pointed to Andrew as he said to Faith, "What's he doing?"

Faith looked over at Andrew. "He's trying to figure out how the window works. I think."

"Is he really?" Cody said, sounding approving. He went over to the window where he crouched down so he could look out at Andrew's level. "What's up?"

There wasn't room for both of them to stick their head and shoulders out, particularly now as Andrew had managed to wriggle an arm out. "Do you see this?" Andrew said, reaching up to rub his finger along the top of the frame. "There is a hinge up here. It allows the window to open outward. Once the windowpane has been opened fully the hinge locks to become a brace to keep the pane from falling back against the frame." He grunted. "I do believe for this mechanism to work properly it would have to be very strong."

"I guess," Cody said. "I've never thought about it."

Andrew wriggled a bit more. "I certainly hope they are."

There was an ominous sound to that statement. "Why?" Faith demanded.

Andrew hesitated, then he said, "Because I do believe I am stuck."

"Oh, for heaven's sake!" Faith said.

Cody rocked back on his heals. There was a suspicious twitch to his lips that suggested he was fighting the urge to laugh. He managed to keep a straight face as he stood up to assess the situation. "Andrew, you need to arch your back and roll your shoulders. Make yourself as small as possible, then inch back and forth. That should work. I'd hate to have to cut your t-shirt off you so we could grease you up to let you slide out."

Andrew grunted. "I'm damned well not about to be disrobed by you, my friend!"

At that very moment the door opened again.

This time Faith's worst expectation was fulfilled. Ava the Tyrant Lizard walked in.

And heard Andrew's half-amused comment.

"Nor by anyone else, I should hope," she said tartly.

Cody sighed. Horrified, Faith said, "Oh...ummm...ah...Hi Ava."

"Who is this?" Ava demanded, joining Cody by the window.

"This is my—" Faith began.

Cody said, "This is Andrew. He's a computer grad, here as my intern. He's trying to make the decision to go for his masters or look for a full-time job. Andrew, this is Ava Taylor, the COO of NIT."

"A pleasure dear lady," said Andrew from the window. "If you will be patient for a few minutes I will introduce myself properly."

Ava didn't acknowledge this. She said curiously, "What are you doing?"

There was an ominous silence. Faith said, "There was a bird."

"A bird?" Ava raised her brows in a disbelieving way. Not surprising, since Faith's windows displayed a panorama of asphalt parking lot with nothing green in sight. She looked pointedly at Cody.

Faith said in a rush, "Yes, a bird. It...ummm...flew into the window and got...stuck. Andrew was helping it escape."

"I see," said Ava, who looked as if she saw entirely too much. "What was your intern's name again, Cody?"

The intern, still stuck in the window, was wiggling in a determined way and had begun to make some progress, but he wasn't free yet.

"Andrew."

Ava waited a heartbeat, and then another. Her brows rose. "And does Andrew have a last name by any chance?"

"Of course," said Cody.

Faith realized Cody had no idea what Andrew's last name was because she'd never used it. Why would she? Andrew was Andrew. Cody was covering his ignorance by staring at Ava as if she'd just asked the dumbest question in the world. Ava was glaring back, resisting the silent intimidation. In a second or two she'd probe deeper and in doing so make it obvious Cody didn't really know Andrew well. That would blow Andrew's cover and make Cody look like an idiot. Faith had to do something.

She kicked Andrew on the ankle, hoping Ava wouldn't notice.

Andrew said loudly, "Ouch!" which tore Ava's attention away from Cody for the moment.

"Are you okay?" Faith said. She leaned close to Andrew to say more quietly, "Tell Ava your last name. Quick!"

"When I am able too free myself of this insidious device," Andrew said, his tone indignant, "I will introduce myself properly. However, until that time I will tell you, dear lady, that my surname is Byrne."

Ava absorbed the somewhat flowery language. She observed Andrew with considerable interest. "And what is Andrew Byrne doing down here in Faith's office supposedly rescuing birds in distress instead of being up in your office, Cody, working with you?"

Almost out of the window, Andrew stilled.

Cody leaned against the edge of Faith's desk. He looked

relaxed, but the muscles in his jaw had tightened and his mouth was a hard line. "He was here because I sent him down here. What is your point, Ava?"

Ava raised her brows. "Nothing. Except that I'm having difficulty accepting that a young man who gets himself stuck in an office window would be of any benefit to NIT."

"Are you questioning my judgment, Ava?" Cody demanded. He sounded cool. His raised brows suggested that this was a mild disagreement between colleagues. The flash of fire in his eyes said otherwise.

Ava must have read the anger in his eyes as clearly as Faith had, but she wasn't backing down. "Had you taken the time to clear this through me—as you are supposed to!—you wouldn't have placed yourself in this position, Cody."

He crossed his arms over his t-shirt covered chest. "And what position is that, Ava?"

"You've exposed your very poor management skills," Ava said, with surprising heat.

"No!" Faith said. "It's not—"

"Hell and Devil confound it!" Andrew said, popping out of the window like a cork out of a champagne bottle.

"You see," Ava said dryly, to no one in particular.

Andrew brushed himself off, then sauntered over to Ava, his mouth curved in a disarmingly rueful smile. "I fear I have not created the best impression."

Ava shot him a glance that said he'd got that right.

Andrew replied with a direct look, his eyelids slightly lowered. The faint smile slowly widened as he took Ava's hand, held it for a moment, then raised it at the same time as he bowed over it.

Ava blushed and looked away, clearly rattled.

"I trust," Andrew said in a low voice that was as smooth forty-year-old scotch and just about as lethal, "that I will have the opportunity to redeem myself in your eyes."

Ava collected herself. She drew her hand from Andrew's slowly, as if she really didn't want to, but knew she had to. "I am sure you are a very fine young man. But NIT has no need of another computer programmer—"

"I've asked him to work with Faith, to make sure that the software problems we've had over the last few weeks don't reoccur," Cody said, interjecting quickly.

"How nice for you, Faith. Your own computer jock." Ava shot Cody a frigid look. "I still do not think that an intern is necessary and I would have said so if I had been asked." She smiled sweetly at Andrew. "It has been interesting meeting you, Andrew. Please remember. Redemption is not easy to achieve."

She walked out of the office, annoyance in every tense muscle in her body. Andrew followed her, poked his head out the opening to make sure she was out of range, then quietly shut the door. "That one," he said, "is dangerous to know."

# CHAPTER 20

"Do you not long for daylight and the open when you are trapped in this building all day?" Andrew said as he followed Faith into the NIT suite. It was Wednesday morning and office life had begun an inevitable slide from fascination into routine.

Faith tilted her head to one side, considering the question as they walked through the bullpen to her office. As she dumped her purse into her bottom drawer, she said, "No."

Andrew wandered over to the window where he'd presented himself to Ava Taylor so spectacularly two days before and gazed out, longingly. The sun was shining. The temperature was a balmy seventy-two degrees and there was a freshness about the day that always seemed to come first thing in the morning. "I should be tending my fields to ensure my plantings are healthy and free of pests and weeds."

Faith heard the wistfulness in Andrew's voice and rejoiced. Though they'd agreed he would stay in her time only until the weekend, she knew Andrew. If he wanted to stay longer he'd work on her until she agreed it would be okay. On Monday and most of yesterday he'd been intrigued by the gadgets and comforts of her time. She had begun to fear that she would have to work very hard to convince him that he had to go back to his own.

What she needed to do now was push the wistfulness into frustration and that into determination and action. As she locked her desk drawer, she said, "Fields take care of themselves, don't they? All you have to do is throw in a few seeds and poof! You have plants that grow and grow until they're big enough to harvest."

"Ha!" Andrew turned away from the window. His eyes were sparkling with the enthusiasm of the expert. "I fear you would make a poor farmer with an attitude such as that, Faith. The earth needs sustenance, just as you and I need it. I practice crop rotation to enrich the soil, though many of my neighbors do not. It is a process that requires thought and study, but I believe my acres yield far more than those of other farmers. That is why I am able to sell my excess to the merchants in Boston town and to employ hired men to assist me in my endeavors."

Faith settled down in her chair and logged-on to her computer. "Sounds like you work smart, Uncle Andrew. That's the hallmark of a good manager." While the machine was powering through its start-up rotation, she added, "A pity you couldn't be as effective in this time period."

He frowned. Propping his jean-clad hip on the edge of her desk, he crossed his arms over the black t-shirt he wore. "I would appreciate an explanation of that comment, if you please."

Faith opened her e-mail program. "Umm? What was that, Andrew?" she said, pretending to be focused on work and not their conversation. As he opened his mouth to explain, she said brightly, "Oh, right, not effective." He nodded. His frown had deepened to a thundercloud. Faith almost laughed. "Well, I guess what I was trying to say was that in the past you are an expert and successful. You understand your business and you make excellent decisions.

Here you have just begun to learn and you would have to work through a long process just to achieve the success you have in your own time."

She opened e-mails and dashed out replies while Andrew considered that.

Finally he said, "Here I am not likely to be set upon by the henchmen of Mary Elizabeth's father because my politics do not match his and he resents me courting his daughter."

Faith abandoned her e-mail. She swiveled her chair so she could face him. "If you were not forced to stay close to me, you would probably find that there are plenty of men like Mary Elizabeth's father around. Behaviors don't change just because the year has."

Andrew considered what she'd said. Then he laughed. "You're telling me that I need to go back and face George Strand, are you not?"

Faith grinned back at him. "I am asking you to think about it." She pointed to her doorway. "Now, I need to get some work done and you need to look busy and effective. Go fiddle with the spare computer station out in the bullpen."

Andrew looked out the door. His expression was glum. "Computers are tedious."

"For some of us, not others." She pointed to the door again as she said firmly, "Now, go."

He went.

The morning sped by with few interruptions. The bullpen was quiet, with only the normal low buzz. No computers needed health care. Andrew successfully entertained himself without entertaining her staff at the same time. When the phone rang just after noon, Faith stretched and let her focus slip away from budget figures before she answered.

It was Cody. "Hi. I've reached a frustration point and need a break. Want to go for a walk?"

"How about eating instead."

There was a moment of silence, possibly while Cody consulted his watch or looked at his computer clock. "Oh yeah. It's noon. Time for lunch. Now you mention it, I am kind of hungry."

Faith could hear the surprise in his voice and her heart warmed. When Cody was deep into a project he lost track of everything. His ferocious ability to concentrate was one of the fascinating things about him.

"I'll be down in ten minutes."

"I'll let June know I'm leaving and I'll organize Andrew."

Cody sighed. "Yeah, Andrew. Okay. I guess." His voice lowered, became husky. "Though I'd rather have you all to myself."

Faith laughed. "And when does that ever happen around here? I'll see you in ten."

Cody agreed, rather wistfully, and hung up. Humming to herself, Faith walked out of her office.

And froze.

Andrew was on the Internet. On a site about the history of Boston and its regions.

That was bad enough, but standing behind him, looking over his shoulder at the screen was Ava Taylor. Judging from the set of her shoulders, she was not pleased.

"Andrew. I'm going to lunch in ten minutes. When I get back I'd like you to create a spreadsheet that contains the specifics of each computer in this area, including the model, operating system, RAM, ROM, and any other details—"

"Like the number of times each computer has gone down since Sue Green's accident," Ava said, nodding approvingly. There was considerable enthusiasm in her voice.

Andrew looked up with a frown. "I believe that promises to be a dreary task."

Faith shrugged. "Assembling data often is, although it is absolutely necessary if you want to come to a balanced decision." She looked down at the computer screen and added, "If you want to research American history on the net, do it on your own time."

"I completely concur," Ava said with relish.

Faith headed back to her office to get her bag, leaving Andrew to log off the Internet and prepare for lunch. She had just unlocked her drawer when Ava marched into her office. Glancing up, she saw Ava close the door. Warning bells went off in her head.

"Does Andrew always slack off like that?" Ava said without preamble. She advanced to the center of the room, invading Faith's space, dominating the small area.

Faith slung her purse over her shoulder. One hand resting on the bag, the other crossed at her waist and holding on to the strap, she prepared to defend herself. "There isn't much for him to do."

"My thought exactly," Ava said with considerable relish. "What I saw this morning confirmed my belief that an intern is neither necessary nor useful. I did like the way you handled him, though. You must let me know how well he responds to your direction."

"Of course," Faith said. She glanced at her watch before she added, "Is there anything else you'd like to discuss, Ava?"

"I think I heard you say that you have a lunch engagement?"

Faith nodded.

"I won't keep you, then. Is it with Cody Simpson?"

Faith nodded. "And with Andrew."

Ava contemplated this, the expression on her sweet, rather doll-like features considering. Then she said seriously, "I know you're close to Cody, Faith, but, girl-to-girl, he's not reliable, you know." Faith didn't reply. Ava retreated to the door where she paused, her hand on the knob. "Not only does he refuse to work as a member of the NIT team, but he clearly is willing to manipulate other employees to further his own agenda. I do hope you will bear that in mind when interacting with him."

"I think you're wrong about Cody. I trust him and I know he would never do anything to harm anyone who works for NIT, or the company itself."

Ava pursed her lips as if she was about to say something, then the door opened and she had to jump away. She glared at Cody, as he stood revealed in the doorway. "Cody. We were just talking about you." She looked over at Faith. "Remember what I said. We'll talk later." She swept out of the office.

Cody raised his brows. "What was that all about?"

Faith sighed. "Ava being Ava. Shall we go?"

They discussed the incident over lunch. Andrew grumbled about the data digging, but Cody and Faith were both adamant that he needed to appear to be doing something useful. Ava, they agreed, would jump at any opportunity to criticize Andrew's performance. It they weren't careful she might even be able to get him fired before the week was out. Andrew grumbled some more, but finally accepted his fate.

Faith watched him pick up a fry, then dip it in ketchup, before he ate it. Andrew had ordered fries with his lunch every day this week. He was fascinated by them, the crisp outside covering the soft inside, the faint taste of oil, the sugar sweetness of the ketchup that turned an ordinary vegetable into a candy. He loved everything about fries, including wiping his greasy fingers on a napkin made of paper. Faith had the uneasy feeling that he'd be instructing his cook on the basics of deep frying potatoes the moment he returned to 1772.

Cody was watching Andrew eat his fries too, but he wasn't paying much attention, since he didn't know that fries were a special treat. There was an abstracted expression in his eyes that told Faith he was deep in some puzzle-solving universe of his own.

She went back to worrying about changing history and Uncle Andrew's cholesterol count.

"Weird woman," Cody said suddenly. Faith looked at him, a question in her eyes. "Ava Taylor, I mean."

Andrew laughed. "Aye, that she is." He worked the paper napkin over his fingernails, fastidiously cleaning the edges. "She puts me in mind of a snake, always slithering around where no one can see her until she is ready to strike."

Faith shivered.

Cody nodded. "Interesting. She doesn't slither around me, though. She's right there, in my face. She has this crazy idea that employees need structure and a predictable environment. When I first started she tried to get me into a routine that included office hours and meetings—dozens of meetings on stupid things like the cost of paperclips. I told her—politely, I might add—that meetings for the sake of meeting were a waste of my time and I wasn't going to participate. I don't think she believed me. When I missed the first one, she sent me an e-mail telling me I was expected at the next and then a reminder of the date and time." He shot Faith a rueful smile. Andrew might not even have been there. "I managed to lose that message somehow." His smile grew into a grin. "In fact, when Ava suggested I'd ignored it, I told her it had probably gotten lost in transit. So she checked the server and, you know, there was no record of it at all."

Faith's eyes widened. "Cody are you saying what I think you're saying? You went into the server and you trashed her message?"

He nodded, still smiling. "Yup and every shadow of it. No record of that e-mail existed, except in her out basket. It simply disappeared into the ether. She was livid."

Beside her, Andrew was chuckling softly, but Faith didn't know whether to be amused or terrified for Cody. "So what happened?"

He shrugged and laughed. "She took to phoning me to remind me about meetings. Since I don't always answer my phone when

I'm working on a project and I collect my voicemail only off and on, I've managed to miss most of them. She hasn't given up, though. The woman is stubborn."

Faith began to laugh. "Focused, Cody. You should be able to relate. Ava is as focused on her path as you are on yours."

"Could be." He shook his head, bemused by a person he couldn't understand. "Enough of my issues with Ava. Andrew, any problems come up this morning? Do you need any tips to make you look good through the rest of the day?"

As office politics went, the battle Ava was waging with Cody over meeting attendance was pretty minor. As long as Cody did the creative work he'd been hired to do, Faith was pretty sure Ralph wouldn't care if Cody avoided meetings related to office organization. Ava would continue to be infuriated by his absence, but how much harm could she do with Ralph on Cody's side?

Bringing in an intern into the company under false pretenses was a very different matter, though. If Ava found out that Andrew was not what he was supposed to be she wouldn't hesitate to use the information. How far she would go, Faith didn't know, but at the very least she could damage Cody's position, and his reputation.

Because of her, Cody might lose his job.

"Hey." Cody stroked the back of Faith's hand to get her attention. "Time to go." He smiled at her. "We've already been out of the office for an hour. Ava's going to be furious."

Faith stared at him, loving his quiet confidence, worried about the danger she might have put him into. "And you don't care."

"Not a bit," he said cheerfully.

Feeling as if his voice was caressing her, she smiled at him, but inside part of her wondered if he was underestimating the damage Ave could do. "Andrew's right, she is like a snake, slithering around in the background. I want you to be careful, Cody. I think she's capable of being vindictive."

He tipped her chin up. His eyes were dark, their expression amused. "You've got that one right. She's probably added luring you into bad company and corrupting you into chronic tardiness to my list of sins."

Faith laughed. Put that way, Ava didn't sound quite so intimidating.

Cody bent toward her. He might have kissed her then, but Andrew cleared his throat, reminding them both that they were in a very public place. Cody smiled that sexy little half-smile and took her hand. There was no reason they couldn't walk back to the office, together, as a couple.

With Uncle Andrew as their chaperone.

# CHAPTER 21

Faith opened her fridge door and contemplated the contents. With Andrew visiting it was fuller than usual. The meat drawer contained a package of chicken breasts and one of steak. There was asparagus, broccoli, and green beans for vegetables to be cooked and served with the meal, plus three kinds of lettuce, tomatoes, and yellow peppers for a salad. She'd discovered that Andrew was an eager-eater. He devoured an immense amount of food, but never seemed to gain a pound. She figured he must have a metabolism that burned energy with the same abandon as a jet airplane.

Since Faith couldn't bring herself to view food with the kind of lusty enthusiasm Andrew did, she chose the low fat chicken breasts. Deciding she would stuff them, she also pulled out a package of deli cheese slices.

Andrew wandered into the kitchen from her little project room where he'd been doing his typing exercises at the computer. He found the package of chicken breasts in its disposable hard foam tray and picked it up. As he had yesterday and the day before that, he ran his finger over the plastic wrap with a kind of amazement. "Is this for our dinner, then, Faith?"

Faith put broccoli and green beans on the counter, to the right of where the chicken breasts had been resting before Andrew picked them up. She shut the fridge door. "Yup."

A gleam of enthusiasm entered Andrew's eyes. He bared his teeth in a wolfish grin, dropped the package on the counter, then poked his thumbs into the plastic wrap and tore it apart in a sweeping gesture of manly authority. Faith leaned against the counter and watched him. As he exposed the poultry with considerable satisfaction, she shook her head. "It doesn't take much to entertain you, does it?"

He laughed and poked a chicken breast. "I understand why you cannot have chickens outside your door for eggs and meat. You do not have the space. I must own, I do not recognize this city for the place where I lived. The size..." He shook his head as he abandoned his contemplation of the raw poultry, then he washed his hands in the sink. As he dried them, he looked out the window. "You have a pleasant garden, Faith. The trees are large and well grown. They hide the fence that divides your property from those of your neighbors. Your flowerbeds contain plants that I have never seen before and are pleasing to the eye. But you no longer have enough land on which to place a kitchen garden of any size. I could not grow my vegetables here or pasture my cattle. And I can walk to the next house in the space of a heartbeat."

"Well, not quite a heartbeat, Andrew. My neighbors aren't that close." Faith began to slice pockets into the chicken breasts.

Andrew flashed her a grin. "Well, perhaps I do exaggerate."

"A little," Faith murmured. With the pockets done, she too washed her hands, then reached for the cheese slices. "Would you mind getting that square pan out of the cupboard by the stove, Andrew?"

While he hunted around, Faith found a can of cream of broccoli soup that she planned to pour over the chicken to make a sauce. As she plunked the can on the counter, Andrew hauled out a pan. "Is this it?"

"That would be the one."

He turned it in his hands, viewing it from all angles. The pan was nothing special, just an aluminum square with sides two inches high. It had a few dents, and dark spots in the corners. Inexpensive to start with, it was practical but not particularly pretty, yet Andrew handled it with the reverence of a priceless artifact. "You have so many things in your time that are different from the ones in mine. This pan, for instance, is made with a metal that is light yet durable. If such a thing were created in my time, it would be made from cast iron and would weigh considerably more."

Faith switched on the oven to heat it up, then wiped the counter before she attached the can of soup to the electric can opener. "In your time you'd be cooking over an open flame. If you used my little aluminum pan the food would scorch. I can use it because my oven provides a regular, even heat."

Andrew nodded as Faith set the can opener in motion. "All these gadgets you have in this century," he said, watching the can whirl around, its lid gradually cut away from the sides. "I hunger for them when I'm in my own time."

"I hunger for my supper," Faith said. She placed the chicken breasts into the aluminum pan, then dumped the condensed soup over top and set the pan into the warmed oven.

"I could make a fortune inventing some of the things you have."

Faith tidied the counter, throwing away packaging, recycling the soup can. "There was a man in sixteenth century England who invented the flush toilet. Look how long it took before anyone thought it was a good enough idea to do something with it. Ideas have their time, Andrew, and your world isn't ready for electric can openers and condensed soup."

There was an edge to her voice that Andrew caught. "You've

got something eating at you, girl. Spit it out or we'll be bickering before the night is through."

Faith threw the cloth into the sink. Then, with a sigh, she sat down at the big, round table. "Andrew, my life is such a mess."

He sat down beside her and said, "There now, isn't that so for all of us? Why don't you tell me about it?"

"Ava is after Cody."

Andrew's jaw tightened and the expression in his eyes hardened. He nodded. "Aye. I am not surprised. Have I not said the woman is a snake?"

Faith rubbed her eyes. "Liz calls her a tyrant—" She broke off, feeling guilty. Dinosaurs hadn't been discovered in Andrew's time.

Andrew didn't seem to have noticed there was supposed to be more to the sentence. He'd been dealing with Ava all week. Apparently describing her as a tyrant struck a chord. "Miss Elizabeth is correct in her assessment. I believe conflict between Cody and Mistress Taylor is as inevitable as conflict between England and its colonies in America." He shot Faith a speculative look. Faith gave him back a blank expression. Andrew laughed.

Faith sighed. "The conflict between Ava and Cody is all about total control of the NIT organization. Ava lusts for it. All Cody wants is to manage his time and his area his way. If Ava would just leave him alone, everything would be fine, but she won't be satisfied with anything less than complete domination."

"It is the way of all tyrants. It is what King George of England desires. He and your Ava Taylor would understand each other very well."

That made Faith laugh. "Don't ever say that to Ava. I'm sure she'd be deeply insulted." Andrew's eyes gleamed. Faith realized she'd just handed him another clue about his future. She hurried on. "I don't think Cody realizes she will do pretty much anything to get to him, including using you and me. She has already guessed you're not the expert you claim to be and she figures that if she knows, Cody must know."

"She is quite correct in that assumption."

Faith shot him an impatient look. "Yeah, but I think she plans to use you to get at Cody. Andrew, you have to be careful. It's Wednesday night. We have two more days to go. No more Internet. No more goofing off."

Andrew assumed an offended expression. "I do not know the meaning of your term, 'goofing off,' but I believe you to be using it as a derogatory description of my behavior."

"I am."

"I trust you will accept my sincere apology for any errors I have made during these past several days and my deepest promise that I will do nothing to endanger Cody Simpson, a man for whom I have the greatest respect and affection."

Uncle Andrew had puffed up like an angry rooster defending his flock of hens. Faith figured he'd received about as much of her message as he was likely to acknowledge. All she could do now was keep her fingers crossed and hope for the best. She nodded glumly. "Thanks."

He eyed her shrewdly. "I think Mistress Taylor's desire for domination is not your only concern."

Faith thought about that. He was right. Ava scared her silly, but her own relationship with Cody had become such a tangle she didn't know how to sort it out. "Cody doesn't know about you, about all of this." She waved her hand in the direction of the living room. "All he knows is that you are my weird cousin who has phobias. He helped me out, blindly. He trusts me. Now. But I haven't told him about you visiting and Mom going back into the past. I don't know how he'll take it."

"Consider this, Faith. When I arrived I must have looked and sounded like a madman. And yet, Cody accepted me and he has been more than patient with me since. Trust him, Faith. Tell him.

He cares for you. Have confidence that he will accept you for what you are."

Faith thought about Cody, his curiosity and interest. He had an open mind, it was true, but then a mental image of her father's face intruded into her thoughts and she shook her head. Asking any man to accept the reality of time travel, instigated by individuals who were able to project a light across the centuries, was dangerous. "I don't know, Andrew. What if he thinks I'm crazy and doesn't want to date me anymore? I think I'm...I really like him. He means a lot to me. On top of that, we work together. Relationships that go bad can create a huge strain in the office. Ava has already told me that if it's him or me, I'm the one who will be expected to leave NIT. I've got a lot at stake here."

"Aye, you do, girl. As do I." Andrew paused, waiting a moment then two for emphasis. "I have realized that I am in love with Mary Elizabeth. Yet I have never told her I am a Traveler and a Beacon too. I hope she will accept me, but even if she does, her father will do his best to see that we do not wed as he hates me for my politics."

Momentarily diverted, Faith said, "You're a Beacon? Do you have a visitor from the past or one from the future like Mom?"

"From the past." Andrew's mouth hardened into a dangerous line. "My many times great grandmother. She lived in Boston town in the early days of the settlement. She was a devout, religious woman, with a quick intellect who discussed the Scriptures with her friend Anne Hutchinson, and others of like mind. When John Winthrop and the Puritan leaders accused Mistress Hutchinson of heresy, they also accused our ancestor. Her husband, a poor sort of man, denounced her and sent her away from their home. Then she was convicted and banished from Boston. She had nowhere to go but the vast wilderness and there she eventually found my light. She has made a home for herself now, but she still comes from time to time for food and shelter when the weather is bad."

Faith eyed him curiously. "Are you the first Beacon, the one who began it all?"

He shook his head. "There were others before me, and in Scotland and England too."

"I had no idea."

"Nor I, until she found me. Her name was expunged from the family records by her brute of a husband." He looked at Faith, a brooding expression in his eyes. "I could not turn her away, even if Mary Elizabeth rejects me because of my abilities. I am what I am, Faith, as you are what you are. Not all men—or women!—will accept us or understand our powers, but I have hope of Mary Elizabeth and I believe Cody will as well."

"I almost told Cody last week, but I chickened out when you arrived."

Andrew put his hand over hers. "Tell him soon, Faith. He deserves to know." He smiled. "You deserve to know how he will react. Waiting will only make the telling more difficult, the hearing more shocking."

"You're right." Faith smiled. Absurdly, she was scared at the thought of confiding in Cody, but she was excited too.

"And I will tell Mary Elizabeth when I return. If she still wants me I will brave her father's wrath and ask him for her hand."

"Good luck."

Andrew smiled rather devilishly. "You as well."

# CHAPTER 22

"*I* have come to a decision."

Andrew liked to make serious pronouncements when she was in the middle of a traffic nightmare. Like now, as she approached an intersection toward the end of a green light. There were half-a-dozen cars on the opposite side turning left. She knew at least two or three were going to try to sneak across between the point when on-coming traffic stopped for the yellow and when the yellow flicked to red. The trick was to get into the intersection before those left-turners gunned it to make their turn, or to be far enough away that a safe stop could be made when the light went yellow.

Faith was used to a quiet morning commute with only the radio news for company. She could focus on surviving the rush hour gauntlet and preparing for the day ahead. Andrew was a sociable guy, however, and every morning since he'd arrived he'd chatted non-stop from her house to the office. It was now Friday morning, the fifth day he'd come into work with her. Faith was beginning to develop the knack of tuning him out.

She was a few feet away from the intersection now, too close to stop without the car behind rear-ending her. She kept her foot on the gas and entered the intersection.

"I am going to ask Mary Elizabeth tonight."

"What?" One of the left-turning cars surged into the intersection, directly into Faith's path, a second one hot on its bumper. "No!" She hit the break pedal.

"You think I should not?" Andrew said, frowning.

"Andrew, I…" The driver of the second car hit the breaks too, while the first one stepped on the gas. Faith squeaked between them as the light went red. Crisis over, she glanced over at Andrew. "What were you saying?"

"I have decided to go back tonight. There is a subscription ball in Lexington. All of the best families will be there. George Strand is sure to attend and to bring his family. It would please me to claim a dance or two with my Mary Elizabeth."

"And you'll tell her then?"

"Aye. And ask her father for her hand if she agrees."

"A ball. This sounds like a pretty big deal. Why didn't you tell me before we started on our way to work? You could have gone back this morning."

"I did not decide until just now. I had to weigh all of the alternatives."

Faith checked her mirror, then zipped into a narrow opening in the outside lane. "I'll take you home. You can go back, make sure everything is okay on your farm, prep for tonight." They were about halfway to NIT. If she turned around now she would be at least a half-an-hour late for work, but she would find some way of covering it with Ava. She could even work late tonight.

Sure that was it. She'd trade off the time she missed this morning for some at the end of the day. It was perfect. Who would complain—

"I'll stay," Andrew said.

Faith's fantasy of a productive, unstressed slide into the weekend evaporated. She sighed.

Andrew said, "I have responsibilities I cannot shirk. I will go this afternoon after we return from your workplace."

"Responsibilities? What are you talking about?"

"The report you required me to create." He sounded miffed, as if she had failed him in some way.

"Report?" Her memory clicked in. "You mean, the one on the status of all of the computers in the bullpen?"

"Aye, that would be the one."

A make-work project. He was going to stay for the whole day because he hadn't finished a make-work project? She didn't know whether to be outraged or proud.

Both emotions were irrelevant. Andrew had decided he was going to remain a while longer. She'd just have to deal with it.

The morning passed quietly. Andrew worked on his project, laboriously typing in the information he'd assembled. Cody came down for lunch a little after noon and they celebrated Andrew's decision to return home with deli sandwiches and toasted his announcement that he would be asking Mary Elizabeth to marry him with cans of diet cola.

An hour after they returned from lunch Andrew delivered his report to Faith with a flourishing bow that would have made most men look silly. Andrew, however, had a trick of laughing with his eyes as he performed the bow that took away pretension and added charm. Faith accepted his work with appropriate solemnity and was surprised to discover that it actually contained useful material.

By mid-afternoon she felt like a runner on third, staring at home, knowing that the batter up had a ninety-five percent hit rate and homered six times out of ten. Two hours left and Andrew would be leaving NIT for the last time. She could hardly wait.

She was cleaning her desk, prioritizing the week's unfinished tasks, when June walked into her office. "Angela's at it again," she said.

*Angela's at it again.* With those few, simple little words Faith's day dissolved into disaster. "Her computer?"

June nodded. "Yeah. Andrew's working on it now, but Angela's going on vacation next week, so she needs to make sure she's up-to-date."

"I'll call Cody." Faith was already picking up the phone.

June looked puzzled. "It's okay. I'm sure Andrew can handle it. I just wanted to let you know what was happening."

Faith punched out Cody's extension and nestled the receiver between her shoulder and ear. While the phone rang, she smiled at June. "Thanks for the tip. I appreciate it."

June glanced at the phone. Still looking puzzled, she nodded. Then with a shrug she left. The phone rang three times. "Come on, come on. Be there!" On the fourth ring, just before it tipped over into voicemail, Cody answered. "Angela's computer is down. Andrew is fixing it," Faith said without preamble.

Cody responded with just as much unspoken urgency. "I'll be right there."

He must have run all the way. Faith beat him to the bullpen by only a couple of minutes. She stood behind Andrew, watching him open folders in the control panel with the same kind of aimless desperation as a person trying to find a diamond ring in a haystack. This was bad. This was really bad.

It was painfully obvious to June, Angela and every female who had paused to check things out as they passed by, that this boy didn't have a clue how to handle his toy.

When Cody arrived he squeezed her hand reassuringly as he monitored Andrew. In a casual way he asked Angela for background details, then gently prodded Andrew out of the chair and took over.

Faith breathed a sigh of relief. She put her hand on Cody's shoulder and said, "Come and see me when you're done."

He smiled briefly, but his focus was already deep into the computer's malaise. Faith went back to her office.

The next thing she knew her door was shutting with a decided snap. She looked up to find Ava standing with her hand on the knob, looking like a triumphant Amazon warrior, except that Liz and her mother claimed the Amazons were an ancient myth, not a reality.

Ava was very real, though, and so was her triumph. Faith's stomach knotted. Intuition told her that whatever was making Ava so very happy was not going to please her.

She was right.

Ava strode into the room, her eyes glittering. "I have him."

Him was either Andrew or Cody. Faith would place her bet on Cody. "What do you mean?"

"That intern of his, Andrew. He's an idiot."

"I don't think he's that bad." She held up the report. "He did excellent work on analyzing the computer prob—"

Ava put her hands on her hips. "He's a fraud. He knows no more about computers than I do, and that isn't saying much."

Faith dropped the report on her desk. She swallowed hard. "Ava, I—"

Ava showed her teeth in a malicious smile at odds with her doll-like features. "Either Cody Simpson knows Andrew is a fraud or the good Dr. Simpson isn't the computer whiz he claims to be. Either way, I have him."

Faith stared at her, appalled.

Ava swept on. "I don't think Simpson can cope. He's behind in his projects, you know. He's costing us money and he's doing nothing to deserve that big fat salary he's being paid. Ralph doesn't seem to mind that Cody isn't making any progress, but when I tell him Cody Simpson can't be trusted and why, he's going to want to make sure that Simpson delivers." She laughed. It wasn't a nice sound. "That means Dr. Simpson won't have a free hand. No more skipping meetings. Or giving verbal reports that consist of 'it'll get done'. He'll have to put the status of his work in writing. Weekly, at least. Daily, preferably. Oh yes, I have him now. Cody Simpson will regret foisting his phony intern on this company."

Faith stared at Ava. Her eyes glittered with the fury of a fanatic, while the tension in her body told of emotions on the edge of explosion. Ava would carry through with her threats. She would take away what Cody most valued about working at NIT, an unstructured environment and creative freedom. She would make his working life miserable.

She would make him quit, all because he had helped Faith out.

Faith couldn't let that happen. She couldn't betray him that way. She took a deep breath, then plunged into the murky depths of Ava's plotting. "Andrew is my cousin."

"He'll regret...What did you say?"

Faith swallowed hard. Ava's cheeks were red with emotion. Her eyes bored into Faith and her mouth was a straight, hard, line. She'd heard what Faith had said and she'd caught the implication. She was not happy. "Andrew is, well, he's the family problem. He never sticks at anything except, ah, playing computer games. The family thought, we thought—I suggested!—that maybe if he came into NIT for a week or so and learned what it was like working with computers, he'd pull his life together and go back to school. Get a degree. Make something of himself. I asked Cody to take him on as an intern. He said he would."

Ava's eyes had narrowed as she saw her quarry slipping away, but at the end of Faith's blurt of information she began to smile. "No problem. I've still got him. He's shown considerable irresponsibility in taking on a person with no skills whatsoever. He should have checked Andrew out. Ralph won't like this."

Faith took another deep breath. Forced it out. Sucked in a second. Then plunged deeper. "He did. He interviewed Andrew."

"You know, Ms Hamilton, I'm still not convinced. Had Simpson done a proper interview he would have learned of your cousin's inadequacies."

This was it. The muck at the bottom of the pit had her fast. There was no way out. "I knew that Cody was having a hard time doing his own work and fixing the computers down here, and I played on that. I coached Andrew on what to say to Cody to make him think Andrew would be useful. It's not Cody's fault Andrew couldn't cut it. It's mine."

Ava bought the explanation. Her eyes glittered with a thwarted rage that needed an outlet somewhere. She held out her hand. "I am disappointed in you, Ms. Hamilton. I thought you were a team player. Well, you've shown me differently. Give me your office keys, please."

Faith stood frozen. Ava's hand twitched, demanding those little pieces of metal that were the symbol of the regular world Faith had always longed to succeed in. To surrender them to Ava was the end of her dream of fitting in, of being normal.

Her eyes locked with Ava's. She reached into the pocket of her slacks, found the ring, pulled it out. Then hesitated. She didn't want her dream to end this way, at the hands of Ava the Oppressor.

Ava's hand twitched in a 'gimme' motion.

Faith still hesitated. Could she do this?

Of course she could if it meant protecting Cody and saving his job. She dropped the keys into Ava's outstretched hand.

"I am going to see to it that you are fired." Ava's fingers curled over the metal, then she pulled her hand back with a flourish, snatching Faith's dreams away at the same time. "For some reason Ralph Warren has a soft spot for you. But when I tell him what you've done, you'll be finished here." She swept out of the room, triumph in her thrust-back shoulders and the tilt of her head, fury in every staccato step.

Faith sat down at her desk before her knees buckled. Ava might or might not be able to follow through on her threat, but her last comment showed her insecurity. She could plan and plot, but ultimately Ralph made the big decisions.

That cheered Faith a little, but not much. She'd been an accidental participant in Ava's battle with Cody all along. If Ralph decided to keep her on it would probably be because he'd decided to fire Cody, which wasn't what she wanted at all. No, the best she could hope for was that Ralph fired her. End of job at NIT. End of dream of being normal.

Tears of anguish welled up. She shut her eyes tight to keep them at bay. She didn't want Cody or Andrew or anyone in the bullpen to see puffy eyes and tear streaked skin and wonder why she'd been crying. They'd ask questions, questions she didn't want to answer. The people she supervised would feel sorry for her, or angry with NIT, neither of which would do the organization any good. Andrew would assume she was upset because of her need to succeed in the real world and would feel guilty that he'd been the cause of her loss. And Cody?

Cody would fight for her. He'd storm out after Ava and he'd face her down in a battle so huge the whole place would shake. Two tyrannosaurs fighting over the fate of a rodent-sized mammal.

The image brought a hiccup of brightness to the gloom she was feeling. She opened her eyes and rubbed away the tears with her knuckles. To help her through this Cody didn't have to do battle for her. In fact, she didn't want him to. This was her fight, not his. But the knowledge that he would defend her, the belief that he cared for her, the way she had come to care for him, was a balm to the pain she faced at the destruction of her dream.

Sooner or later Cody would have to confront Ava. The glee in

Ava's voice when she figured she had him cold had proven that, but he couldn't do it over Faith, or when he was filled with anger on her behalf. He'd have to fight Ava over his own issues.

She took a deep breath. When she came in on Monday morning it would probably be to retrieve her personal things from the office, but Ava would make sure she couldn't get into the computer files, so she'd better clean them up now, while Cody and Andrew were still busy in the bullpen.

Turning to her computer she did a quick scan of her e-mail, deleting the 'personal' folder, then she went on to her document files and dumped her few private ones into the trash. As she shoved the mouse around and fiddled with computer files, thoughts of Cody filled her. He had a wickedly sharp intelligence and he always noticed things, even though he didn't seem to at the time. It was going to be tough to keep him in the dark about this, but she had to, at least until she had come to grips with her own feelings.

Her files were in the trash now. She stared at the little icon, her mouth twisted into a smile that was bitter rather than amused. More important than her files, the virtual trash can also held her dreams. She moved the pointer onto the icon. Her finger rested on the mouse, hesitated, then clicked. A dialogue box came up, advising her that the files would be deleted permanently, giving her the opportunity to change her mind. She stared at the screen, aware of time passing. The choice had to be made. Yes or no. Decide now.

She swallowed hard, acknowledged the knot in her stomach that was making her feel sick, and the cold sweat that had turned her body icy. Then she clicked okay and the files were gone.

Reaction set in. She stared at the screen for what seemed like a long time, but probably wasn't, searching for the despair she expected to feel. It wasn't there. What was filling her was a kind of relief.

Relief? Really? Couldn't be. Or could it?

She had hidden behind the goal of being normal for so long that she had forgotten what mattered in her life. A loving family who supported and cared for her. Success in her chosen profession, because she reached for the heights and wasn't afraid to take risks. A man who was her partner in all things, who loved her with an intensity that understood and accepted her for what she was. Nothing more. Nothing less.

Instead, she'd been aiming low, telling Andrew to stay away, building a relationship with Cody that was based on a lie—or at least an omission—all because she was afraid people would find out she wasn't normal.

Well, that was about to change. She logged-off the computer with a sense of finality that was empowering. It was time for her to come out of her protective burrow and show Cody just exactly who she was and how she felt about him. It was time for commitment.

The screen went dark. Faith grinned. Commitment wasn't something that could be rushed, though. She'd make a weekend of it.

She'd start tonight, after Andrew went back to his own time. She'd show Cody that she wanted him, that the passion they'd almost shared after the Mountain Madness concert was real and only the beginning. She'd seduce him. Coax him into bed, give him herself, let him see parts of her she'd kept hidden.

She straightened the papers on her desk, recycling some, sorting others, putting file folders back in the cabinet. Tomorrow night she'd implement the second half of the commitment plan. This part was tougher, scary where tonight's agenda was pure joyous anticipation, for she would have to tell him about her special power. How he reacted would decide their future together.

To make sure Cody accepted her, she'd pull out all the stops. She'd invite him into her world in a way that was as seductive as the passion they were going to share tonight. Candles, she mused, getting into the planning. Warm lighting, flowers, Celtic or new age music to give an 'otherworldly' quality. A special meal using the fragile, hundred-and-fifty-year-old china she saved for Andrew's visits that had to be washed by hand.

She shoved the drawer into the file cabinet. It closed with a slam.

A new dress to signify change and a beginning. She began to hum. The dress would have to be fancy, the kind that shouted it was for a special event, not every day wearing. Heels, definitely spike...

The sound of footsteps had her turning. Cody was there, in her office, closing the door. He stood, legs apart, arms loose by his sides, body straight and tall. His features were set in hard, concerned lines, and he appeared ready to take on whatever danger presented itself. She smiled and the worried expression in his eyes eased.

"I saw Ava leave here looking like she'd just won the lottery." His gaze swept her office, rested momentarily on her bare desk, then on the blank computer screen, before it came back to her face. "What happened? Are you okay?"

A quick stab of pain came, then was gone. Faith sauntered over to Cody. She linked her hand with his, raised it up so she could hold it in both of hers while she smiled into his eyes. "Everything is fine. More than fine. Andrew has been fired, but since he was going home tonight anyway, it doesn't matter."

She was very close to Cody. She could feel his tension. His body was responding to her, but he wasn't quite ready to let go of the problem at hand.

"Your desk is clear and your computer is shut down, like you're leaving."

Butterflies took flight. She smiled enticingly and moved a little closer. "I am. Andrew has to leave and I'm going to drop him off.

That means I'll have the evening free. Want to come pick me up? About seven o'clock?"

That little half-smile she loved chased the concern from his eyes. "I'll make a reservation at Mel's."

She couldn't resist it, she traced the shape of his mouth with the tip of her finger. "No. Not Mel's. I want you to take me to your place."

Understanding smoldered into life. Just to make sure there was no confusion, she reached up, caught his head between her hands, and pulled it down so she could kiss him.

There, in her office. A teasing, tempting kiss that told him exactly what she had in mind for the evening. He let her play for a time while he eased his arms around her, then he caught her hard against him and kissed her with a passion that had a promise of its own. When he released her, he laughed. "Go," he said. "I'll see you at seven."

She grinned back at him. "I'm looking forward to it."

# CHAPTER 23

here was an elation about Faith he'd never seen before, as if she was living life for the first time. And yet, beneath the laughter there was a fierce edginess that smoldered, waiting for an opportunity to explode. When he'd picked her up at seven sharp and she'd told him that Andrew had gone home to see Mary Elizabeth, Cody told himself she was just relieved that Uncle Andrew had decided to resolve his relationship with his girlfriend. And yet...

Something else had happened today. He could see it in the shadows in her eyes and the way she brooded when she thought he wasn't looking, as he drove them both to his place on Beacon Hill.

So what was it that was bothering his Faith? The obvious answer was Ava's dismissal of Andrew. In itself that was no surprise. What was amazing was that Andrew had survived until Friday before he was caught. Though the man was absolutely fascinated with the little things of twenty-first century life—Cody could still laugh at the scene in Faith's office when Andrew got himself stuck in the window—his complete absence of knowledge about computers was really strange. Andrew was of an age to have grown up on computer games and even if his family hadn't had the money to invest in a computer of their own, back in the days when a PC cost about the same as the family car, he would have had friends who had computers or seen them at work.

Come to think of it, what exactly did Andrew do? And where did he live?

Yes, Andrew had a lot going for him as a major irritant, but Cody didn't think it was Andrew who had caused that underlying intensity in Faith tonight.

So that left her job or her boyfriend.

Cody liked the idea that he could be important enough to Faith to influence her moods. This afternoon in her office she'd told him she wanted him to take her to bed tonight. At least, he thought at the time that was what she had in mind when she said she wanted to see his place and then kissed him, there in her office, where she worried about every damn little thing. He could be wrong though. She might just want to check out his apartment to see what kind of place he had. Or maybe how well he kept up that place.

The thought of that had him in a cold sweat as he drove along the Longfellow Bridge, heading across the Charles River from Cambridge to Boston. Faith was so neat, so careful about how she kept her house and he was so untidy. He forgot to put his clothes away and he didn't make his bed. Not only did he get preoccupied and not put things away but his place was dusty. He lived in Beacon Hill, a city neighborhood surrounded by major arteries. The roads were busy, the traffic was constant. There was air pollution and some of it seeped into his apartment as dust. It was inevitable.

As he turned onto Charles Street he cleared his throat. "Faith, about my apartment." He risked a glance at her. She had been looking out the window at the river, but as he spoke she shifted in her seat so she could see him better. She smiled at him. His heart did a flip. He plowed on. "It's old."

"Most of the houses on Beacon Hill are." There was amusement in her voice.

"It was remodeled into apartments thirty years ago. I'm on the top floor." He turned off Charles onto his street.

"So have you got a great view?"

He found a space, pulled in and from long experience expertly maneuvered the car so it was tight against the curb. "Yeah, I do. I can see the Charles River from my bedroom window."

"I like the sound of that," Faith said, opening her door.

Her voice was warm, rich, and inviting. Cody felt himself heat up as he followed her out of the car.

He took her hand as they walked from the car to his building.

She looked around thoughtfully. "Which house is yours?"

"The one with the stone planter by the steps. My downstairs neighbor likes to fuss with stuff that grows. I think he's a closet gardener."

Faith laughed. "A useful person to have around."

As they reached his house, he tried to see it from her eyes. Would she notice the trim around the doors and windows had been freshly painted? Or that the iron railings on either side of the stairs were free of rust? Would she appreciate the way the stone steps had aged over the decades, so that there was a dip in the center of the treads?

The apartment was his home, but not in the way Faith's house was her home. He slept here—sometimes—he worked here—sometimes—it was big enough for his needs. He didn't love the place, the way Faith loved her old farmhouse, but it was his and he wanted her to like it.

Because if she liked his house, it meant she liked him. Right?

They reached those old, worn steps without her saying anything. Cody told himself it didn't matter, but he began to wonder if she was going to ask him to turn around and take her back to Lexington. "Are you ready to come in?"

The look she gave him almost melted his socks. Oh, yeah. This was going to work.

His apartment took up most of the third floor and included a loft that had originally been part of the attic. Standing in the hallway, he hesitated. "Faith."

She smiled at him in a warm, encouraging way that said she cared about what he had to say.

He wanted to tell her that he'd do anything for her to keep her in his life, but he didn't know the right words. He'd tried to show her by helping out with her strange relative, Andrew. He knew that she'd never let her home get into the state his was, with dust and clutter everywhere, so he wanted her to know that it didn't have to be that way. That he was open to change.

Maybe she'd figured that out already. Still, he couldn't take the chance that she might misunderstand. He cleared his throat. "Before we do, ah, I want to, ah, prepare you."

She looked astounded. Then she laughed. Crossing her arms over her breasts, she leaned against the doorjamb. "Sounds like we'll be here for awhile. Okay, shoot."

"My place is big, but it's cluttered."

She nodded. "Got it."

"I probably have spiders."

"Oh horrors. What else?"

"It isn't perfect."

She pushed away from the door to take hold of his shoulders. Then she shook him gently. "So what?" she said. She raised one hand to his cheek, cupped it lightly, then gently traced the line of his jaw to his mouth. She watched his expression, her gaze softening, her eyes darkening. As her thumb moved across his lips, he touched it with the tip of his tongue, then nipped it gently.

Faith laughed. His feelings for her burned hot, demanded an

outlet. He put his hands around her waist, then drew her close so she could feel him. Her hand slid down from his face so she could grab onto his shoulders and her lips parted. Cody couldn't resist. He lowered his head so he could plunder those lips in a kiss that said just how important this moment was to him.

They were both breathing hard when he pulled away at last. "I've been wanting to do that since I picked you up."

Her smile blazed. "Me too."

"Then let's go inside." She nodded and he reached for his keys.

The layout of his apartment was simple. The door opened into a small foyer that contained a built-in cupboard and an armless chair with a padded seat and wicker back. As soon as they entered, he saw the jacket he'd been wearing yesterday draped casually on the chair. He stared at it in horror until he noticed Faith's lips twitch. Good. She wasn't offended by the sloppiness. Still, he ushered her deeper into the apartment as quickly as he could.

To the left were two bedrooms and a study. The doors were closed, thank heavens. That meant she wouldn't see the workbench he'd put in the study so he had the space to take apart computers, or the clutter of books and files in the first bedroom. The second was respectable enough, though. Like any normal bedroom it contained a double bed and a dresser. He never used it.

To the right were the living room, dining room and kitchen. They were reached through open archways, with no doors to shield them from her eyes. He hoped they passed muster. Ahead of them was a staircase that led up to the loft where the master bedroom suite was located.

Maybe he could convince her to start the tour up there. It was worth a shot.

She headed straight for the kitchen, poking her head into the living and dining rooms on the way. He followed, looking critically over her shoulder. He didn't use them much, so both rooms were burdened with a minimum of clutter. The kitchen scared him though. It was his main living space and a personal disaster area. "Faith? Could we, you know, look at this another time?"

She turned her head, tossing him a look so full of mischievous amusement, that he felt his heart fall to his feet then bounce back up again. Oh God. He wanted that look to stay. To see it again, and again. She sauntered into the kitchen, her gorgeous long, thick sunshine hair swinging along with her stride.

"You promised me the full tour, and I'm holding you to it." Then she reached the kitchen. "Oh, my."

His kitchen was a nice room. The cooking area was spacious, with plenty of counter space. A big island contained the stove and dishwasher. The breakfast nook was a bay with large windows that let in the sunshine. It was his favorite part of the apartment and it showed in the papers piled high on every part of his teak dining table.

He held his breath as she looked around her curiously, ran her fingers across the polished marble counter, touched the surface of the stainless steel fridge, walked over to the piled-high teak table.

And ignored the mess as she looked out the window at the view.

Cody realized he'd been holding his breath. He let it go as he followed her over to the breakfast nook. "There's only me," he said, a little desperately.

Still staring out the window, she said, "I'll bet this room is flooded with sunshine in the morning."

Relief swept through him. Everything was going to be okay. He reached out to smooth a lock of that fabulous hair away from her face. "Why don't you stay the night and find out?"

Her eyes widened and her breath caught, then she seemed to soften. It seemed like the right moment to cover her lips with his, just her lips. If he touched her anywhere else he wasn't sure he'd be able to control himself long enough to take her up to the loft and into his bed.

Because no matter how desperately he wanted to make love with her, he didn't want to seduce her. He wanted her to be a partner in their lovemaking—and everything else in their lives. He wanted a friend. He wanted an ally. He wanted Faith.

Oh, God, this was killing him.

She stood perfectly still, while her lips fed hungrily on his. When he could stand it no more he caught her head between his hands then he hardened his mouth on hers, forcing her lips open, sliding his tongue between them, deep into her mouth. She made a sound that was the sexiest whimper he'd ever heard and opened to him.

He knew that he was very close to losing control. He wanted to strip away the clothes that hid her from him. He wanted to see her body. He wanted to have her naked beneath his hands. Oh, man, did he want her naked. They would touch, they would play, they would love.

But he couldn't do it unless she wanted it as much as he did. He wouldn't convince her. She had to ask.

Was he nuts, or what?

When he dragged his lips away from hers he figured that was the hardest thing he'd ever done. He wasn't even quite sure his reason for doing it made any sense. He just knew he had to.

She looked bemused, then her gaze sharpened. She turned away from him to inspect the cooking area.

Disappointment flooded him. It appeared that she wasn't as hot for him as he was for her. Damn. Had he misread her signals that badly?

He was still wrestling with the puzzle when she tossed her golden mane and began to move.

She headed for the phone. Now he was really feeling miserable. She was calling a taxi to take her home. Or maybe her sister. Or— oh hell—her mother. "Faith, you don't have to—"

Leaning against the counter, facing him, she smiled. Holding up one finger to ask him to wait, she said into the phone, "Yes, I'd like to order two pizzas, the works. Yes, that's right. What was that? Oh, the hungry man size. The address?" She raised her brows. Numbly, Cody told her and she repeated it into the telephone. "And when should we expect delivery? Thanks." She hung up. Holding his gaze with her own, she pushed away from the counter. "We have half-an-hour. Care to give me the rest of the tour?"

"There's only my bedroom left."

"Uh-ha. That's what I figured."

As he took her hand to lead her up to his loft, he decided that sounded pretty much like an invitation, one he'd be happy to act on. "The master suite is my favorite part of the condo. There's a fireplace, a huge walk-in closet, and a great big bay window that overlooks the Charles. It even has a little alcove for a desk and a computer. " He knew he was babbling and she'd see it all in a minute anyway, but he needed to break the tension that was growing with each step they took up the staircase.

"I thought you said the kitchen was your favorite room."

He had said that. That's what babbling got you. He scrambled for secure footing. "It is, during the day, that is. At night—"

He broke off, appalled. He sounded like an advertisement for sex. Faith was sure to be offended.

She laughed. "Cody, are you as nervous as I am?"

It was a good thing they'd reached the landing, because he stopped dead. "What do you mean?"

She swallowed, then smiled shyly. "I want to make love with you. I've wanted to since before Uncle Andrew came to visit. But with him in my house and following me around everywhere I—"

He kissed her and this time he didn't hold back. He gathered her up in his arms and showed her, with his mouth and the size-able bulge in his pants, that he wanted her too.

By the time he released her, she was holding on to his shoulders. She put her head against his shoulder for a brief moment, then she straightened. Her tongue flicked out to moisten her lips as she reached for his shirt and started to undo the buttons. Each time her hands brushed his skin little shafts of pleasure shot through him. If he let her continue he was going to explode all on his own. On the fourth button down he covered her hands with his and held her away. "Let me," he said. He could hear the raspy edge in his voice and it appeared Faith could too, for she smiled as she slid her hands in a seductive path to his shoulders.

He made short work of his shirt, then took his time with the blouse she was wearing, a sexy confection of lace and silk that hugged her curves. The jut of her nipples was clearly visible and he couldn't resist taking one into his mouth, while he cupped her other breast with his hand.

"Cody, that is really…" His fingers found her nipple and tightened. She groaned. "…really nice. Where is the bed?"

"Soon," he muttered.

Her fingers dug into his shoulders. That only increased the pleasure he was getting from touching her, even through the thin silk. But if it was good now, what would happen if he stripped off her shirt?

She was everything he had imagined. Her skin was softer than the fine material and the nipples that thrust into his hands were warm. They tasted of flowers and desire when he took one into his mouth.

Gasping, Faith reached for the button at his waistband, then she pushed at the fabric. "Cody," she said, "you are driving me crazy. Take me, now!"

That sounded like a really good idea. He was about ready to burst and if Faith was too, then what was stopping them?

Some perverse devil made him say, "Not a hope lady. You come on my terms, when I'm ready to drive you over the edge. Not before."

She laughed. "Oh wow. I don't believe this. You're making me wait? I don't think I can."

"If I can, you can." He knelt down, reaching for her waistband, the way she had reached for his. "Put your hands on my shoulders."

She trembled as she did what he asked. He pushed her pants down until he could see her underwear. It was bikini style, a hot red that made him smile when he looked up at her. She smiled back, shyly, he thought, but the message was clear. She'd put the undies on for him, so he would enjoy taking them off.

He peeled them down her hips slowly, taking pleasure in the smooth, warm texture of her skin, the way she trembled with every touch. Then he made her step out of the puddle of pants and underwear on the floor and open her legs.

When he kissed her there she gasped and cried out. He used his teeth and his tongue and his hands until he felt her go over the edge in her first climax. Then he swept her up in his arms and carried her over to the bed.

She smiled and reached for him. "What about you?"

He laughed and stripped out of his clothes as quickly as he could. Then he stretched out beside her and stroked her breasts. "I'm going to make you fly again, then I'm going to come inside you."

"Promise?" she said, her lips curled in a sultry smile.

He straddled her, letting her feel his erection while he nibbled her mouth, nipping her lips with his teeth, stroking them with his tongue. She arched against him, her fingernails busy tracing thin lines along his back. He kissed his way up her jawline to her earlobe, and enjoyed her little squeak of pleasure as she began to squirm against him. He held her steady, making sure she was ready for him, then he entered her.

She gave a little groan that sounded like a purr of feline pleasure as he anchored himself. "Oh, wow."

She said a lot more than 'oh wow,' when he began to move. She arched and writhed and said his name over and over again. Their coupling seemed to last forever until he tipped her over the edge and followed her down.

The intercom phone rang two minutes later. He groaned. "The pizza."

"Good timing," Faith said. She bit the tip of his chin. "I'm starved."

# CHAPTER 24

"Oh my God. That is some dress. Faith, you look fantastic!"

The dress that Liz was gushing over was a dark red sheath that burned with an enticing fire. Cut square across the bodice and held up by narrow ribbon straps, the lustrous fabric was a sensual silk that moved when Faith moved and slithered against her skin in a feather-light caress. The hem almost reached mid-thigh, showing off the length of Faith's legs.

As Faith twisted this way and that in front of the mirror, Liz said enthusiastically. "Cody's going to love it." She grinned a knowing, very female grin. "He'll drag you off to bed without bothering with dinner."

"I hope so," Faith said, remembering the before pizza, after pizza, dessert and midnight sex from the night before. "But I'm going to tease him a little. Make him wait while we eat. And then, when we're both so hungry we can't hold back any longer, I'll take him to bed and tell him who Uncle Andrew really is."

"Whoa! What did you say?"

Faith turned away from the mirror. "Cody helped me out this

week and it almost cost him his job. He deserves to know who I am." She took one last look in the glass and saw Liz frowning at her.

"What's this about losing his job? Is this Ava the Tyrant Lizard in action?"

Faith headed for the changing room, Liz trailing along behind. "Yup. I'm going to buy this, then let's have lunch. I can do my grocery shopping afterward. I'll tell you what happened while we eat."

They went to one of the sit-down restaurants in the mall. The menu was packed with standard items labeled with cute names to make them seem different, the service efficient. Liz managed to wait until they had ordered before she pounced. "So give. What has Ava been up to now?"

Faith stirred cream into her coffee. "One of the computers went down on Friday afternoon. Andrew didn't know how to fix it."

"Uh-oh." Liz sat back. They were in a booth, sheltered from the other patrons of the busy restaurant. She picked up her coffee mug. Holding it between her hands, she watched her sister. "Let me guess. Ava arrived on the scene, figured out Andrew was a fraud and started to roar."

"Something like that." Faith sipped her coffee. Then she put the cup down with a sigh. "She cornered me in my office and gloated that she was going to get Cody. She said he'd foisted Andrew on the company and that was grounds for dismissal."

Liz sucked in her breath. "What did you do?"

"I told her the truth." Faith shrugged. "What else? I couldn't let her destroy Cody."

"The truth? The real truth?"

Faith laughed at the astonishment in Liz's voice. "Not the complete truth, just enough to clear Cody. Can you imagine how she would have reacted if I'd told her Andrew came from 1772?

She wouldn't have believed a word. No, I told her Andrew was my cousin and that I'd begged Cody to help me out by bringing him in as an intern."

The waitress arrived with their meals, a chicken salad sandwich and fries for Faith, soup and a salad for Liz. After she'd topped up their coffee and departed, Liz said, "That still leaves Cody vulnerable. After all, he agreed to it, knowing that Andrew didn't have the skills to do the job."

Faith popped a chip into her mouth and chewed. "I told her that I lied about Andrew's skills, that I conned Cody into agreeing. She knows that Cody and I have a thing going outside of work. She probably figured I blinded him with sex."

A spoonful of soup halfway to her mouth, Liz regarded her with a fascinated expression. "So what did she do?"

"She fired me."

Liz put the spoon back in the bowl, the soup untasted. "She what?"

"She fired me." Faith laughed at the amazement on her sister's face. "And before you ask, no, I'm not upset."

"But your job at NIT is so important to you!"

"Cody is more important," Faith said simply. She picked up the sandwich half, looked at the toasted bread, the curly leaf lettuce, the chopped chicken, mixed with celery and mayo. "You know, Liz, I've been living my life on Dad's terms, not mine. I assume people will react a certain way because that's how Dad reacted. I desperately wanted to succeed in business because I believed it would make me succeed in Dad's eyes. It didn't. All that happened was that I got in the habit of being everything someone else expected. When Ava Taylor started at NIT I followed pattern and turned into someone she wanted as an employee."

"You didn't, you know," Liz said. "You were always complaining about Ava, resisting her demand that you conform."

Faith took a sip of coffee while she considered that. Finally she shook her head. "I don't think so, Liz. I wanted to fit in so badly I allowed her to manipulate me into going out with Cody even though I was afraid of becoming involved with him. Then, because I thought Cody wouldn't understand, like Dad never understood, I told Andrew to stop visiting. But Andrew came back anyway and Cody helped us without asking why. He just did it, because… because he loves me, I hope. I know it's because he believes in me."

"Hold it! Go back a step. You hope Cody loves you?"

A smile that was a little shy, a little triumphant, dawned on Faith's lips and in her eyes. "I sure do, Liz, because I'm so deeply in love with him."

Liz sat back, her face a portrait of delighted surprise. "Oh, wow!"

Faith's smile turned dreamy. "I trust him Liz. That's why tonight I'm going to tell him about being a Beacon. I think he'll accept me for what I am."

Liz reached out, squeezed her sister's hand. "Faith, I'm so happy for you. But…" She hesitated. "What if he doesn't?"

FAITH SHOULDERED open her front door. She was loaded down with the bag from the dress shop, another containing new shoes to go with it, and two bags of groceries filled with supplies she planned to use to make the perfect dinner for Cody. She'd chosen a menu that wouldn't need much preparation, so she did a bit of quick prep work, then put away the food. She checked her watch. The afternoon was creeping to a close. Time to wash and change for the evening.

She sang in the shower. Tonight she was going to tell Cody about her ability. That frightened her, but it was also a relief. Cody would not abandon her just because she was a Beacon. She was sure of it.

Well, almost sure of it. Her stomach did nervous flips while she dressed in the flirty little sheath that screamed 'I want you!' and butterflies danced as she swept her hair back into a sophisticated knot that begged to be taken down. After another quick look at her watch, she headed for the kitchen. She wanted to have the table set in the dining room and the appetizers in the oven before Cody arrived.

She had just put a tray of sausage rolls in the oven when she heard an impatient bellow. "Faith, finally! You are home! Where have you been?"

She froze. After a moment she carefully closed the oven door then cautiously followed the sound of the voice. "Andrew?"

He was standing in the middle of the living room, his expression angry but determined. Though he was wearing one of his best suits, a burgundy silk coat with wide lapels laced with gold thread at the button holes, a white brocade waistcoat, and black silk breeches, Faith noted that the silk of his coat and breeches was dusty, as if he'd rolled around on the road a time or two. Then there was his face and knuckles. "You've been fighting."

"This morning," he said grimly. "Where were you all day? I've been trying to come forward since noon."

"I was out shopping." Frowning, she studied him. Whoever he'd been fighting had certainly landed a few good blows. An enormous bruise, high on one cheekbone was already turning black and blue and affecting his eye, which was swelling shut. "How many this time?"

With a little groan, he sat down at one end of her sofa. "There were two."

Her dismayed glance moved lower, to his hands. There she could see smears of blood. Since his face and body showed no evidence of cuts or scratches, she guessed the stains came from one or more of the other guys. "I hope you gave as good as you got."

He grinned at her, then winced as the movement affected his injured cheek. "Those men will think twice before they make another attempt, but it was George Strand who set them upon me and I do not doubt that he will send others in their place."

Faith sat down on the edge of the recliner. "Andrew, what happened?"

"I stole a few private minutes with Mary Elizabeth last night at the ball. I explained to her about being a Beacon and traveling to the future." He paused and smiled faintly. Faith had a sudden mental image of Andrew locked in a passionate embrace with his eighteenth century lady.

"She believed and accepted. My joy knew no bounds! I asked her then and there to marry me. She agreed. We decided I would visit her father this morning to formally ask for her hand."

"Let me guess, her dad was not pleased."

"He was furious. He ordered me out of his house and before I knew it I was being set upon by two of his men, intent, as they said, upon teaching me a lesson."

"I know you want to marry Mary Elizabeth and that George Strand is her father, but the guy's contemptible," Faith said. She was furious that Andrew had been treated this way. She went to the kitchen for an ice pack.

He rested it against his cheek cautiously. "Aye, he is that. After I sent his men back to him with their tails between their legs, I returned to my farm to decide what I must do. Strand made it very clear that he would not willingly allow his daughter to join her hand with mine." He stood restlessly and began to pace. "If Mary Elizabeth and I are to wed, it will have to be by an elopement. And after we elope—will I be able to bring her back to my farm? Or will her father steal her away from me? Or make her life miserable?"

"If she loves you, Andrew, and she is with you, her father's anger will hurt, but it will be countered by the love you give her."

He paused at the window, staring out into the front yard at an ancient maple that was a relic of the original woods where he'd found Faith's beacon. "That may be, Faith, but I cannot be sure." He paused, then added, "More important, nor can Mary Elizabeth. She is a fine young woman who respects her family, particularly her mother. I would not be the one to drive a wedge between them."

"I'm sorry, Andrew." Faith went over to him to give him a hug. "What a mess. Is there anything I can do?"

He nodded. "I wish to use your computer."

"Why?"

"Does it matter?"

Well no, it didn't. Unless…"That depends. If you want to play computer solitaire, be my guest. If you want to use the Internet for research, the answer's no."

He glared at her. "I need to know what happens to George Strand. I can find out on the Internet."

"Not necessarily. And it's not allowed, Andrew. You know that."

"Not only is the man one of the King's chief agents in Boston, but he is a bully and a brute. I must know what happens to him."

Faith knew George Strand's fate. Everyone in the family did. He would die in the service of King George, shot by a patriot during the Revolutionary War. Shot by the son-in-law he refused to acknowledge. Shot by Andrew.

There was no way Faith was going to let Andrew on the Internet, because he was right, he probably would find out what had happened to George Strand and then what?

"You can't, Andrew. What happens if you discover he lives another forty years and makes his daughter's life a misery each and every day? What would you do?"

"Take her away from him!" Andrew said, putting his hands on his hips in an authoritative way.

Faith shook her head. "Then you would be changing history.

Andrew, you cannot search out your own future. It is too dangerous!"

He glared at her. "I will do this."

"No, you will not."

Now at an impasse, they glared at each other. Andrew was the first to look away, but he was far from defeated. He allowed his brows to rise in a thoughtful way. "Your clothing is even more revealing than most in this century," he said. "I assume this scrap of material is for Master Cody's pleasure?"

She eyed him warily, wondering where he was headed with this. "That's right."

"Have you told him about the Beacon?"

"No. I was going to do it tonight." Even as she said the words she realized that Cody would be arriving in less than an hour expecting an intimate dinner and a quiet evening. He certainly wouldn't want to be joined by a confrontational Uncle Andrew.

"I will help," Andrew said, looking pleased with himself.

As well he might. He knew very well that Faith wanted to be alone with Cody when she told him about her special ability. He probably assumed that she would cave into his blackmail and allow him on the net, just to be rid of him.

Think again, Uncle Andrew. "I'll call Cody and put him off while we sort this out."

Andrew's lips pursed in annoyance. "I'm not going back without the information, Faith."

"Andrew, you must! You know that." With that she left him to consider the realities of the situation and went into the kitchen to rescue the appetizers then call Cody.

His voicemail answered. Frustrated, she left a message asking him to call her. Then she paused and thought. Somehow she had to get Uncle Andrew back into the eighteenth century before he snuck in some research on the net. How? She needed help and a whole lot of support.

She phoned Liz's cell. Her sister and Andrew had always gotten along. Maybe Andrew would listen to her.

Liz's voicemail answered too. What was it with people? Did no one answer the phone these days? She left an urgent and slightly hysterical message, then dialed her mother.

This time she was in luck. Chloe answered on the third ring. "Mom? Andrew's here and he says he won't go back until he finds out what happens to George Strand. Can you come?"

# CHAPTER 25

There were three vehicles parked in the drive at Faith's house. Cody recognized her car, but not the other two. He frowned, wondering if he'd misinterpreted her invitation. When she'd slid out of his bed this morning, she'd talked about spending the night at her place. Somehow, he'd been certain she had planned a one-on-one evening. He'd been so sure that he'd used the day to shop, not one of his favorite occupations, but a necessary one.

He parked to one side of the drive so that the other cars would be able to leave, hopefully just after he arrived. Then he retrieved the large bouquet of roses and orchids from the seat beside him and checked his pocket before he slammed the door. Taking a deep breath he headed to the house.

He knew there was something wrong the instant Faith answered the door. She was wearing a red dress of some soft, shimmery fabric and he allowed himself a moment to admire the way it hugged her curves and showed off her long legs, before he set his mind to solving the puzzle set before him.

"Hi," she said. She glanced over her shoulder, her expression worried.

She was standing in the middle of the doorway, blocking his entry. He smiled at her in a reassuring way and stepped forward, forcing her to move back and open the door wider. Her reaction was reluctance and again she glanced inside the house. He thrust the flowers at her. Once more, good manners and habit forced her to react. She took the bouquet, stared at it in a bemused way for a moment and then held it close and inhaled.

"I bought them for you," he said. "I hope you like them."

As if she had drawn strength from the fragrant scent, she smiled as she looked up. "I do! Oh, Cody, you weren't home! I called you, maybe half-a-dozen times."

He moved closer, touched her shoulder and gently eased her away from the door, which he closed behind him. With the door shut, the normal outside sounds disappeared and he could focus on those inside the house. There were voices coming from somewhere in the rear, a woman's voice, then another and a male voice followed, after a moment, by another male voice. A piece of the puzzle fell into place. Apparently Faith's family had decided to visit.

Faith heard the voices too. "I didn't plan for them to come tonight."

Cody took her arm at the elbow and guided her across the hall. He had a vague idea of taking her into the living room where they could cuddle on the couch while she described whatever crisis had caused this family gathering. "Do they often just show up?"

Faith shook her head and opened her mouth to speak, then shut it again as her father's voice bellowed, "I told you this would never work! Just when it looks as if she's got a decent man interested in her, this…this madman from the past shows up. It will always be like that. No normal man would accept a lifetime of this kind of nonsense."

Faith went completely white. She shot a quick, horrified look at Cody. The flowers in her hand shook as she shivered. Fury raced through Cody. He still didn't know what was going on, but the need to solve the equation gave way to a far greater need to protect his woman. He strode toward the kitchen, aware that Faith was trailing behind.

A woman's voice—Faith's mother, Cody thought—was saying bitterly, "Not every man is as narrow-minded as you are, Daniel!"

"Mom!" said Liz.

Then Cody burst into the kitchen.

They were gathered around the kitchen table. A plate of appetizers, probably meant for him, sat in the center. Daniel and Chloe were glaring at each other, while Liz huddled protectively beside her father and Andrew calmly ate one of the appetizers, which looked like a sausage roll.

It was Andrew who saw Cody first. "Ah-ha," he said around the sausage roll and pointed at Cody. Everyone else focused on the doorway and suddenly there was silence.

That suited Cody just fine. He shot Daniel an angry stare as he caught Faith's hand, deliberately linking himself to her. "It's a good thing I'm not a normal man, isn't it, Hamilton?"

Having swallowed the sausage roll, Andrew pounded his fist on the table. "Well said, sir!"

Daniel rounded on Andrew. "He has no idea what he's talking about."

Faith trembled. Cody wanted to kill her father. Instead he tightened his grip on her hand and drew her closer. "Don't I? How do you know? You've been out of her life for years. How do you know what she will or will not tell me about herself?"

Daniel said furiously, "I know because her mother didn't tell me until after we'd been married for…"

"My mistake, Daniel! I thought you cared enough about me—about our family!—to…"

"And Faith is just like her mother," Daniel concluded, ignoring his ex.

"Faith is not her mother and I am not you. Don't put your own twisted feelings on Faith and me."

Though Daniel continued to glare at him, there was doubt mixed in with the outrage now. Beside Cody, Faith stirred. She squeezed his hand, then eased away from his hold. She held the flowers out. "Mom. I need to find a vase for these. Can you hold them for a minute?"

Chloe said, "What lovely flowers, Cody," for all the world as if they were not in the midst of an emotional scene of monumental proportions.

Cody watched Faith. Her movements were jerky, but growing smoother with every task performed, as if the ordinary jobs steadied her. Out of the corner of his eye he could see Daniel fuming. Andrew was eating more sausage rolls. He passed the plate to Liz, who shook her head miserably.

Almost everyone at the table was dressed in normal warm weather clothes. Liz was wearing a spaghetti-strap dress patterned with flowers in yellow and blue pastels. Chloe was also clad in a summer dress, although hers covered more skin than Liz's did, while Daniel had on a red golf shirt and black twill pants. Andrew, however, was dressed as if he was going to a costume party. Although the temperature had to be nearly eighty, he was wearing a suit coat made from a slithery fabric that looked like silk. The color was a splash of dark red and the fancy garment sported wide lapels and buttonholes embroidered with gold thread. Under the coat was a shirt with a thick fall of lace at the wrists and around his neck was a tie with more lace, held in place by a tiepin that looked suspiciously as if it was made from a sizeable diamond.

Cody had wondered about Andrew since he met him a week ago. The odd way of speaking, the childlike amazement for everyday items, the lack of knowledge about things that should have been as familiar to him as his fingertips. Seeing him now, dressed in clothes that made him look like a wealthy country gentleman from an eighteenth century print, only added to the mystery about the man. Moreover, those expensive clothes of his were dirty. There were tears in the lace at his wrists and Andrew was sporting a bruise that had already developed into a hell of a shiner.

Whatever was going on here, Andrew was the key. Cody was prepared to stake his life on that.

With the flowers in the vase, Faith turned to her family. "Okay. This needs to be resolved—tonight. Mom, Andrew needs guidance. He's here because he wants to use the Net to get it. I think we need to tell him what he wants to know."

Outraged, Daniel said, "You're not allowed to!"

Faith sighed. "That's part of the mystery, isn't it?" She opened the fridge door. "Maybe we have to tell Andrew. Maybe he's supposed to know." She plunked a brown paper package onto the counter, hauled out a plate and ripped open the package. Inside were two large cooked lobster tails. She sliced the shells open and used a fork to pry the meat loose.

"But—"

"For once you might listen to your daughter and take her feelings into consideration," Chloe said. "We know how to handle these things. You abandoned us long ago. You have no say in this matter."

Faith shook her head as she cut the lobster meat into bite-sized pieces. She had the look of a woman at the end of her patience.

"I'm with Dad," Liz said. "He's still part of this family."

Cody touched Faith's shoulder. She looked up, startled. "What would you like me to do, Faith? Do you want me to go?" He didn't want to leave, but he wasn't sure Faith would appreciate him around while her family took pot shots at each other.

Her response was quick and certain. "Oh, no Cody, no. Tonight you stay. Please."

He couldn't say no. Hell, he didn't want to say no. Not only did he want to be here to support Faith, but her family's conversation was intriguing.

"Daniel Hamilton is no more entitled to be one of us than George Strand is," Andrew burst out angrily. "They are both cold, uncaring men who would rather see their daughters unhappy than acknowledge that they must live their lives their own way."

The group around the kitchen table erupted in a heated debate.

Faith shook her head again and loaded the lobster onto a plate. She put it on a tray, then added cutlery and a jar of seafood sauce, working, Cody could see, as quickly as she could.

"All of this is getting us nowhere," Daniel said.

Faith turned around. "You're right, Dad. Listen up, all of you. I invited Cody over tonight to be with me. Me. Alone. This," she indicated the people assembled at the table, "isn't exactly what I had in mind when I planned the evening. Right now Cody and I are going out to the backyard where we will drink some wine and eat some lobster and talk—alone—while the rest of you discuss what needs to be done." She took a bottle of wine from the fridge where it was chilling, then grabbed two glasses from the cupboard.

As she handed the wine and glasses to him, Cody smiled. His heart leapt when she smiled back. He had no idea what was going on, but he was pretty sure he was about to find out. Whatever it was, it had split her family and a part of him couldn't help wondering if Daniel Hamilton was right. Another part kept fiddling with the bits of information he had, trying to put the puzzle together.

She picked up the tray and smiled at him. "Okay, let's go."

As he followed her out the door, he heard Chloe Hamilton say, "Andrew, you have to go back. Mary Elizabeth is waiting for you. You will marry the girl and have—"

"Chloe!" Daniel Hamilton bellowed in outrage.

Chloe continued on without pause, "three children. And you will adopt your sister's family when she dies." The rest of what she said was lost as the back door slammed behind them.

But what he'd heard was fascinating.

THE EVENING WAS clear and still warm from the day's sunshine. Mature maple trees shaded the lawn and flowers bloomed in the borders. Insects buzzed and the occasional bird chirped. A squirrel dashed across the grass, intent on a food-finding expedition. The scene was restful, and even here, on the outskirts of a major city, it was possible to imagine what the land must have looked like when this was a prosperous farming area.

Faith set the tray onto a wrought-iron table near the house and arranged two of the matching chairs so they were close together. Cody put down the glasses and opened the bottle of wine. While Faith laid out plates and cutlery, he poured, then he held her chair while she sat, a little act of courtesy that was old-fashioned and somehow appropriate under the circumstances.

Faith held her glass of wine between her hands, rolling it back and forth while she tried to figure out how to explain the unex-plainable. Cody spooned seafood sauce onto his plate, then dipped a chunk of lobster tail into it and ate. He said nothing, waiting until she was ready to begin. She wasn't sure whether to be grate-ful, resentful, or worried. Maybe she was all three at once.

Tonight was the second time her father had shown up on an evening when she planned to tell Cody about herself. The second time he'd undermined her nerve by reminding her of the disaster her parents' marriage had been, all because Chloe was a Beacon, as she was.

Yesterday she'd decided it was time to commit to Cody. She

had already given him her heart and last night she offered him her body. Did she have the strength to present him with her trust tonight?

She didn't want to tell him what she was. She was afraid of seeing an expression of polite amazement on his face, or, worse, watching helpless as he walked out of her life. It would hurt too much. Over the past few weeks she'd come to depend on him. When he wasn't around she wanted to be with him. When he was with her she wanted to explore his mind, touch his body, hear him laugh, feel his kiss.

She sighed, took a sip of her wine, and said, "My life is always like this."

Cody smiled faintly. "You mean your family regularly comes by to bicker and fight?"

Faith laughed, though she could hear no humor in the sound. "No. Andrew shows up, just like that," she said with a snap of her fingers. "He usually comes on Friday night to shower and prepare for the weekend. He's quite a ladies' man, you see, probably because he is clean and smells of my cranberry soap. Or he was until he met Mary Elizabeth and decided he'd found the love of his life. But he doesn't necessarily have to come on Friday nights. In fact, I'm never sure when he will show up."

"Where does Andrew live?"

This was it. The moment when she retreated or went forward. Decision time. She sighed again and drank more wine. "Cody, he used to live in the old farmhouse that my mother and sister live in."

Cody frowned. "He used to live there?"

Trust Cody Simpson to catch the important part of the sentence. "Yeah, used to. He doesn't live there anymore because he's dead."

Cody sat back, startled. "Are you telling me Andrew is a ghost?"

Faith shook her head. "No, oh no. Andrew is very much alive.

But Cody, he lives in the year 1772. He's a Traveler—that's what we call people who can move back and forth in time."

"He travels through time," Cody said, enunciating each word as if to clarify the meaning in his mind.

"Yes! He travels from his own time to mine because of me—I'm a Beacon. Somehow, and I don't know how, he can see me or sense me. He says it's like a light in the woods on a night with no moon or stars. He comes toward that light and when he reaches it he is here with me in my time. I don't understand it. Andrew doesn't either. We just know it happens."

Cody put his glass on the table. "What you're describing sounds impossible."

This was it. He was about to tell her that she was a nut case and he didn't want anything more to do with her. "It does, doesn't it? Look, Cody…" She could hear her voice crack and struggled to control raw emotions. She was shaking now, so she put her glass on the table too. Staring at her hands, she said, "It's an ability that runs in my family. My mother is both a Beacon and a Traveler. Her mother, my grandmother, was only a Beacon, but my great-grand-mother was a Beacon and a Traveler too. Not everyone in the family has it. My sister is completely normal. She says she wishes she had the ability, but I know she doesn't, not really. Why would she want it?"

"Because it's fascinating," Cody said. "Faith, there has to be a scientific reason for this!"

Faith looked at him gloomily. "Probably. It's not exactly some-thing we talk about in a casual way. One of my ancestors was accused of being a witch in seventeenth century Salem because of her ability to travel. Another was exiled from Boston because of it. Being different—being this different!—can be dangerous."

Cody stared at her for what seemed like an eternity, then he reached out. He touched her cheek, stroking gently in a gesture that conveyed awe and incredible tenderness. "And you told me."

"Yes," she whispered. She was unprepared for his response, but could feel a sense of wonderment bubbling deep inside, contained now, but ready to rise to the surface as it grew and expanded.

"Faith, I am honored." He slid his hand into her hair to draw her close, then he kissed her with that same tenderness and a triumph born of awe.

Dizzy with sensation, Faith found herself curled on his lap, her body melting into his. What had he said? *I'm honored.* I'm honored? Had she heard right?

When the kiss ended she said, "Cody, you're not...I don't know...frightened by my ability?"

Drawing his thumb along her lips, he laughed. "Frightened? Faith, I'm intrigued! You have people from the past coming into your life all the time. What a privilege."

She pushed on his shoulders, arching her body back so that she could see his face. "Does that mean you want to continue being with me?"

He looked surprised. "Yes, of course! What did you think, that I'd dump you because—"

Faith felt her skin heat as she nodded.

"Why?" Cody said, frowning. Then understanding dawned. "Oh. Your father."

"My mother told me that she'd hidden her ability for years because she knew my dad wouldn't understand. Eventually he learned of it though. At first he though she was crazy, then he thought it was just plain weird. He wanted her to stop doing it and when she couldn't, he decided it was because she wouldn't." Her voice lowered almost to a whisper. "He said she'd made her choice and it wasn't him."

Cody smiled and kissed her lightly on the chin. "Faith, whatever makes you the person you are is okay with me. As long as Andrew doesn't show up when we're making love, he can visit as often as he wants."

Faith laughed, a little shakily. "Cody, are you sure?"

"You bet." He stroked the length of her long, bare leg, exposed by the short skirt of the shimmery red dress, and grinned like a buccaneer at her quick intake of breath. "If I can handle your father, dealing with Andrew will be a snap."

She put her head on his shoulder and snuggled close. She was shaking, from a release of the tension she had been holding on to for so long. Cody's arms closed around her, keeping her safe. No matter what was to come she truly believed that he was willing to accept her for what she was. It was a wonderful feeling.

"Hey," he said, after a minute. "I've got plans for tonight. Have some of that lobster, enjoy a glass of wine and fill me in on what's up with Andrew so we can figure out how to get rid of him and the rest of your family."

Faith laughed and left his lap for her chair, reluctantly. While they nibbled on the lobster and drank the wine, she told him about Andrew, Mary Elizabeth, and her father, George Strand, and the role Andrew would play in George Strand's fate. Cody listened patiently, sitting relaxed in his chair, one ankle propped over the other knee.

"Now Andrew is frustrated. Every time he tries to make points with Mary Elizabeth her father turns on him. He wants to know if his trouble is worth it. He wants to know if he marries Mary Elizabeth, what part her father will play in their lives, and he wants to use the Internet to find out."

"This is an amazing story," Cody said. He looked over Faith's shoulder, lost within his mind as he thought over all she'd said. She observed him quietly, enjoying the concentration on his face and the way he absentmindedly twirled the wineglass as he thought. Something akin to contentment washed over her. Being with Cody was really all she wanted. Yes, she liked her job and yes as a Beacon she was an important component in a whole time travel system, but if she thought she would lose Cody because of either part of her life, she would find some way to let them go.

Quite simply, Cody Simpson had become the most important element in her world. She wanted him, she needed him, and she loved him so very much. She would be his friend, his partner, his lover. There would be times when she would protect him or help him, others when she would give him his space. Now that she'd confessed her greatest secret, she would also have to tell him that she'd probably lost her job and wouldn't be back at NIT after Monday, and she'd have to explain it in such a way that he didn't feel responsible or upset. She'd work on that. It would probably be okay. After all, he'd taken the news that she was a Beacon extremely well, considering how bizarre the whole thing sounded.

She came back to herself with a start to find that he was watching her, his expression tender. "You were far away. Where were you?"

"Thinking about you." His smile deepened. Faith thought of their lovemaking the night before and she realized that she really, really wanted more of it. As soon as possible. "So. Got any ideas on how to handle Uncle Andrew?"

"When we came out here your mother was telling Andrew that he was going to marry Mary Elizabeth, have a bunch of kids and adopt some others. Maybe she's already given him what he wants to know." He shook his head. "We may have a problem if she did, though. We're dealing with the paradox of time travel here. Is the past the way it is because the individual traveled to the future, found out what happened, and therefore acted in a certain way because he knew he was supposed to? Or will the past be changed and rewritten because the person came to the future. Which one is right?"

We. A little shiver passed through Faith. Shock. Delight. It didn't matter. She loved the way he was joining his life to hers and her heart was singing because of it. "Is there no algorithm to explain it?"

Cody shot her a wry look, unaware of the little moment of blissful pleasure he'd given her. "Science doesn't believe time travel is possible. No, there's no algorithm that I know of."

"Then you'll just have to write one, won't you?"

He laughed. Glancing down at his glass, he swirled the wine, then he looked up. "Would it bother you if I did?"

"Only if you published it in a scientific paper the academic world rejected out of hand and you made yourself a laughing-stock." She stared at him intently, hoping to make him understand. "Because you would, you know. No one believes in the Beacon except those who are part of it. That's why we don't tell just anyone about it."

He caught her hand and lifted it to his lips. "Your secret is safe with me."

"I know," she whispered. Then she cleared her throat. "Cody. Let's go sort this thing out and get rid of everybody."

"Yeah," he said, smiling at her over their joined hands. "I'm with you."

# CHAPTER 26

The kitchen had turned into an armed camp when they went back in. A truce had been reached, or perhaps something closer to a stalemate. The bickering had stopped, but Chloe and Daniel were eyeing each other with wary hostility, while Liz looked lost. The food on the serving plate was gone and Andrew was standing at the counter opening a bottle of wine with practiced ease. He poured a glass then raised it to the light to examine the clarity of the ruby red liquid. Apparently satisfied, he brought the glass to nose level, swirled the wine, sniffed, then sipped. He raised the glass in a toast. "An excellent claret, my dear Faith. I congratulate you."

Chloe smiled and winked. Faith began to feel hopeful that they might be able to sort out this current family crisis fairly quickly. "Mom, how much did you tell Andrew?"

"Only what it was necessary for him to know," she said calmly. Daniel snorted with ill-disguised contempt. She ignored him. "That he will marry Mary Elizabeth because George Strand will not be able to keep them apart. He poked and prodded me, wanting more, but I won't give it to him."

Andrew put the glass on the counter and headed for the refrigerator.

Cody squeezed Faith's hand, then he wandered over to the counter and leaned against it sipping his own wine while he watched Andrew slap a packet of well-marbled rib steaks onto the counter. He raised his brows. "There's only enough for two."

Andrew grinned. "I'm hungry. I broke my fast before I called upon my future father-by-marriage, but I was unable to eat again after that thieving representative of an unjust king set his henchmen upon me."

"A patriot, are you?"

Andrew cocked his head. His eyes gleamed. "Aye, I am. But here now, you know that word and what it means. Is it famous—or infamous?"

Cody laughed. "The paradox of time travel. Were events caused by the knowledge that they happened? Or did they happen and all of history may be changed if they do not occur as they were supposed to."

"Aye, I see you've got the way of it."

Daniel said indignantly, "You told him about yourself."

"Yeah, Dad, I did. Do you think things between us would have worked out better if I'd pretended to be something I'm not?"

Andrew jerked his head in Daniel's direction and said confidentially to Cody, "Don't mind the old man. He's always disliked me. The first time I came to visit..." He shook his head, remembering. "What a scene. I turned up in the middle of a dust-up between them—"

"Who?"

"Why, Faith and her father, of course. Over an exam she'd taken." He propped his hip against the counter, absently echoing

Cody's stance. "Silly thing to bicker about, but there you are. They were hard at it when I arrived, Daniel mad as flame because the girl hadn't made the top mark in her class. Not living up to her potential, he called it." He smiled and swirled the wine in his glass as he looked over at the people sitting at the table. It was clear they could hear what he was saying, and he knew it.

Daniel's eyes were narrowed. He'd erupt soon, but he was waiting to see just how far Andrew would take it. Faith was standing near the table, but separate, not part of either group. She was white and her body was tense. Cody reached over and grabbed her hand. He drew her to him, then he wrapped his arm around her waist and brought her close so that she was nestled against his chest and between his legs. She leaned her head back against his shoulder in silent surrender, and for comfort.

"I'd been out in the woods that day," Andrew continued. He smiled, his expression almost meditative. "Avoiding my chores, even though I knew I'd get a hiding when my old man caught me. The light, when it came, was blinding. I had to go to it. I had no choice. It was filled with desperation and hopelessness, and a despair so strong it cried out with need. It begged for my assistance. I could not help but give it."

"Are you telling me that I caused my daughter to become a Beacon?" Daniel said dangerously.

Andrew smiled at him, drank more wine, made him wait. Though Daniel's eyes were glittering with a fury that was all the more potent for being tamped down, Andrew didn't rush. "Do you remember my arrival, Daniel?"

"I do. You were dressed in a dirty shirt and breeches and you smelled of sweat and horse manure. Your hair was long and loose and you were carrying a tree branch. Even though I could see you were young, you were stocky and well-built. You held that tree branch the way a man who plans to beat another does."

"I remember too," Faith said. "I was crying. I'd failed you yet again, Daddy. When Andrew arrived I—" Cody kissed her neck, diverting her momentarily. Daniel's eyes widened in shock, then narrowed. The red in his cheeks deepened. The dark, remembered emotions that had been threatening to overwhelm Faith fled. There was a laugh in her voice when she said, "I thought he was my avenging angel."

Cody put his glass on the counter so he could wrap his other arm around Faith and pull her more securely against him. "Well, Daniel, it looks like you are the reason that Faith is a Beacon. How do you feel about that?"

"It's nonsense!"

"I think the lad may be on to something." Andrew held up his glass and squinted at the light as it splintered through the wine in shafts of fire. He spoke in a casual way, as if what he was saying really didn't matter, though they all knew it did. "In the family we've never questioned why it begins, it just is. But if you think about it, there's always some strong emotion involved the first time a person travels or leads someone to them."

"Then I might be a Beacon too," Liz said wonderingly. "I haven't been one up until now because I haven't had the emotional need to become one?"

Andrew replied to her, but he smiled his wolfish smile at Daniel. "Aye, could be. Mostly the Beacon is born when a person is just reaching the adult years, but it has been known to happen when a person is older."

Daniel whitened as Liz brightened with excitement. After all these years Andrew had found a way to use the club he'd never had a chance to wield when he first met his distant descendants.

Cody ignored this exchange. He'd been thinking about the possibilities and the whys and hows of the beacon ability. "Then it might be something hormonal? A body chemical that triggers some kind of inherited receptor in a recessive gene?"

Andrew stared at Cody as if he'd spoken in a different

language. Which, perhaps, he had. Shaking his head, Andrew said, "I leave the aye or nay of that up to you, Master Scientist. I've done my part. Now then, Faith, would you grill me one of these fine cuts of beef? I believe Mistress Chloe has provided me with as much information as she will allow. I want to go back to claim my Mary Elizabeth. And I want to do it on a full stomach."

"You would want to become a Beacon?" Daniel said, turning to Elizabeth. "You want to be a freak like Faith is?"

"Here now," Andrew said warningly, his features hardening.

"Daniel Hamilton, shame on you!" Chloe cried.

Trembling, Faith tried to slip out of Cody's embrace. He kissed her hair, tightened his hold. "Seems to me," he said, outrage and contempt clear in his tone, "that the freak in this family is you, Daniel. Not your daughters. Not your wife. You."

Faith stilled. Liz gasped. Andrew laughed.

Daniel surged to his feet. "This is ridiculous!"

Faith took one of Cody's hands, then the other and kissed each before she shifted them aside so she could leave the shelter of his arms. "You're right, Dad, all of this is ridiculous. There are no freaks in this family, only people with passionate emotions that develop in different ways. Why it happens doesn't matter. That it happens, does. I've spent most my life trying to be what I'm not. The perfect student. The best daughter. An ordinary office manager. I'm not any of those things, I never was. All I am is Faith Hamilton, a girl who did her best in school, who loved her daddy, but was never quite sure she had his love in return. An office manager who worked really hard for her company, but who wasn't even considered for a senior position when it came up. A woman who was attracted to a man, but figured she wasn't good enough for him because she was different.

"A woman…" She turned, caught Cody's hand, and smiled at him. "…who took a risk and discovered that being different was okay."

"More than okay," he said, his voice husky.

Daniel's color had returned to normal, but he still looked disgruntled. "That's all very nice, but—"

"You know, Hamilton, I'm getting tired of you. Lay off Faith."

Chloe pointed a finger at her ex. "Cody has a point—"

"I know you're going to be my father-in-law and I'm trying to be polite, but you're making it extremely difficult."

"What!" squealed Liz, clapping her hand over her mouth to muffle the shriek and giggle that followed.

Faith echoed the word, but more faintly. "What? Cody? Are you proposing to me?"

He blinked, then smiled that rueful half-smile that made her hot right down to her toes. "Yeah, I guess I am." He patted his jacket pockets, found what he was looking for, then pulled out a blue velvet box. "This isn't quite how I envisioned this evening." He gazed around the room at the faces of Faith's family. Liz, bright with delight, Chloe bemused, Andrew grinning so widely that there was danger his bruised face might split. "But..." His gaze fell on Daniel's shocked expression and hardened.

He flipped open the box and took out a ring. The massive diamond glittered under the hard kitchen lights. Faith stared at it, mesmerized.

"Faith, I know I have lots of flaws. I tend to focus too intensely when I'm working and I'm not very neat. I like my freedom and I don't do the corporate schmoozing thing very well. I know you're dedicated to NIT, and that's okay—"

"I'm not dedicated to NIT, Cody. I work there. Well, I used to work there until Ava fired me."

"As long as you don't make me do the social climbing—" He paused. "What did you say? Ava fired you?"

"She tried." Faith laughed. "She has to check with Ralph first."

Unexpectedly, Daniel spoke up. "Is the woman mad? Why fire

one of her best employees? Was it office politics? Did she think you were after her job?"

"Daniel, be quiet!" Chloe said indignantly. "You are interrupting Cody."

"He is, but it's a good question," Cody said. He raised his brows. "Was it office politics, Faith?"

"Sort of. She wanted to fire you, Cody, not me, and she was going to use Uncle Andrew's visit as the excuse. I couldn't let her do that."

"You sacrificed your job for me? Faith!"

She put a finger on his lips to silence him. Shaking her head, she said, "My job at NIT doesn't matter, Cody. You matter. I love you. I couldn't let Ava the Oppressor take you down. You love the work you are doing at NIT. I want you to keep doing it as long as you choose to."

"Wait. Back up a step. You love me?"

She nodded, smiling. "A minute ago, you listed your flaws. You didn't list your greatest strengths—your open mind and your trust. When Andrew arrived you didn't ask who he was or why he was dressed so strangely—"

"My clothes are perfectly respectable," Andrew said.

Faith ignored him. "Or why he had to go everywhere I did, although I'm sure you wondered about all those things and more."

"I did," Cody said.

Faith nodded. "Yes. I needed help and you gave it to me, for no other reason than I needed it. You helped me see that two people who were very different could still work together as one. I think, if I hadn't already been in love with you, that Uncle Andrew's visit would have tipped me over the edge."

"Glad I could be of service," Andrew said, toasting them with his glass before he drank.

"Shut up, Andrew!" Liz said.

"Shhh," said Chloe, to silence them both.

Cody cocked head and raised his brows. "Are they always like this?"

Faith laughed, a little shakily. "Always. You have to learn to ignore them."

Cody looked at her parents and sister, then his gaze landed on Andrew and lingered. When he looked at Faith again, he smiled that sexy smile that had such a devastating effect on her. "Or out-do them." She looked at him questioningly and he laughed as he dropped to one knee. "Faith, we began because I lusted after your gorgeous body—"

"What! Have you and my daughter had...had..."

"Sex, Daniel. The word is sex," Chloe said. "And while I'm not a fan of casual—"

"Will you let him finish?" Liz demanded.

Faith raised her eyes heavenward and shook her head. Cody grinned. "But we're here now because I fell in love with your heart and your spirit and everything that makes you so special. You honored me tonight by trusting me with your secret. Will you honor me further by agreeing to become my wife?"

Liz moaned with satisfaction. For once the others were silent. Faith smiled down at Cody. "You look very silly on the floor, you know."

"So much for romance," he said dryly.

She laughed and dropped down opposite him. "Yes. Oh yes, Cody." She took his face between her hands and kissed him. The ring slipped from his fingers and bounced free, landing on the floor with a tinkle on the hardwood.

"Good thing Faith doesn't have a dog," Andrew observed. "Those two half-wild hounds of mine would have been upon that ring in an instant. One of them would have had it in his belly by now."

265

Faith and Cody broke apart. Cody picked up the ring, kissed it, then put it on Faith's finger. "Can we get rid of them?"

Faith laughed. She touched the ring tentatively, possessively. "Yes, but not yet. I am so happy! I want to celebrate. With you, with my family. I want to pick a wedding date—"

"Soon," said Cody.

"Small," Daniel said.

"And ask Liz to be my bridesmaid—"

"You bet," said Liz.

"Am I invited too?" Andrew demanded.

"I hope you'll be my best man," Cody said, easing into the spirit of things.

Faith's eyes sparkled. "Oh, yeah." She smiled and tilted her head, adding softly, "And then, Cody my love, after we've eaten and drunk and laughed as a family, I want to take you away and talk to you about our honeymoon."

He caught her meaning immediately. He curled his mouth into a smile filled with promise. "My place or yours?"

"Doesn't matter." She laughed softly. "As long as we're alone."

"Are they talking about sex again?" Daniel demanded.

Andrew reached into the cupboard for glasses. Chloe headed for the refrigerator. As she opened it, she said tartly, "Oh, for heaven's sake, Daniel. Grow up. Faith is an adult woman. There's nothing wrong with her being intimate with the man she loves."

"After they're married!"

"Yeah, right. Get real, Dad," Liz said. "Mom, what can I do to help?"

Cody said, "It will always be like this, won't it?"

Andrew handed around glasses of wine.

"It'll only get worse when we have kids of our own."

Cody paled. "Oh, man."

"A toast!" Andrew said, holding up his glass. Everyone stopped.

"To Cody and Faith. May their love span the centuries and bring them the happiness they deserve."

They raised their glasses, each of them smiling, even Daniel. "To Cody and Faith!" they chorused.

And drank.

*The End*

# CLAIM TIME FOR LOVE

## FORWARD IN TIME, BOOK TWO

*A*ndrew stepped through the center of the beacon into Faith's kitchen. She was standing by the stove and she wasn't alone. Her sister Liz, mother Chloe, and father Daniel were seated at the table where her lover and now fiancé, Cody, was opening a bottle of wine.

"Andrew!" Faith frowned. "Is there a problem?"

"Of course there's a problem or he wouldn't be here," Daniel said, disgust in his voice.

Cody finished pouring a glass of wine and brought it to him. There was amusement in his eyes. "Your timing is impeccable, Andrew. I can hardly wait to see how my parents react to you."

"Oh!" Faith put her hand to her mouth. "They'll be here in a half an hour!"

Andrew sipped his wine as Cody went back to pouring. "I'll not stay long enough to be introduced to your excellent parents, Master Cody, my friend. I've a request to make and then I'll be on my way."

Cody picked up two glasses and handed one to Faith. "Since

268

you didn't know that we were having a family introduction and wedding planning session tonight, is there any particular reason you decided to visit?"

He couldn't lie to Cody, whom he admired. "It is Mary Elizabeth. Her father has locked her in her room and he is feeding her only the barest of necessities. He has found a suitor for her, but she refuses to accept the fellow's offer of marriage. Strand wishes to starve her into obedience."

"That's terrible!" Liz said.

"You can't tell him anything," Daniel said.

Faith opened the oven door and pulled out a cooking tray filled with sausage rolls. "Unfortunately, he's right. The less you know about your future, the better."

Chloe sighed. "You have to be patient, Andrew."

"Patient! How can I be patient when the lady I love, a gentle kind lady who has done nothing wrong but to be born the daughter of a great beast of a man, is being abused by one who should be her steadfast protector?"

There was silence, then Cody said slowly, "That is a problem. I suspect the answer is less than you desire, Andrew. And more than you would allow, Daniel."

Faith slid the sausage rolls onto a waiting platter, then held it out to Andrew. He took one and munched. The ease of food preparation was one of the best things about the twenty-first century, he reflected. Along with vehicles that moved swiftly along paved roadways and information machines that held all the knowledge of the universe within their depths. "Let me use your computer, Faith. I need to know the date of my wedding."

"You already know it's in New York City," Chloe said. "Why do you want to know the exact date?"

"New York City is far distant and the man Strand wants to affiance Mary Elizabeth to is a colonel of Dragoons—"

"Jonathan Bradley," Chloe said, thoughtfully. "He becomes a viscount."

"He is to be a lord?" This was getting worse and worse. "No wonder her brute of a father is so determined to force her into wedlock. I will have to steal Mary Elizabeth away, but to get her to New York without being captured by Bradley and his mounted soldiers is well nigh impossible!"

"I've wondered about that," Cody said.

"If I know the date, I will know if I should try to spirit her away by sea or try the longer, slower overland route. I will also know when we must escape her father's clutches." He looked around, deliberately making eye contact with each of them. "Don't you see? Everything hinges on that date. Everything."

**CLAIM TIME FOR LOVE**
**Available in eBook and Print**

ALSO BY LOUISE CLARK

**The Forward in Time Series**

Make Time for Love

Claim Time for Love

Discover Time for Love

A Turbulent Time for Love

**The Nine Lives Cozy Mystery Series**

The Cat Came Back

The Cat's Paw

Cat Got Your Tongue

Let Sleeping Cats Lie

Cat Among the Fishes

The 9 Lives Cozy Mystery Boxed Set, Books 1-3

# ABOUT THE AUTHOR

Louise Clark's time travel romance series, Forward in Time, includes both contemporary and historical settings, as well as humor, passion, and hot heroes. Her experience writing both contemporary and historical romance made writing a time travel series a natural. As well, her love of travel meant the books are set in different locals, from historic Boston to the badlands of the American West, and beyond.

For up-to-date information on her latest release, please visit www.louiseclarkauthor.com